ORDER AND CHAOS
BOOK TWO

GRAVEN
IDOLS

JESSICA DALL

Graven Idols

Order and Chaos™: Book 2

Copyright © 2016 by Jessica Dall. All rights reserved.

First Print Edition: August 2016

ISBN-13: 978-1-940215-75-4
ISBN-10: 1-940215-75-7

Red Adept Publishing, LLC
104 Bugenfield Court
Garner, NC 27529
http://RedAdeptPublishing.com/

Cover and Formatting: Streetlight Graphics

CHAPTER ONE

BRIER WINCED AS ANOTHER ROUND of gunfire echoed outside. Her hold on the plate in her hands tightened. Having only a few chips along the porcelain edge and a couple of scratches on the gold inlay, the plate was one of the few that had survived the Augarian battle intact. The last thing she needed was to shatter it because the soldiers in the city had decided to play with their new toys that had arrived in the last supply wagons. Releasing a breath, Brier picked up her dishcloth and started scrubbing the remaining spots on the plate a little more roughly than was warranted.

Once the plate was as clean as she could make it without stripping the gilding off entirely, Brier turned for the cabinet just in time to see a tiny blond blur in a gray dress barreling straight for her legs.

"Rosette!" Brier took a half step back, one hand lifting the plate out of harm's way as the other went out to steady the girl, but the seven-year-old had already ducked behind Brier and pressed her face into Brier's skirts.

Her voice floated up, muffled by the fabric. "Nico's mad."

Brier looked toward the kitchen doorway, where a tall man stood at the threshold. With his blond hair slicked back and well-fitted rich clothes, Nico looked more put together than anyone else still living in the palace. When they met Brier's, however, his stormy brown eyes showed he was just as close to losing his composure as the rest of the palace dwellers these days.

She twisted to look down at Rosette. "Not your doing, I hope?"

"He was already mad." Rosette's face disappeared into Brier's skirts again.

After another glance at Nico's tense expression, Brier forced Rosette back a step—ready to send the girl off whether or not Rosette's powers had played any part in Nico's mood. She dropped her voice. "Why don't you find Palmer for me? Tell him I'm having headaches again."

Rosette frowned as though she knew Brier was trying to get rid of her, but she nodded and scampered off through the far door, holding the skirts of the too-big dress out of the way. Brier shook her head at how out of place Rosette looked, even dressed like an Augarian girl. But then again, Brier wasn't sure Rosette had truly fit in anywhere they had taken her so far. By all accounts, Rosette had lived on the streets of Tetii before meeting Brier and Palmer. Perhaps it was some of that wildness still shining through—the spark that made Rosette Rosette.

"That girl is a menace." Nico's voice broke Brier out of her thoughts.

She released a breath through her nose and turned back to look at him. Nico's tone had already told her they were in for yet another argument. "Good morning to you, too."

"I found her in my things again."

That certainly sounded like Rosette, Brier had to admit. She gave a tight smile and turned to place the plate in the cabinet. "I'll make sure she doesn't have anything of yours."

"Why is she even still here?"

Brier tried to keep the smile in place as she faced him again, her temper bristling at his tone. "Where do you think she should go, exactly?"

"Back to wherever she came from." Nico motioned vaguely toward a wall. "Do we really need trouble like her around on top of everything else?"

"She's a little girl."

"And when did she become our problem?"

"She isn't your 'problem,'" Brier said. "No one's asking you to take care of her."

"Really? Because *someone's* letting that brat run around here, and it certainly wasn't my decision."

Brier's skin prickled as her powers attempted to flare with her irritation. She forced them back down, clenching her fists to quell the tingling in her palms. She'd already unwittingly destroyed half the city. The least she could do was to keep herself from leveling the rest because Nico was getting to her. Again. "She's less of a brat than some people I knew at her age."

Nico's jaw twitched at the less-than-subtle barb. "At least I had a reason for being here. You've yet to explain your sudden fondness for strays."

"Strays?" Brier lifted her eyebrows.

"You could let her and Tash go wherever the hell it is they belong—"

"Palmer was an acolyte." Brier's tone turned sharp. "He's lived in the Augarian as long as you have. Longer, actually, since he didn't come sweeping in thirteen years ago with his vainglorious father—"

"This isn't about my father." Nico's voice dropped low, deadly.

"Everything in this city right now is about your father," Brier spat, making no effort to temper her venom at the thought of Orris Adessi. "If he hadn't locked me in that room to try to take control of my powers—"

Nico placed his fingers at his temples. "I know."

"—and then tried to *burn me alive* when his first plan didn't work too well—"

"I know," Nico repeated, a little more forcefully.

"—we wouldn't be in half of this mess to start with!"

"I'm not my father!" He dropped both of his arms to his sides.

"I never said you were," she snapped.

"But you're punishing me for his iniquity."

She scoffed. "I'm not punishing you for anything."

"Really? Because it feels like you are."

"Not everything is about you." Her voice rose as if she were a child nearing a tantrum. Fighting with Nico seemed to slowly be turning her back into her six-year-old self.

"No, lately it feels like nothing is." His petulant tone said he wasn't far behind her in their quickly devolving argument.

Brier did her best to keep her voice somewhat level. She wasn't six. She hadn't been six for close to thirteen years. "I'm sorry, Nic. There are a few things happening right now that are a little more important."

His teeth clenched. "Like Tash and that girl?"

"Like trying to keep the world from ending," she said, dreading

Nico's dragging Palmer into it. Most of the time, each man seemed willing to pretend the other didn't exist.

"We're still engaged, aren't we? Last I checked?"

Words caught in Brier's throat. She supposed they still were. Technically. They hadn't truly discussed what they were since everything had happened. That was just one more topic that had been swept aside for more important things to deal with. Especially when who she'd been on her last birthday—when their fathers had announced their betrothal—seemed lifetimes away from who she'd become. "What does that have to do with anything?"

"I should register some sort of importance with my own future wife, don't you think?"

Brier huffed, not sure she could bear having this fight. She pressed the heels of her hands to her temples. "I can't do this right now, Nic."

"Do what?"

"This," she snapped at the challenge in his voice.

He tensed, looking ready to snap right back at her. Then his anger drained out, and his face turned hard. "Fine."

She groaned internally, much too acquainted with those moments when Nico closed himself off entirely. "Nic…"

He turned on his heel and stormed out of the kitchen. Brier debated going after him, but they both needed a chance to calm down, anyway. Nico wouldn't bother to speak again, no matter what she did, until he got past his own bad mood. Not after that kind of "fine."

An especially loud blast went off in the piazza, making what glass they still had in the windows rattle.

"Will you all stop it?" Brier shouted up at the daylight, as if any of the soldiers would hear her.

"Next time there's an army to face, you'll be glad my boys have those." General Gully's deep voice near the far door made Brier start.

She spun to face him. "How long have you been there?"

"Not long, Little Miss Chaos." The giant of a man strode into the room. "But thank you for keeping your yelling indoors while the men practice with their harquebuses."

Brier bit her cheek to keep herself from snapping at the pet name he had given her. He'd already seen her yelling futilely at the sky and had likely heard some of her fight with Nico. He would brush off any outburst as her being upset at Nico rather than attributing it to her rightful annoyance at the incessant guns and asinine pet names. She forced her voice to remain level. "Wouldn't their time be better spent rebuilding the rest of the city?"

"There's not much reason to rebuild a city you can't hold." He rubbed the top of her head as he passed, moving for where the kitchen knives were kept. "We've kept the city going so far. I'll keep doing what is best for it. You don't have to worry yourself."

Brier gritted her teeth, unable to move her jaw freely as she answered. "Of course. If you'll excuse me."

"Go ahead and lay down," he said, his back to her as he went through the kitchen supplies. "We'll be done soon, so you can rest then, I promise. I'm sure you've had a long morning."

Irritation at his patronizing tone made energy shoot to Brier's fingertips. The burst of her powers took chips out of the tile under her feet before she reined in her temper again. Gully didn't seem to notice. She clenched her fists and turned for the door. If she had to talk to one more person before she could force her anger back in check, there wouldn't be a city for anyone to rebuild.

CHAPTER TWO

A FAINT TINGLE HIT THE BACK of Palmer's mind, snapping him out of his thoughts. It took a second to place. Someone was coming. Who, though, he couldn't discern. Not through the odd haze that had been affecting his visions for weeks. He frowned. Despite how much he had worked to suppress them before, the flood of information was too overwhelming to filter through half the time. Having his powers so weakened felt crippling.

Standing by the large desk in his room, Palmer leaned to look out the window. He spotted the line of wagons making their way around the cracked marble of the piazza. He released a relieved breath. At least supplies were the good kind of newcomers. Gods knew they had been inching toward starvation rations day by day.

Grabbing his coat, he headed out the door. Far too often, if Palmer didn't hover as they took inventory, the soldiers conveniently forgot the palace residents when dividing new supplies.

Little footsteps followed him as soon as he turned toward the stairs to the side door. Those, he didn't need a vision to decipher. Slowing, he waited for Rosette. "Saw the wagons?"

"And Brier sent me to find you." Rosette hiked up her skirt to catch him. The fine fabric jerked as she ran. All in all, Brier had done a good job fashioning the dress into something Rosette-sized, but Palmer couldn't help but find the full formal skirts absurd on the little girl—former Augarian fashion or no.

Then again, he hadn't gotten entirely used to the fine clothing Brier had fit him into, either, with his silk shirt and embroidered satin jacket. "What for?"

"She *said* she had a headache." Rosette stopped in front of him, pouting. "I think she just wanted me to go away. She was talking to Nico again."

"No wonder she has a headache," Palmer mumbled.

"What?"

"Nothing." Palmer forced a smile. Rosette had already developed her own dislike of Nico Adessi. Palmer didn't need any more reasons for Brier to think that was his influence. "Do you want to see what's come this time?"

A bright smile appeared as if the pout had never existed, and Rosette darted away with more energy than Palmer ever remembered having. Glancing over his shoulder, he did his best to get a quick read on Brier's location. The feeling was only slightly less muddied than everything else he felt lately, but he tracked her moving across the piazza. Alone. And from the energy she was putting out, she cared to keep it that way. Letting her go, he turned after Rosette.

By the time he made it outside, the girl was already getting herself into trouble, ducking under and around the wagons as one of Gully's men tried to catch her—of course without coming too close. Even that was brave of him, honestly. Most of the soldiers refused to come within twenty yards of Rosette lest they begin vomiting blood or something equally horrific.

Still, relief flooded the soldier's face as he spotted Palmer. "Mr. Tash, we need to catalogue what has arrived."

Palmer nodded and bent to look under the nearest wagon just in time to see Rosette slip something into one of her pockets. "Rosie."

She looked at him, empty hand dropping innocently to her side.

Palmer didn't bother calling her on it. "Let them unload. Come stand with me."

The pout returned, but she moved toward him, her hand slipping one last thing between the slats of the wagon when she thought Palmer wasn't watching. He shook his head. Fine dress or not, Rosette hadn't entirely moved past her pickpocketing days.

He returned to the step by the side door as Rosette moved beside him.

7

He rubbed her thin arm, hoping to calm her—and keep her in place. "We can watch from here."

She shrugged.

Leaning closer, he dropped his voice. "And we won't grab anything else until they're finished."

She looked up at him, her blue eyes going wide as if she had no clue what he meant. Palmer looked back out at the wagons. It would have been far too easy to underestimate the girl, if he hadn't known better.

Raised voices carried over the noise of unpacking. Palmer tensed, eyes scanning the wagons. At the far edge, three red-coated soldiers were blocking a group of dark-haired people Palmer didn't recognize. He glanced at Rosette. "Don't move."

As he maneuvered toward the commotion, the voices became clearer.

"This is a restricted area," one of the soldiers spoke, his Latysian accented though perfectly constructed. "You must depart immediately."

"Signore, we're hungry. There's no other food in the city." The voice froze Palmer in place. He shifted, trying to see around the line of men.

"This is a restricted area," the solider repeated, his short words becoming even more clipped as his patience seemed to wear thin. "If you do not depart immediately…"

Palmer caught glimpses of the people—four men and a woman, it seemed, all dressed in near rags—standing on the other side of the soldiers. As one of the soldiers shifted back an inch, his hand going to the hilt of his sword, Palmer got a clear look at the thin, mousy man standing at the front, still trying to state his case. Palmer's throat tightened. The man was thinner than the last time Palmer had seen him and looking worse for wear with patchy stubble blending in to dark splotches of grime across his face and neck. Still, he was familiar enough to strike Palmer dumb. *Egidio.*

Before Palmer could force the name out of his mouth, feet scraped marble and a soldier shouted. A dagger glinted as one of the larger men in the back moved. Swords came free. A crate clattered to the ground as the men unloading the wagons turned toward the commotion.

Palmer pushed himself into the middle of it. "Wait. Stop!"

Shockingly, the swords pointed at him wavered, and the men forcing Egidio and his companions to the ground paused. Unsure what he'd intended to do once in front of a dozen armed men and a group of rough-looking strangers, Palmer froze.

The arguing soldier recovered first. "Mr. Tash—"

"Palmer?"

Palmer met Egidio's confused brown eyes, and a knot formed in his stomach.

"Mr. Tash," the soldier cut in before Palmer could answer. "We have the situation handled. Please return—"

Palmer found his voice again. "I know that man. He used to live here."

"The general has given specific orders that no one is to enter the city without his approval."

"I believe we've been here longer than the general." Palmer did his best approximation of Brier's "who are you to dare question me" voice. Adding, when it didn't seem to work quite as well for him, "I could get Signorina Chastain, if you'd rather discuss this with her."

Palmer couldn't imagine Brier would be any more enthusiastic about letting more people into the Augarian than General Gully was, but invoking her name sent a flash of fear through the soldier's eyes. The man had seen the Augarian battle, watched buildings crack open and blood rain from the sky with the rest of them.

The soldier's eyes scanned the new group suspiciously before he addressed the soldiers who had run to join the commotion. "Search them for weapons. Special attention there." He pointed at the three men Palmer didn't recognize. The soldiers had forced the men to their knees as the first soldier looked back at Palmer, face hard. "You *will* be held responsible for any trouble they cause."

Palmer nodded and looked back at Egidio and the others as the soldiers searched them. Slowly, the realization that he was being left with five people—four of whom he'd never met, including one who was potentially dangerous—set in. He reached for his powers on instinct, attempting to gather any information about them he could get. All that came through the haze was a deep, gnawing hunger. Palmer could hope that full stomachs would fend off any other outbursts from the group, especially from the two largest men the soldiers were only now letting up off their knees. Egidio had never been the aggressive type, and because

9

both the smaller man and the woman were even shorter than Palmer, he didn't consider them much of a threat. The large, surly-looking men, however...

"Palm?" Egidio's voice broke into Palmer's survey of the group. "What are you doing here?"

Palmer looked back at his old friend and realized Egidio was studying him as closely as Palmer had been the others. Palmer ran his hands over his velvet-lined coat, suddenly aware how unreasonably well-off he looked compared to the group standing in ripped, threadbare clothing. The woman—she couldn't have been older than Palmer—didn't even have a blanket over her thin smock, let alone a proper gown or coat to guard against the cold.

"Why don't we go inside?" Palmer motioned, managing to keep his voice level enough to pretend the situation hadn't fazed him in the slightest. "We can talk where there's food and heat."

Brier pressed her lips into a thin line and stepped over what used to be part of the temple's front wall. Her breath caught as she took in what was left of the temple. Even living with the state of the palace day after day, she had been avoiding seeing the destruction she had leveled on the temple. That loss said something damning in a way the rest of the city couldn't. The previously grand vaulted dome had fallen in, revealing open sky above and marble scattered across splintered pews. If she hadn't known the rubble was marble, she would never have even guessed it was. The blood that had rained from the sky had stained the white a rusty brown. As she looked around at the carnage, she couldn't help feeling as if she should have stayed away.

She picked her way up what had once been the center aisle and found a pew that remained partially intact. She carefully pushed her skirts under her—fully aware the fabric would come away stained—and took a place on the dirty kneeler, clasping her hands in front of her.

But the action didn't offer any sort of comfort. Before everything that had happened, she'd gone to services regularly. Like everyone else, she'd learned—and never questioned—the Augarian pantheon, but she'd never felt called to a religious vocation. Now she wished she could find a shred of absolution in the kind of faith she'd witnessed in the Seers who truly believed they were serving the will of the gods. But then if the only "gods" were actually people like her, absolution would be a long time coming, no matter how fervently anyone believed. She couldn't save the souls of the pious any more than she could save her own.

"Not the place I'd expect to find you of all people."

Brier's eyes flew open. She twisted, looking at the man standing near what remained of the doorway.

"Don't you know it's dangerous wandering around this city alone?" He smiled at her. "Monsters running amok, by all accounts."

Recognition hit her hard, knocking the breath out of her. "Leo?" She pushed herself up off her knees. "Leone Adessi?"

"Hi, Chas." He held out his arms.

She moved back down the aisle and hugged him, willing to overlook the less-than-loved nickname. Pulling back, she searched his face, which was slightly thinner but remarkably similar to his cousin Nico's. "What are you doing here?"

"I came in with the supply wagons." Leone motioned behind himself with his thumb. "I was staying out with my uncle at his vineyard... my mother's brother, of course. Not Nico's fath—"

"Of course," Brier cut off the clarification.

"And that lot was finally getting tired of me," Leone continued, not seeming bothered in the slightest by her interruption. "So I figured, rather than go find another relative to bother, I'd see what had happened here. You know, they're saying that the dead walk and monsters live in the Red City now."

Brier frowned. The words sounded oddly familiar, as if she'd heard them before, inside her own head. "The Red City?"

"Blood apparently rains from the sky"—he smiled as though it were all a joke. He had the luxury of believing it was—"and has painted the city red to show its corruption. I was rather disappointed to see things really just look a little rusty. They make it sound like it's a crimson horror from the talk out in the countryside."

Brier looked out past Leone's head at the red-brown tint the dried blood had left over the destroyed city. How Leone could sound so unconcerned while standing in the middle of the formerly grand, vibrant city that was now primarily inhabited by ghosts, Brier couldn't fathom. But then, it had been that way before—Nico and all of his friends sitting around, entirely indifferent to anything they didn't find entertaining. Apparently, without visible monsters in the street, the shell left of the old Augarian wasn't amusing enough to merit interest. She forced what she hoped was a pleasant smile. "You said the supply wagons were here?"

"A whole line of them. Though I'm not sure even they have enough with them, looking at this place." He glanced at the piazza. When he turned back to Brier, his easy demeanor had dimmed slightly. Some sort of emotion was caught behind the carefree smile. "I'm sorry that after making it all the way back here, you have to live like this."

Brier furrowed her eyebrows questioningly.

"I heard you'd been found, in one of the letters I got out at my uncle's. About how you'd been rescued from kidnappers?"

Brier didn't bother to confirm or deny it, not sure what account Leone had heard about her months-long journey from Ruhegipfel, where she'd been trained, back to Latysia.

"I was glad to hear it, Chas. We were all worried about you. Nico went just about mad after you disappeared, thinking you were dead."

Brier's jaw tensed. She did her best to hide it. "He seemed sane enough when I returned."

Leone shrugged. "You know my cousin. He can turn his affectations on and off as it suits him most days."

Brier nodded, trying to think of a response.

"But no," Leone continued before she could. "He went out into Latysia not long after you were kidnapped and didn't come back for days. Was gone long enough that people were starting to worry he'd... you know." Leone dragged his thumb along his throat as if he were cutting it. "I still have no clue where he went. As far as I know, no one does."

Brier swallowed. "He never said where he went?"

Leone shook his head. "Came back nearly a week later and acted like he had no idea what any of us were talking about when we asked about it. Though, you know him..."

She did, better than most. And there was no getting Nico to talk

12

about something he didn't want to. Brier forced a tight smile, reticent to dwell on those thoughts. "Do you know how many wagons there are? We've been running low on just about everything for days now."

"Half a dozen, maybe? I only joined them just outside the city, so I haven't been around long. Had to pay them far more than I should have to get them to let me in." Leone looked back at the piazza. He released a breath, shaking his head for a moment before he turned back to Brier. "They really did a number on this place, didn't they?"

They. It sounded so refreshing. So much less accusing than "you." *Didn't you?* She looked back at him and offered something much more like a real smile this time. She slid her arm into the crook of his and interlocked them with one another the way she had when they were younger. "Come on. Let's see if we can find that cousin of yours."

Leone let her lead without comment. "We were nearly mugged coming through town, you know. Latysia's all but deserted. Nothing but street gangs and feral dogs as far as I could tell."

Brier swallowed and felt her chest tighten. The destruction inside the Augarian was bad enough. She tried not to think of just how low once-bustling Latysia had fallen. "Most people left for the country, I'm told. The ones who could afford to when you did. The one who couldn't... well, they went when there wasn't anything left."

Leone nodded, looking around. "I'm surprised Nico's let you stay here."

Brier blinked. "Let me?"

"It would have to be safer sending you off to the country, as well. I know I wouldn't want my fiancée wandering around with the city like this."

Brier frowned, unsure how to answer.

Leone didn't seem to register her hesitation. He looked around the hallway as they stepped through the north door. In better shape than the halls on the south side of the palace, the hallway had panes missing out of the windows and long cracks running through beautifully painted walls. Brier could only imagine what Leone was making of it. In true Adessi form, his face didn't show a thing.

Something crashed. The sound of metal hitting tile echoed up a stairwell.

Leone glanced at the doorway. "Kitchen staff still clumsy?"

"There is no kitchen staff." Stomach tightening with a fresh wave of apprehension, Brier detoured and headed down the side staircase to one of the narrower halls that ran under the main palace. She ducked through another short archway and stopped dead at the sight of the large, unfamiliar man standing behind a counter. Pressure started behind her eyes. Her sight went fuzzy, but a hand on her wrist snapped her back to reality. She glanced down at Leone's hand and stiffened her arms to stop him from pulling her back.

"Chas." He tightened his hold on her.

She looked back at the stranger. "Who are you?"

The tall man looked up from tearing apart a stale loaf of bread and ran his eyes over her. He smirked. "Who do you want me to be, *principessa*?"

"Brier," Leone hissed.

Palmer appeared from behind a counter, followed by four more unfamiliar bodies in rags. Brier's eyes locked onto Palmer, their connection flaring to life as she projected her voice into his mind. *What in the name of all that is holy is—*

"Brier," Palmer said, looking flustered. He pointed to one of the shorter men standing to his left. "Do you know Egidio? He was at your birthday party last summer?"

Brier glanced at the dark-haired man's thin face and had to wonder about Palmer's sanity. The man standing next to Palmer was just as filthy as the first, and his bruises and dingy, ripped clothes told Brier he'd been in more than his share of brawls. No one like that would have made it to the door of an Adessi-funded party, much less have spoken to her. *Palmer—*

"We lived at the temple together," Palmer continued. "And these are his... friends."

Leone leaned closer to her, dropping his voice. "Brier, you should go upstairs."

"I'll handle it." She held up a hand. If one more person tried to tell her what she should do...

Leone recoiled slightly, as if she'd tried to strike him. She couldn't blame him. She'd never used that tone of voice with him, let alone

14

snapped when he was just trying to make sure she didn't get hurt. He didn't know everything that had happened.

"Where'd he come from?" Palmer asked, coming up behind her.

Brier looked at him, frowning at the expression Palmer was giving Leone. "Him? What about them?"

"Brier," Leone said, jaw tense, "go upstairs."

She clenched her fists.

"Does this concern you?" Palmer answered him before Brier could.

"More than you can imagine." Leone looked back to Brier. "Who is this?"

Something metal hit the tile floor as two of the men in the kitchen fought over what little food was left in the kitchen. The headache at the base of Brier's skull built. She tried to fight the noise. Whispers in her mind mixed with the angry voices all around her, turning into a deafening cacophony. The whispers cut off just as Palmer snapped something at Leone.

Brier didn't try to follow what had been said behind the unholy noise. Taking a deep breath, she forced her powers back and cut Palmer off mid-sentence. "Get those people out of here. We don't have enough supplies as it is."

Palmer hesitated for a split second as if thrown off before turning back to her. "Are you making *him* leave then?"

"He's not some street rat," Brier said, quietly enough not to be heard over the full-fledged fight in the kitchen.

"Neither's Egidio."

"He's certainly destroying our kitchens like one." Leone sneered at the group. "If that's the company *you* keep—"

"Leo, stop." Brier fought to keep her voice passive.

Leone kept on. "I don't know who you think you are—"

"Leo—"

Glass hit the floor. Brier jumped, her hand flinching open as the voices in the kitchen rose. A low rumble started under their feet as her energy spiked.

Bri. Palmer grabbed her wrist, tightening his grip to the point of near pain.

Brier jerked away from him, but his intervention had been enough to head off whatever wave of energy she'd unwittingly started. The rush of everything wouldn't let her calm down enough to thank him. "Get those people out before something happens." She turned away, grabbing Leone's shirtsleeve to make sure he didn't stay behind—not certain if she was cautioning Palmer about the strangers or herself.

CHAPTER THREE

Palmer's jaw refused to unlock as the last of Brier's skirts disappeared up the stairs, trailing the new Adessi. Things couldn't possibly have gone well with Brier showing up before Palmer had figured out what he was thinking himself, but her showing up with yet another Adessi in tow had made the situation much worse.

"Ask Signore *Duca*." The deep voice pulled Palmer out of his thoughts.

He turned to see the largest man rip a bottle of wine from between two other men. Palmer stared them down until they stepped away from each other. From the looks of the cabinet doors hanging open or off their hinges, to the scattered pots, the man hadn't stopped the fight soon enough.

"Palm." Egidio stepped forward cautiously, his eyes darting around as if he expected an attack, making him look more like a mouse. "Is everything all right?"

"Fine," Palmer lied, scanning the rest of the group. The two other men had begun jostling for the wine—though not as violently as before—while the woman had chosen a place in a corner, where she was alternating scratching at her arm and picking at the stale loaf of bread Palmer had given them. None seemed to be an immediate threat. He looked back at Egidio. "Did he just call me a duke?"

"Well..." Egidio glanced down at Palmer's clothes.

"I didn't have anything to wear," Palmer said defensively.

"And you're friends with..." Egidio looked at the empty hall.

"That's a long story." Palmer shifted his weight, trying not to think too hard about the situation.

Egidio had never been particularly wealthy, especially when compared to the bulk of the families that sent their sons to study at the temple and university in the Augarian. That was likely why he and Palmer had become friends in the first place. But as the son of a moderately successful merchant, Egidio had outdone parentless Ward of the Church Palmer by far. Egidio should have left Latysia months ago, long before the city fell. How he'd ended up in rags while Palmer was living in the Augarian palace dressed in clothing that cost more than many men made in a year, Palmer wasn't sure he wanted to know.

He cleared his throat. "There are usable rooms in the old temple dormitories, if you all needed a place to stay."

"*Principessa* told you to throw out the riffraff?" The largest man watched Palmer closely, eyes challenging.

"Just a little crowded in here with the soldiers," Palmer said, hoping the veiled threat would be enough to get the man moving without actually having to call in any of Gully's men. If he could keep Brier separated from the group long enough for him to figure out what had happened to Egidio, maybe he'd actually be able to make some sort of plan. Rash decisions had never turned out as well for him as they seemed to for other people. He only hoped Egidio's choice in companions was more trustworthy than his instincts said they were.

Palmer and Egidio had never been especially talkative. For as long as they had been friends—ever since Egidio had visited Latysia to train as an acolyte six years ago—Palmer could count the number of their long discussions on one hand. As he got the group settled into one of the generally intact brick rooms in the old dormitories across the piazza from the palace, however, even their usual short talks were missing. The awkwardness and mistrust hanging in the air seemed to keep most of them silent. By the time Palmer had them settled enough that it didn't seem they would have a problem for the rest of the afternoon, he hadn't learned much more than the others' names. The apparent leader, Jacopo, and equally intimidating Bruno were both at least half a foot taller than Palmer, with shoulders that were twice as wide. Brother and sister, Tomer and Peony, were much shorter and younger than thirty-something-looking Jacopo and Bruno, and the siblings weren't as surly as the big men. In fact, Peony acted terrified of just about everything. Her brown eyes remained wide enough that they seemed to take up half of her dirty tan face, and Palmer didn't think she'd uncrossed her bony arms since they had left the kitchens.

Palmer offered a smile, but the expression only made her blink with surprise. He turned back to the rest of the group. "Feel free to take any of the blankets or robes or whatever around." Without any rebuilding happening in the dormitories, Palmer imagined the space hadn't been entirely picked over yet. He tried to think if there was anything else to say, but the men had already stopped paying attention as they circled the room, so Palmer just excused himself.

Peony continued to watch him. Egidio rocked forward as though he intended to follow, but something seemed to hold him back. Chalking it up to one more thing he wasn't sure he wanted to know, Palmer decided not to waste his time trying to understand the wedge that had forced him and Egidio apart. He turned for the piazza. An argument awaited him in the palace—and he doubted Brier would remain silent about Egidio's group remaining in the Augarian.

You get to keep your friends. Why don't I get mine? he grumbled in his head, then sent a quick prayer he hadn't sent that to Brier. He'd certainly managed to contact her over farther distances before. Of course, that had been when their powers had been working and they hadn't been arguing half the time.

Maybe we *should leave Latysia,* he thought, not for the first time. But if he suggested that, he would have to answer the obvious question: *And go where?* He'd yet to work out any sort of answer to that.

Palmer pulled off his coat as he crossed the threshold into the palace, even if it wasn't any warmer inside the roofless grand hall than out. His body barely registered the cold as he forced his powers to attempt to find Brier.

"Signore?"

The voice distracted him before he could pinpoint her. Palmer blinked to clear his vision, looking at one of the workmen who had remained to help rebuild after most had gone home for spring planting.

"We found these under a wall of the old library." He held out two thin books. Their covers were blackened with soot but in otherwise-remarkable condition for having survived on the side of the palace that had burned. Palmer had assumed any books they hadn't already recovered had long since turned to ash in the pit that had once been the original Augarian library. The workman watched him expectantly. "They said you were buying books?"

"Oh." Palmer shook off his thoughts and went for his purse. Simply *having* a purse still felt slightly foreign. Still, it was better to use some of the gold that had been recovered in the rubble to pay the workers for things that shouldn't leave the Augarian than to have them slip out to the black market in Latysia. And the workers honestly deserved it more than the rest of them sitting around day after day. He pulled out a couple of coins and offered them in exchange for the books. "Thank you."

The worker smiled, pleased with his windfall for the day, before heading back off to wherever Gully had him stationed.

Palmer watched the man go and released a breath. Maybe the books would at least head off the worst of the argument ahead. Brier always seemed most like her old self when she was working in the new library they had put together for her. Or at least the "self" he'd known.

Pushing those thoughts out of his mind as best as he could, Palmer glanced inside the two books he'd bought. One seemed to be a religious text he vaguely remembered having read in one of his classes at the temple. The other looked much older, something from the old ancient-studies shelves, maybe. More out of hope than anything, he turned for the little library, even as the faint buzz of energy told him exactly where Brier had gone. No, he wouldn't be lucky enough to find Brier in the one place they could have had a rational conversation. He would have to try to get her away from two Adessis.

Brier settled down in the room Nico had claimed for himself on the mostly standing side of the palace. She took a sip of the brandy Leone had brought with him from his uncle's, then smiled as the warmth rushed through her. She'd forgotten how good it felt to not worry about anything. Perhaps that had been her mistake. Liquor had always made things around the palace endlessly more enjoyable. It likely would have made sitting around the countryside in the middle of winter while they were walking miles back to Latysia more fun, as well.

"It's absurd." Leone motioned widely from where he was sitting in a chair across the room. "I mean, there are Seers running normal services, of course, but these doomsday cults? You've never heard the crazy things they're spewing."

"You have?" Nico poured himself another glass from the bottle on the nightstand.

"Well…" Leone shifted in his seat. "One of my cousins, Bianca, she ran away to one—had her convinced the world was ending. She was quoting this deranged former Seer even when her father dragged her back home from whatever little camp she'd been living in out in the middle of the countryside."

"And you think I should go out to the countryside with all these doomsday prophets about?" Brier blinked, trying to keep her eyes focused.

Leone waved away the point. "We wouldn't be going near any of those. There are plenty of people *not* preparing for the end of the world. You two could make it a proper wedding tour, if you wanted."

Brier stiffened, but Nico just leaned back against the headboard next to her and gave an easy, "Maybe."

She finished off the rest of her glass as tension worked its way back through her shoulders. Whether Nico was keeping up appearances in front of his cousin or had decided to let their argument go, Brier didn't know. Either way, that would be the end of that fight. At least until the next time everything bubbled up again. Nico Adessi didn't apologize, but at least he never expected her to, either. Nothing was ever too big to hope it couldn't just be ignored forever, after all.

The rest of the brandy hit Brier's head, and her vision blurred for a second, making the world black then cloudy. She squeezed her eyes shut and only opened them again when the room in front of her was back in focus.

"You all right, Chas?" Leone asked.

She managed a smile. "Fine. Just some good stuff you brought."

Leone smiled back, and his answer got lost under a faint buzz of energy in her ears. A second later, she recognized the feeling of Palmer getting closer. "Great," she murmured as he knocked.

Leone cut off midsentence as he looked at the door.

"I'll get it." Brier pushed herself off the bed, her legs barely catching her as she stood. She giggled, holding still as she regained her balance.

"Bri, sit down." Nico shifted toward her.

"I'm fine." She followed the wall to the door and managed to get it open as the world continued to shift.

Palmer frowned. "Hi..."

She waved weakly as she rested against the doorframe.

Palmer started to talk then made a face. He studied her quickly. "Have you been drinking?"

"Can't slip anything by you." She pushed a strand of hair out of her face, unable to stop the sarcasm dripping from her voice as reality fought its way through her pleasant drunken haze.

Palmer frowned and glanced into the room behind her. "Could we talk for a minute?"

His tone told her everything. She paused, her hand still by her head. "You didn't make them leave."

"Brier—"

"I can't do this right now."

"Bri—"

"Palmer." Her voice turned a little too shrill as she fought to hold on to the loose, relaxed feeling. "I'm actually having a good time for the first time in months. Could you just... let me right now?"

Nico moved to her side before Palmer could answer. "Problem?"

"It's fine." Brier closed her eyes as her relaxing night inched closer and closer to a full-fledged fight. "Just give me a second."

"Everything all right?" Leone's footsteps told her he'd moved behind her, as well.

"Fine," she said, gripping the edge of the door to swing it shut. "We'll 'talk for a minute' tomorrow, all right?"

Jaw going tight, Palmer held up something. "Would you like me to drop these off in the library at least?"

She blinked to force her eyes to focus again. As recognition hit, she straightened slightly from her slouch against the doorframe. "You found more books?"

"A worker did." He dropped his hand to his side again. "He brought them to me."

She reached out to take them, but her body tipped forward, and the motion swung the door with her. Palmer went to steady her, but Nico already had an arm around her waist, as if he had expected her to slip long before she had. Her arm went on top of his as a giggle escaped her mouth, coming from nowhere. She waited for the world to stop shifting. "I probably should sit down."

"Yeah, I said." Nico pulled her back against his hard chest. She blinked. The sensation of being held against him was oddly foreign but pleasant—she liked it a little too much.

Palmer searched her expression. "Are you all right?"

"She's been drunk before, Tash," Nico said. "I think we have it handled."

Palmer looked up over Brier's shoulder at Nico, giving her a chance to recover.

She shook her head to clear it and tried to track down what was off. Nico didn't affect her like that. Not just by grabbing her. Not when they'd been sneaking across the hall to each other's rooms since they were six. The world shifted, and she let it go. She needed more liquor and to go back to how she'd felt five minutes ago. Soul searching wasn't helping.

Whatever silent standoff the men were having passed, and Palmer motioned with the books. "I'll just put these in the library, then, I guess."

"Thanks," Brier managed as she started to shut the door again. "We'll talk tomorrow."

CHAPTER FOUR

ALMER RELEASED A DEEP BREATH, calming his mind, trying to force the tension to leave his body. Even if he didn't need sleep these days, the sessions—relaxations, meditations, whatever they should have been called—were nearly as good. But the tension wouldn't leave. Something, a grain of irritation, wormed its way into his mind and wouldn't leave him at peace. Unfortunately, he knew what that *something* was. What he'd seen earlier hadn't merely been Brier not being herself—if being with one Adessi had been doing that to her, he could only imagine what two would do—it had been the entire energy hovering around her. Something was wrong. He simply couldn't see what the problem was, even with it hovering just in front of him.

Giving up on his attempt to relax, he sent his mind back out to check on her. At least that he could do. Pain started behind his eyes, but he ignored it. After continuously checking on Brier and the five across the piazza all evening, he'd been pushing his powers more than he had in weeks. Apparently, his body wasn't enjoying it. He closed in on Nico's room, frowning when he came up empty. She'd fallen asleep there hours ago—or passed out, depending how much the Adessis had kept her drinking. The knot in his stomach he'd been ignoring all evening pulled tighter. *She must have finally woken up at some point and wandered off.* As uneasy as the entire situation had left him, Palmer couldn't believe Nico Adessi would actually have let anything happen to her. The man was an ass, but he had already risked his life to save her once. Palmer supposed he could at least respect that. He moved his focus, leaving Nico's room to check hers and then the library.

The vision hit him, bright, colored, clearer than any he'd seen in months. Fire. The library fireplace. Something dark leaning over it. A blurred shadow he couldn't quite make out. His feet were moving before he could think, taking him out of bed, into the hallway, and to the staircase.

Around the corner, on the ground floor, the library door gaped open in the darkness. Orange firelight flickered through the hole, mockingly welcoming. Still, Palmer slowed, approaching cautiously. He leaned to look past the threshold and froze.

The dark shape squatted, huddled by the fireplace. A thin book hung open, pages flapping as a small hand held it by the front cover. One of the brittle pages caught, and the fire worked its way up into the book. Tilting its head, the shape watched, seemingly uncaring as the fire crept closer and closer to its fingers. A face came into focus in the growing light.

"Brier!" Palmer found his voice as he rushed forward.

She looked at him, uncomprehending. He jerked her upright, and she stumbled. The fire caught the book's spine and licked her fingers. With a gasp, she dropped it.

"Gods—" Releasing his hold on her, Palmer reached for the poker. He flung the rest of the manuscript from the rug into the fireplace before it could set the rest of the library alight. He panted, stomping out the last few embers before he spun to face the woman behind him. He couldn't keep the panic from his voice. "What the hell was that?"

Brier's eyes flicked to him from where she rested, half supported by the couch. Her eyebrows furrowed. "When did we get here?"

"What?" Palmer frowned, his breathing slowly returning to normal.

She pushed herself to standing. Not fully able to catch herself with her own momentum, she stumbled forward then straightened again.

"Are you *still* drunk?"

"No." She shook her head, the movement seeming too loose. She paused, hands out to balance herself. Her face contorted as she considered it. "Maybe. Very possibly."

He moved closer to her, taking in her loose hair, rumpled clothes, and pale face. "What did you think you were doing?"

"I... fell asleep, I guess." She looked toward the doorway. "Not here, though. I was with Nico. Unless I went back...?" She paused, biting her lip as she tried to work it out. "Maybe I blacked out before I fell asleep? I don't normally—"

"You weren't sleeping." Palmer shook his head.

"I just woke up."

"You were sleepwalking then." He motioned back to the fire. "Trying to burn down the library while you were at it."

"What?" She followed his point. Her face blanched at the sight of the book. She started toward it as the paper crackled and the cover curled in the fire. "Oh!"

He caught her wrist before she could get too close. "Nothing we can do with that. Leave it."

"I would never..." She looked at him. "You know I would *never* do that."

As his hand began to tingle, he turned her palm up and looked at the angry red skin of her burned fingertips. He wrapped his fingers around them, letting the gold light heal the burn before she could flinch away. At least that power seemed to work fine. He would take what he could get for the moment.

Brier's mouth twitched as a low panic seemed to make her vibrate. He moved his hand to her back, trying to calm her as his own mind raced.

She finally looked back at him. "What book was it?"

Palmer couldn't say he had taken a good look at the cover while trying to get it back into the fireplace. He shook his head, opening his mouth just as he noticed the second book lying on the floor by the desk under the window, several pages curled under from the weight of the cover. He motioned with his chin, not quite trusting to release her again. "One of the ones I just brought in, it looks like."

Brier took a shaky breath. "I'm sorry. I don't know... I have no idea how..."

Palmer pulled her to his chest, and she let him hold her tightly as he tried just as hard as she was to sort out what had happened.

Brier stared out the window, her back to Palmer. She'd done her best to sleep, or at least to pretend to sleep, but as pale-blue light began to glow over the tall Augarian walls outside, the entire exercise seemed more and more futile.

She swallowed, listening to Palmer's slow but shallow breathing. Sitting against the headboard, he was fully awake, not even in one of his false-sleep meditations. She knew the difference—and he would know for her. She released a breath. "Are we going to keep pretending I'm asleep?"

"It's barely morning," he answered without so much as a pause to *pretend* he was surprised she'd spoken. "You could try to rest a little longer."

Still wrapped in her cocoon of blankets, she finally turned toward him. "I don't think either of us would have to be omniscient to know that isn't going to happen."

He opened his eyes and looked down at her. "Are you all right?"

"You should know the answer to that," she murmured, not expecting an answer. He didn't give one. She wet her lips. "Do you know what happened? Last night."

Palmer shook his head. "I've been trying to see something— anything—about it, but I keep coming up blank. You know how my visions have been."

She did. More than she ever wanted to, really. Even as she pushed him away, she could still feel him. They were two pieces of one whole, and maybe that was why she couldn't bring herself to face him half the time. She could try to pretend when she was alone—or with Nico. She couldn't with Palmer. Not when she saw her own thoughts reflected on his face.

"I'm sorry," she whispered.

"It wasn't your fault. You didn't know—"

"No, for everything." She forced herself to meet his dark eyes. "I don't mean to be awful to you."

His eyes slid away. "You haven't been."

"You're still a bad liar, Palmer Tash." She managed a smile before reality came closing back in on her. "What do we do, if we don't even know what's happening to me?"

Palmer pressed his lips together. "Do you remember anything about last night? Before... waking up?"

Brier swallowed as she replayed the evening in her mind—so many parts of it came up blank. Nico had still been annoyed but was pretending not to be. Leone had continued on blindly about leaving. She'd gotten drunk enough to start losing bits and pieces of their conversation. "I drank far too much—enough to black out, obviously—but that's nothing that hasn't happened a hundred times before. Not that I can remember."

The tingle at the back of her skull told her Palmer was trying to see what was in her mind. It quickly turned to pressure as something forced him out, and the pain began to form behind her eyes. She squeezed them shut. "Please don't."

The pressure retreated, even as the pain lingered. Whispers threatened in the corner of her mind.

Palmer's voice broke through them. "You don't remember anything else?"

"Don't you think I'd tell you if I did?"

"Sorry. Just checking."

She bit her tongue, trying to keep herself from saying anything in response as she pushed herself up to sitting. He didn't deserve to be snapped at after last night.

"Bri." He touched her shoulder and waited for her to look at him again. "We're in this together. No matter what happened, we'll figure it out. Both of us."

She rested the side of her head against her knees as she searched his face, taking in the kind of concern only Palmer seemed able to muster for others. Still, the strain of the past few months showed through the cracks. The uncertainty, hurt, and even anger were beginning to break him just as much as they had her. She started another apology. "I—"

"Would you look at the two of you." The voice cut through the room before she could finish. "Nearly sweet enough to make someone vomit, as always."

Palmer straightened. Brier's entire body tensed as her head snapped toward the blond woman suddenly standing by the window.

"Morning." Cerise gave a half salute, signature smirk in place. "Hope you don't mind, I let myself in."

With both the door and windows closed, Brier could only assume Cerise had passed straight through the wall. Though the woman was trouble—which perhaps was more than fitting for the human form of a trickster god—Cerise's specific set of powers only made her that much more of a concern. If Cerise's set of abilities had been more destructive, the woman might have brought down the rest of the Augarian just for the fun of it.

"What are you doing here?" Palmer stood, tucking in his loose shirt.

"I'm here solely to ruin your love life, don't you know?" The smirk grew as Cerise glanced at Brier.

Palmer shook his head, releasing a breath through his nose. "We have enough trouble around here without you right now, Cerise. Do you have a reason for coming? Or did you just get bored up north?"

"It can't be both?" Cerise finally straightened off the wall, looking exactly the same as she had the first time they had met her, eight months ago in Ruhegipfel. Remaining ageless was one of the benefits of being a shapeshifter, Brier supposed—while the rest of them grew thinner and thinner, Cerise could choose exactly how she wanted to look every day. And she always looked just a little too attractive for Brier's tastes. Looking between Brier's and Palmer's suspicious faces, Cerise smiled. "Goebel wanted to see how things were down here. I volunteered. You know, take the excuse to stretch the old wings and all."

Brier looked at Palmer.

"I'll handle it," he answered.

"Am I an 'it' now?" Cerise arched an eyebrow. "That's rather rude. I've always preferred 'she,' personally."

You're all right to find breakfast? Palmer kept his eyes on Brier.

The task was a better option than staying in the room with Cerise. The woman had the particular talent of finding a sore spot, any sore spot, and poking it until it bruised deep enough for everyone to see. And the gods knew Brier had more than enough sore spots. Brier gave a tight smile. "I'll go see if we have anything for breakfast."

"Oh, don't put yourself out for me." Cerise's smile didn't so much as falter.

Good luck. Brier sent a final glance at Palmer, moving for the doorway before she could give Cerise anything else to tease them about. Stepping out into the hallway, Brier released a breath and smoothed the wrinkles out of her dress before she turned for the kitchens. With any luck, she would have at least a few minutes to gather herself before anyone else found her. Maybe by then she would at least be able to pretend she really had things together.

Palmer watched the door close, taking a moment before he turned back to Cerise. At least with Brier out of the room, he wouldn't have to worry about reining in her emotions. No one knew what shape Brier's powers were in after whatever had happened the previous night, but he had no desire to see what lack of sleep and the ability to blast out walls might lead to with Cerise around.

"She's still having you fight her battles for her?" Cerise rested on the desk by the window. "You'd really think a woman who can demolish cities at will wouldn't need to hide behind a man."

"She had a hard night."

Cerise smirked. "Troubles in bed? I could give you some advice if you're having problems."

Palmer didn't bother dignifying that with a response. "Things aren't great here at the moment, but we're managing. If Goebel wants a report, you can tell him that."

"Is that supposed to be your way of dismissing me?"

"We have more than enough trouble here already without you, Cerise."

She snorted. "Just trying to ruin all my fun, Dad. And after I travelled hundreds of miles to see you."

Palmer shook his head, uncertain how he felt about being called "Dad" by a woman who looked older than him by closing in on a decade, but the quickest way to make the nickname stick with Cerise would undoubtedly be to comment one way or the other. "Easier for you than any of us. You can make yourself a swift next time rather than a raven and make it even quicker, I'm sure."

"A swift?" Cerise arched an eyebrow. "Sacrilege."

"It's still a bird."

"Then why don't you just change into a springhare?"

Palmer shook his head, not trying to follow what she meant. Knowing

Cerise, she didn't actually mean anything. "Anything else Goebel wanted you to do while you were down here? Or is that it?"

"You're no fun when you're doing this whole stern-father thing." Cerise rolled her eyes and straightened once again. "Where's Nicolas? Maybe he'll play with me."

Palmer frowned. "You mean Nico?"

"Unless there's another Nicolas around?"

Palmer debated correcting her. Considering Nico's perpetually bad mood, Palmer doubted Cerise getting Nico's name wrong would make any difference. Palmer still sighed. "It's actually short for Nicodemo." He knew based on what Brier switched to when her arguments with Nico turned ugly.

Cerise snorted. "That's a stupid name."

Palmer couldn't say he disagreed.

"I think I'll stick with Nicolas." Cerise smirked. "Mind pointing me his way?"

Palmer pointed out the door. Cerise would find someone to bother whether or not Palmer answered. At least he could deal with Nico being slightly more annoyed than normal, as little as the two of them truly dealt with each other anyway. "Make a left at the end of the hall. His room's on the right."

"Thanks, Dad." Cerise flashed Palmer a smile and moved for the doorway.

He didn't bother answering. The sooner Cerise let him be, the sooner Palmer could get back to what was important around the Augarian. For the moment, that was getting Brier and Egidio together long enough to convince her to not lose her temper about him staying.

CHAPTER FIVE

B RIER BRUSHED HER HANDS ON her thick skirts, eyeing the fire on the hearth warily. Beyond the cost, it was no mystery why the workers who'd run the kitchen had worn simple clothing. Standing so close to open flame in the full-skirted Augarian dresses left Brier feeling as though she were always three seconds away from being kindling. One misplaced ember, and she would go up. The thought tempted her to try to find the simple homespun skirt she had been given in Lantello—even if Nico seemed apoplectic anytime she began to slide toward the person she had been anywhere but the Augarian. After last night, though… if she couldn't find a way to stop whatever was happening to her, even Nico wouldn't be able to pretend everything was all right.

"I certainly can't," Brier mumbled.

"What?" The voice made Brier start. She realized she'd been wringing her hands and dropped both to her side as she turned. Rosette stood on her toes by the counter, looking more interested in what was inside the bowl on the long preparation table than Brier's mumbling.

"Where have you been hiding, *piccola*?" Brier kept her voice light, as if nothing had happened.

"What are you making?"

Brier smiled. Rosette's easy exuberance made the air somehow lighter. She turned back to stoke the coals. Carefully. "It's just porridge again. Gully's men sent in a few raisins, though."

"They have better things than that." Rosette's frown came through her voice.

"Well, it's what we have for now." Brier's smile faltered as she moved a pot over the coals.

She recalled Gully's explanation in assigning rations. *"I've said, Miss Chaos, it's dangerous to leave a soldier sitting with nothing to do and an empty stomach."*

"You don't think you could send some home?"

"I was under the impression you weren't ready to fight another army yourself?"

She wasn't able to argue with that. If she had it her way, she wouldn't have to be within a hundred leagues of a battle again for the rest of her life. Unfortunately, she couldn't imagine much of the world leaving her alone for the rest of her life.

Finally, her mind registered that Rosette hadn't answered. Checking over her shoulder, Brier found herself alone once again. She shook her head. At Rosette's age, she'd learned the palace inside and out—ducking away through passageways before people could blink and sometimes showing Nico if she felt like it. Rosette seemed to be following in Brier's footsteps.

The pressure returned, and Brier's vision blurred.

Have them... followers? You think...

She caught herself on the counter and leaned forward as she squeezed her eyes shut, trying to force the voices out. They fought her.

...write. He's... those stubborn doubts.

"Brier?"

Someone touched her shoulder, and the voices snapped away.

"Brier?"

The kitchen came back into focus. Panting, Brier gripped the counter. She swallowed and looked at Palmer.

He stood next to her, his tan face worried. "Are you all right?"

Doubting her voice, she nodded.

Palmer started to speak then stepped closer and touched her back lightly as he dropped his voice. "Are you hearing things again?"

She released a shaky breath then noticed the two other sets of eyes watching her from the doorway. She stiffened, and Palmer's hand gripped her slightly, as if he were suddenly worried what she would do.

"I wanted you to meet Egidio again," he said in a rush.

Now? Her mind still wavered in and out even as her eyes settled on the short, dark-complexioned woman standing with her arms crossed as if she were trying to shrink into herself.

Are you sure you're all right? Palmer's voice filtered through to her, oddly muffled.

She nudged him off her as she pulled herself back to her full height, keeping her eyes on the woman. A sarcastic edge soaked in as she spoke. "All of you used to be acolytes, of course?"

"This is Peony." Egidio pointed, face pinched as he looked between Brier and Palmer as though waiting for some hint about what to do.

"She doesn't have anything to wear but that," Palmer said. "I thought you're about the same size..."

She shot him an incredulous look.

He faltered. "It's cold out..."

"I can go back upstairs," Peony said, her voice sounding naturally deeper but unnaturally airy, as if she could barely manage speaking above a whisper.

"It's fine," Palmer said.

The hell it is. Brier clamped a protective grip on the skirts she had just been cursing. *You want me to just give her one of my dresses?*

You... have plenty.

"You want to go find Nico to dress your friend too?" she hissed.

Palmer held up his hands in surrender. "We'll find something, but I wanted you to meet Egidio without everything else happening like yesterday. *He* was an acolyte. And Peony lived in Latysia. Her parents owned an inn, actually."

"Lovely." Brier kept her eyes on Palmer, trying to drill into him the absurdity of what he was doing with just that look.

"I knew your father. A bit." Egidio took an unsure step forward. "From when I'd go to the library, Signorina Chastain-Bochard."

Hearing her full name, including the second title she'd grown up with while her father was the head librarian—the name that had fallen entirely out of use when no one was left in the Augarian to need a title or care—released some of the tension building in the center of Brier's chest. She turned her gaze to the mousy-looking man, sizing him up as best she could under the rags and grime.

"He seemed like a good man, from when I spoke to him," Egidio continued, sounding uncertain. "I'm sorry to hear of his passing."

A fresh stab of sorrow tore through her. She forced it as far back into her mind as it would go. Swallowing the lump forming in her throat, she fought for a response but came up empty as everything in her seemed to shift once again. She turned to Palmer, pulling her shoulders back, though the posture seemed flimsy without the indignation holding her upright. "You can explain them to Gully and the others if you want them to stay. I take it their friends are still somewhere?"

"In the old temple dormitories," Palmer said. "They were still asleep."

Brier pressed her lips together and turned back to breakfast. *I'd have some of Gully's men watch them.*

Palmer nodded, though Brier had the sneaking suspicion he wasn't actually agreeing.

"I could help with that," Peony said out of nowhere, still just barely above a whisper. She motioned to the table with an awkward nod. "I learned how to cook at—"

"I have it."

"You're..." Palmer wisely trailed off without demeaning Brier's cooking skills.

Get them out of here now, and I'll consider finding her a coat or something. Brier held his eyes.

That nod was agreement. Palmer moved back toward the door, and Brier turned her back as the group wandered away. She'd just apologized for how she'd been acting less than an hour ago. If only things would stop happening for a minute and let her catch up, then maybe—

"Why are you mad at Palmer?"

Brier started, uncertain when Rosette had reappeared. She covered her surprise with a tense smile. "I'm not."

"You're angry."

Brier supposed Rosette would know. No use lying to a little girl who could force anger on people. "It's just adult things, *piccola*. Nothing to worry about."

Rosette pursed her lips unhappily but didn't argue. She held out her hands. "Can we have this?"

Brier peered down at what looked suspiciously like cured meat. Her stomach growled just at the thought of it. She dragged her eyes up again and scrunched her nose. "And where did you get that?"

Rosette blinked innocently. "I found it."

"Found it where?"

Rosette shrugged.

Brier gave the girl a stern look but couldn't turn away the thought of meat after so long. She nodded at the counter. "Put it there."

A wide smile broke out on Rosette's face, and she scrambled up to the counter.

After putting the half-made porridge into the hearth, Brier pulled out a knife and turned to the meat—vaguely wondering if she should try to hide what knives they had, because of the new men in the Augarian. She cut a thin slice and turned to Rosette. "You know stealing is wrong."

Rosette dropped her eyes to the red tile floor.

Brier ripped the slice apart and offered half to the girl. "Don't be greedy, and make sure the soldiers don't catch you."

Rosette looked up with a bright smile. The meat became a blur between Brier's hand and Rosette's mouth as the girl snatched it.

"Go on upstairs." Brier nodded to the door then popped the other half of the slice into her mouth. Though a bit too salty, the meat tasted heavenly, and it fought away at least part of Brier's lingering headache. How she had missed meat. Placing the cloth over her hand to protect it from the heat, she pulled the pot of porridge from the fireplace and brought it to the counter. Senora Terzi had done her best to teach Brier how to run a kitchen in Lantello, but those few months couldn't counteract the eighteen years Brier had spent never thinking about the Augarian kitchen staff, let alone doing any actual cooking. She set the cloth beside the pot and took a step back. Brier doubted she would have been able to direct a kitchen properly if she had gone off to the country as the mistress of some villa. Her father had taught her to read before she could walk, but other than that, no one had ever cared that she'd been entirely useless.

She stole another small slice of meat before wrapping the rest and hiding it among a stack of pans. She intended to bring the slices up to share—with everyone, if she had to. She just wasn't going to chance the rest of it walking away before she could make things feel the least bit normal for a day or two.

CHAPTER SIX

L ISTENING FOR APPROACHING FOOTSTEPS, ROSETTE worked her fingers into the seam in the wall to find the grooves then gave it a short tug. It creaked open just enough for her to slide inside. She smiled and started down the dark hallway. Many of the old tunnels and passageways she had found around the palace were still blocked with rubble, but this one, she knew well enough. Opening up above what Brier had called a throne room, the tunnel was the only way to get to the little alcove Rosette had set up and filled with all the things she'd found and decided to keep.

She dug into her pockets and pulled out the smooth piece of red glass she had picked up from a room the workers had just cleared. Placing it next to the other colored glass she'd collected, she watched it glint in the sunlight. The red swath on the floor mixed to purple near her shard of blue glass then a muddy yellow-brown next to the green stone she had found—well, taken. Pursing her lips, she shifted the ring away so the red stayed red and the green remained green. Satisfied, with her rainbow back in place, she sat against the wall and picked up the porcelain doll Brier had given her. Brier had been upset ever since all the new people had arrived last week, but she'd gone through her old things to find another dress for the other woman to use—and that meant more old toys for Rosette.

Unlike the blond doll Rosette already had tucked away, the new one had dark hair curled into tight ringlets around the doll's pale face. The hair was perfect other than being a little flattened on one side, and the new doll seemed to have been lost long before the blond doll was.

Rosette placed them side by side in their little cove so they could be friends. Sitting up in the alcove day after day with no one else to play with was lonely.

The door squeaked downstairs. Rosette frowned, listening to the single set of footsteps. They hadn't done any work on the room since putting up planks weeks ago so the builders could fix the walls. Since then, Rosette hadn't seen anyone else in there. Scooting toward the edge, Rosette peeked through the bars of the banister. The new person Brier liked, Leone, moved inside, checking around before he looked back at the paper in his hands. Rosette's face scrunched up—the worry coming off the man hit her like a wave. Whatever that paper said, it was bothering him. Rosette scooted a little forward and squinted at the paper, knowing it wouldn't help. For all of Brier's efforts, letters looked like nothing more than squiggles to Rosette—squiggles that all jumbled together just to be confusing.

Lowering the paper an inch, Leone released a long breath, his jaw clenching and unclenching, before he ripped the letter down the middle. After a few more tears, he stuffed the pieces into his jacket pocket and turned for the door.

Rosette considered sending some energy out at him, just enough to make him a little sick, so she could catch up and get the paper from him. But then Brier or Palmer would find out, and she would get in trouble. Again.

Pouting, she moved back to her little corner and looked at the pair of dolls. "You both be good and stay here."

The dolls looked back at her with their painted eyes as she returned to the banister and pulled her skirt out of the way so she could climb down the planks rather than going through the tunnel.

The ball hit the ground then the wall before popping back to Nico's hand before he threw it again.

Brier lifted her eyes from the book in her lap. The rhythmic thuds were beginning to rattle in her mind. She never should have pulled the thing out with the other toys she'd given Rosette. "Are you going to get bored of that?"

"Aren't we bored of everything?" He caught the ball, studying it.

"You could take something out of the library." She looked back down at her book. "I have everything catalogued." If she had another mental break and burnt something, she would at least have a proper record of it. It wasn't much consolation, but it was something. And for all the tension still hanging in the air, the group living across the piazza hadn't caused any incidents. Brier had even managed to keep her ire to a minimum when talking with Palmer about them. She supposed he deserved that much since he had allowed her to stay with him most nights to ward off any new episodes. Things did feel somewhat better after a proper night's sleep.

"You weren't in your room last night."

Brier hesitated, looking up to meet Nico's eyes. She had the odd feeling that he had caught what she was thinking. "What?"

"I stopped by." He began tossing the ball again. "You weren't there."

"Oh," she said, trying to think of a response that wouldn't lead to another fight. They'd been doing rather well with that over the past week, as if they'd found some sort of unspoken truce. "I was in the library until late."

"Weren't there, either." He didn't look at her.

Brier swallowed, knowing where the conversation was headed.

"Cerise said you were with Tash. That you've been sleeping there since at least when she first got here."

Of course, Cerise. Brier released a tense breath. The sooner that woman left for Ruhegipfel, the better. "You know how she likes to stir up trouble, Nic."

"So you haven't been?" He finally looked at her, the ball going still in his palm. "Staying with him?"

She opened her mouth but came up blank. Against a straight question, she couldn't lie to his face. Especially not when she didn't believe she'd done anything wrong.

He scoffed, letting the ball roll off to the side, where it disappeared under his dresser. "I don't think it's stirring up trouble when it's telling the truth."

"She tells selective truths to stir up trouble," Brier said. "That's what Cerise is best at."

"And what about that is selective, Bri?"

"Nothing's happened." The words came out of her mouth before she paused, unsure if she really needed to defend herself against the unspoken allegation. Gods knew how many women's beds Nico had been in since she'd met him, and who knew what she owed him in their mess of a relationship. For all the talk of weddings and engagements, it seemed less and less likely that anything would ever come of it. Their relationship had never truly had a title, and calling him *fiancé* certainly didn't feel right when they were already struggling to make it back to whatever they were as friends before.

"You're in his room every night for who knows how long, and you're saying nothing's happening?"

"You've slept in my room plenty of times without things happening."

"We obviously have different definitions of 'things happening.'"

Brier shut the book a little more roughly than necessary. "Well, Palmer's not you."

Nico actually laughed. "And what's that supposed to mean?"

"I doubt he was sneaking girls into his room at thirteen and getting ideas," Brier returned. "You were more forward with me six years ago than he's ever been."

Nico snorted, looking at the wall again.

"And, really, *you'd* hardly be anyone to judge me, even if something *had* happened." The words started falling out of her mouth as every grievance from the past decade and a half began to flow from the back of her mind. "Just because I wasn't there for it doesn't mean I didn't hear plenty about what you were up to around here. And I only got what Firth would tell me half the time, so I'm sure what I know is a fraction of it. There have been plenty of girls you've done more with than we ever did."

"So this is... what? Payback?"

Brier scoffed. "If I'd felt the need for that, do you really think I would have had to wait until now? Firth wasn't telling me those things because he thought you and I needed to discuss our relationship."

Nico started to speak then paused. "Firth, really?"

40

"Just because they weren't going to do anything in front of you doesn't mean I was entirely unpropositioned our entire lives. Though Firth was certainly the most forward with his interest among your friends."

Nico started another question then backtracked. "This isn't about Firth."

"Then what is it about?" She set the book aside and crossed her arms.

"Whatever's happening between you and Tash," he snapped. "I'm not enough of an idiot to not see there's something."

"You don't—"

"I swear if you say, 'You don't understand'—"

"You *don't*."

"I don't understand that you were off with this man for eight months and are still sneaking around with him?"

"I'm not—"

"Are you in love with him?"

The rest of Brier's sentence disappeared in the back of her throat. The bluntness of the question had caught her off guard. From the look on Nico's face, he wasn't any more comfortable having asked it than she was answering it. He actually looked as though he had surprised himself.

The door swung open, and a harried-looking Leone stood in the doorway. He blinked as if Brier's presence had thrown him for a second, before he said, "Sorry, I needed to talk to Nic."

Brier took a breath and forced a smile, trying to hide a little of the too-obvious tension in the air. "Could you just give us another min—"

"It's fine." Nico stood, looking at Leone. "We can talk in your room."

"Nic..." Brier tried.

Nico didn't turn around. After a quick glance at her, Leone followed, leaving Brier sitting alone in Nico's room. Pressing a fist to her mouth, Brier stopped herself from following too. It would do no good. He knew the rest of the conversation as well as she did. And if they had it, that would be the end of whatever fragile peace they'd found in their relationship. There would be no going back.

Her hands shook with the emotion from the fight she hadn't finished. And if Nico tried to pretend nothing had happened the next time she saw him, Brier's head might explode. Spotting the bottle sitting on Nico's dresser, she stood, grabbed it, and popped the stopper out of the neck.

The sharp smell of alcohol floated out, too inviting. At least Nico had left her a sufficient way to ignore the entire situation for the day if he was going to do the same. Not bothering with a glass, she took a long drink. The burn ran down her chest before the alcohol hit her brain, and then the tension began to slowly melt away. She took a seat at the end of the bed. The end of the bed in a room that was certainly not Nico's. Not the room she had known, back when she and Nico had run back and forth across the halls, ducking into each other's rooms just because they could. When everything had been a childish game.

Taking the bottle with her, she moved out into the hallway to find somewhere less depressing to get drunk.

CHAPTER SEVEN

P ALMER TAPPED HIS THUMB ON the desk, doing his best to focus on the book in front of him. The candle flickered dangerously low to the holder. He pressed his lips together. Maybe Brier had fallen asleep in her own room. Or in the library. She had done that once or twice. All the possible reasons for her absence didn't make Palmer feel much better. He sent his mind out, searching her usual haunts. The blankness he found did nothing to lessen his unease.

He shut the book and pushed it away. After blowing out the candle, he waited for his eyes to adjust to the moonlight then stood. If he couldn't relax in his room, he could try to track down where Brier had gone.

Checking her room and the library proved his instincts right. And even Nico wasn't in his room. Palmer pressed his lips together, debating where to try next. He heard wings settle above him and turned to spot the raven sitting on a piece of masonry. Despite being unable to see its unnaturally black irises, which Cerise couldn't change between her forms, he already knew it was her. "Have you seen Brier?"

The raven cocked its head to the side. Palmer waited, crossing his arms. With a caw, it rose and changed before reaching the ground. Cerise's feet hit the marble lightly. She looked down at Palmer, seeming taller than normal. "Girlfriend ran off?"

"I'm just looking for her," Palmer said, clipping the words short.

Cerise gave an unhappy shrug. "I haven't seen her for a few hours. Not since she yelled at me for 'interfering' with your little love triangle."

Palmer furrowed his eyebrows.

"Oh, I'm on your side, Kos," Cerise said, using the nickname she'd surprisingly avoided so far. "I just told her it was doing her no good trying to hold on to both you and Nicolas. Not in so many words, but more or less. Drunk as she was, though, not sure it landed."

Palmer's stomach dropped out. "She was drunk?"

"Smelled like she'd fallen into a tankard. I'm a little shocked she was still standing."

Palmer swallowed, trying to come up with something, anything, about where she might have gone. He couldn't even find an energy signature. "Do you know which way she went?"

"Not sure it would matter if I did at this point. This was two, three hours ago."

Palmer started back toward Brier's room as though it would hold some clue to where she was.

"She's a big girl, Kos. I'm sure she can handle sleeping it off," Cerise called after him.

"I wouldn't be so sure of that." He turned the corner without breaking his stride.

The clouds shifted around Brier's feet as soft light made its way through the darkness. She blinked, her head feeling too heavy as she tried to take it all in. How she had gotten there, she didn't know. Somehow, that didn't seem to matter. All of it made an odd sort of sense, walking on clouds. She looked down, studying the fog. Wisps of near nothing, the shifting ground still remained solid, strong enough to hold her as she moved forward. She lifted her eyes. The world around her seemed dark, wrong, like nothing but black surrounding the path of glowing white wisps. She continued moving one foot in front of the other.

The clouds began to thin as the path in front of her grew smaller and smaller. Finally, she reached a single column rising in a spiral. A staircase. Brier looked behind her. The path she had just walked had disappeared into nothing. With no better options, she tried the first step. The cloud swirled, making her shift flutter around her ankles, but the step remained sturdy.

She started up, testing that each step held her weight completely before taking the next one. Higher and higher she climbed. The temperature dropped. Her skin prickled as a cool breeze brushed over her. She paused, making sure the stairs didn't blow away with it before continuing.

The spiral leveled out and faded into a stone path. She stepped out onto it, glad for something stronger than the wispy clouds under her feet. The first touch of stone, and the darkness around the path retreated slightly, just enough to show the ground with grass growing along either side. It seemed familiar and yet so different.

The sound of water reached her. Brier hesitated, suddenly finding herself on a bridge stretching over a river, its water inky in the dim light. Leaning out to look, she rested her hands on the stone walls. Before she could think, she was climbing up onto the edge, staring out into the rippling darkness. She shivered, her heart racing as the wind whipped her face.

Don't.

The voice made her freeze. Different from the others she'd been hearing for weeks, it echoed from deep inside her. A woman. Someone she knew. But how, she couldn't remember.

You don't want to do this.

Brier frowned, unsure what she wasn't supposed to do. Confused whether it was a thought, an order, or a memory, she just stood there, watching the dark water race under her, lost in the dream.

After finishing a lap of the occupied rooms, Palmer went up a floor. His chest constricted harder each minute he couldn't find her. Sure, his visions had been spotty and he couldn't always find her when she was sulking or had blocked him out, but it had never gone on this long. And she'd never been drunk.

Suddenly, a repulsive energy flickered in his mind. He didn't question it. Moving toward the feeling, he hurried down the hall and up a staircase toward the roof. As he neared the top, warning bells went off in his head. Danger. What, he didn't know, but he ran all the same, hurtling out the door and into the night.

Brier stood on the side of the newly constructed roof, a flat part that hadn't yet been shaped into points. Palmer froze. The moonlight caught her bare, pale skin, making her glow. Her loose hair, her only covering from the cold, fluttered around her back. He snapped out of his shock, nearly shouted, then stopped himself, afraid of startling her. She wasn't moving, but one good start could send her tumbling the four stories down to the piazza. She seemed to be sleepwalking again. He couldn't wake her until he had her off the ledge.

As quietly as possible, Palmer approached. At the last second, he grabbed her around the waist and pulled back. Snapping awake, Brier flailed, throwing them both off balance. She landed on top of him, hard. Palmer grunted but held her for another moment before the situation registered. He slid his hand from her bare waist and tried to straighten them out. He averted his eyes as much as he dared.

Brier looked around then seemed to notice her nakedness a beat behind him. A soft mewl of confusion escaped her before she pulled her knees to her chest, hiding herself behind her legs and cascade of hair. "Palmer?"

He started to speak then closed his mouth again, quickly unbuttoning his shirt. He held it out to her. "Here."

She took it without argument and pulled it on. After buttoning it fully, she stood and looked around. The shirt was only long enough to reach halfway down her thighs, but it at least offered some protection. Her voice shook. "Why are we on the roof?"

"I followed you. I don't know why you were here." He wrapped his arms around his chest. The cold aside, he felt too exposed without his shirt. He nodded toward the uncompleted wall. "I pulled you off the side of the roof."

Her cheeks blanched. She swallowed and turned back to him. "And... you don't happen to know where my clothes went, perchance?"

Heat rose in his cheeks, and he hoped she couldn't tell in the moonlight. He cleared his throat. "I didn't happen to pass them, sorry."

She looked at the edge of the roof, her body trembling. "Do you think anyone else saw me?"

"I... The rest of the palace is asleep, I think. No one else is out to see right now."

She nodded, wrapping her arms tightly across her middle as she shook.

"Come on." Palmer placed an arm around her shoulder, trying to shelter and guide her all at once. "Let's get you back inside."

Brier shuffled forward, dropping her arms to hold the shirt down to her legs as though she could wish it longer. They moved in silence until they'd left the stairwell.

Palmer cleared his throat. "Do you want me to take you to your room?"

"Yours is closer," she mumbled.

He nodded and ducked around the hall before sliding them into his room. Finally dropping his arm from her shoulder, he pulled the door closed behind them. "You don't know where your dress is?"

She shook her head, not meeting his eyes.

"Do you want me to get you one from your room?"

"Just..." She released a shaky breath. "Just stay with me right now?"

He nodded and motioned her toward the bed.

She sat down, a little stiffly, and waited for him to join her before she curled up, burrowing in between the blanket and his side. Her trembling worsened even though she'd left the cold.

It took Palmer a second to realize she was crying. "Oh... Bri..." He wrapped his arms around her. "It's all right. It's all right."

"What's wrong with me, Palmer?"

He held her tighter, rocking slightly back and forth. "I don't know, Bri, but we'll figure it out. I promise."

CHAPTER EIGHT

P ALMER'S ARM PRICKLED BY THE time morning broke. He still didn't move it from beneath Brier as she slept. She had cried herself out at some point during the night, drifting off into a—thankfully stationary—sleep. Palmer's mind raced, trying to piece together what had happened the night before. His jaw locked as he came up infuriatingly blank once again. Even trying to connect to Brier's thoughts, which used to happen purely by accident, was a struggle. With a last push against the odd, springy feeling just past her skull, Palmer had to admit defeat. He released a breath and stared at the ceiling.

"What were you doing?" Brier whispered, her voice nearly lost against his chest.

Palmer froze. He hadn't even felt her wake. Swallowing the lump in his throat, he shifted her just enough to get the feeling back to his arm. The light prickling turned sharp. He flexed his hand but otherwise ignored it. "I was trying to get into your head."

She took a moment before answering. "You couldn't?"

"There's something blocking me."

Brier tilted her chin up to face him. A soft murmur attempted to work its way into Palmer's head, but he couldn't make it out. He frowned. *Are you trying to say something?*

Brier looked at him another moment, then her forehead creased. "Can you not hear me?"

"I hear something but not words. More like... whispers."

Brier's mouth pressed into a thin line, her entire face reacting to the lost connection.

"We'll fix this," Palmer said, his voice more sure than he felt. "We just need to figure out what's wrong, and then we can fix it."

"Should we let Cerise get Goebel?"

Goebel would need a good week to make it to the city, even with Cerise's help, but if anyone would know what was happening to their powers, it was Goebel. He'd been the one who'd known how to train them in the first place. Palmer nodded. "I'll ask her to go after breakfast."

Silence settled back over them. Brier finally shifted up onto her elbow. His mostly buttoned shirt came into view as the blankets fell back. He did his best to ignore the rush of heat that shot through him. Sliding his eyes away, he pushed himself up to sitting. That sort of attention was the last thing Brier needed at the moment.

He looked at his dresser and debated getting up to put on another shirt himself, but he remained in place. He started his questioning gently. "Do you remember anything? From before you woke up on the roof?"

Brier took a moment before speaking. Her voice came out as barely a whisper. "Nico and I had another fight about something stupid. He stormed out, and I, stupidly, started drinking. I think I might have said something to Cerise at some point? I'm not sure. It all starts getting fuzzy at that point. Then, well, you were there for the rest of it."

Not much to go on. Nearly less than what Cerise had given him, though Palmer was relatively sure it was safe to assume the fight with Nico had led to Brier yelling at Cerise. Palmer sorted through it all for anything he might have missed, for anything that sparked any sort of vision, but he came up just as blank as before. He finally glanced at her again and moved to grab his spare shirt. "Would you like me to get you a dress? It might look a little odd if you have to go out..."

"Thank you," Brier murmured, pulling the blankets toward her chest once again as if she remembered what she was wearing. "I'm sorry for stealing your shirt."

"Nothing to be sorry for." He slipped on his other shirt and buttoned it quickly as he avoided her eyes. "You'll be all right while I'm gone?"

"I won't be drinking." She attempted a laugh that ended up more as a light groan, which she cut off sharply. "You won't be long?"

He nodded as he crossed the room to kiss her forehead quickly. "I'll be back as soon as I can."

She let him go, looking immeasurably small in the middle of his bed. The knot in his stomach resurfaced at the sight. He forced himself out the door and headed for Brier's room.

The room looked untouched, exactly as it should, as he entered, as if mocking him. He moved for the bureau, not letting the thought sit. His eyebrows rose as he swung open the door. The fuss Brier had made about finding something for Peony to wear obviously hadn't risen from lack of options. More fine, richly colored fabric filled the bureau than Palmer had ever touched in his life. Before coming up against Orris Adessi's more murderous tendencies, Brier certainly hadn't been suffering from the family's patronage.

Scanning the choices, Palmer picked out the smallest. He was well aware that Brier had been tying her dresses as tightly as possible over the past few months, to make up for the weight she'd lost on their trek back to Latysia. She hadn't regained much with only the meager rations they'd been receiving from the supply wagons. Even on the smallest dress, though, the folds of fabric had to weigh close to fifteen pounds. How Brier had ever managed to run in one of those things, as she had in the days around the battle, he had no clue.

The door to the room opened. "Brier?"

Palmer took a deep breath and shifted the dress so he could close the bureau. He gave a tight smile as his eyes met Nico Adessi's. "Sorry to disappoint."

Nico's face went hard all at once, his eyes taking everything in. "What are you doing here?"

Palmer glanced at the dress in his arms and motioned with it sarcastically. "Thought I might try wearing dresses for a change."

"All the best," Nico returned, his tone matching Palmer's. "Where is she?"

Folding the fabric as best he could to keep the skirt from dragging on the ground, Palmer moved toward the door. "Who?"

Nico blocked the way. "Who do you think?"

Palmer shook his head, shouldering past the taller man.

"Hey." Nico caught Palmer's upper arm. The contact sent a jolt through Palmer's mind. The image flared to life in the vacuum. Last night. Nico undoing the dress Brier had been wearing yesterday as she flickered in and out of focus...

Palmer pulled back, not listening to whatever Nico had continued to say, as he cleared the image he didn't want to understand. Palmer didn't want to understand, but it made a little too much sense—at least when it came to where Brier's clothes might have gone. He tried to hide the growing tension left over from the vision as he gave Nico a quick glance. "When she wants to see you, she'll find you. Until then—"

"Excuse me? Who do you think—"

"She had a hard night," Palmer continued, certain he sounded snide. "Got drunk after fighting with *you* and somehow ended up unconscious on the roof, with no memory of how she got there or really anything from last night. Drank enough to entirely black out. Something tells me she doesn't especially want to talk to you right now."

Despite Nico Adessi's ability to hide his emotions, he looked as though Palmer had hit him in the gut. Nico's body tensed as he tried to recover. "She wasn't drunk last night."

"She certainly was when I found her," Palmer said. He pushed to test the man. "Did you see her?"

Nico hesitated, long enough to suggest guilt. "We worked things out. After the argument."

Palmer shifted the dress between his arms. "Well, she doesn't remember a thing about that."

Nico's jaw locked. "You sure that's not just what she told *you*?"

"She already had me try to get into her memories to figure out how she ended up outside." Palmer's tone went hard—he couldn't stop himself from twisting the knife. "There's nothing after she started drinking. If you'll excuse me?"

Nico let Palmer move back down the hall. Releasing a breath as he reached his own door, Palmer forced any traces of that short vision from his mind, just on the off chance that would be the sole thing Brier picked up from him. She knew how to lie, and did rather easily, it seemed, when put in a corner. But if she hadn't wanted him to know what she had been doing with Nico... or what it looked like they had been on their way to doing in the clip of a vision, there had to be better ways to lie than to wander up to the roof in the middle of the night, naked. Doing his best to clear his mind, he opened the door to his room.

Brier stood at the window, her arms wrapped tightly around her middle as she stared off toward the Augarian wall. Palmer watched her for a moment, the lingering annoyance slowly shifting back to worry as he took all of her in. Without her full skirts, just how much weight she'd lost since last summer was apparent. Her legs were bone thin, and the roundness of her hips had turned sharp. She looked frail, skeletal. Perhaps he would have to start condoning Rosette's thievery long enough to get both girls looking healthy again.

When she didn't turn, he cleared his throat. "Hopefully this works?"

"Thanks." She barely glanced at it, rubbing her arms through his shirt's sleeves as though she were cold. Maybe she was.

He set the heavy dress on his bed. "I can wait outside if you like?"

She shook her head. "I suppose you've already seen everything there is to see at this point."

"Well." Palmer cleared his throat. "It was dark."

She moved to the bed and ran her hand over the smooth fabric of the dress. "Though, I suppose, if anyone had to find me like that, I'm glad it was you."

Palmer shifted his weight between his feet awkwardly. "Oh?"

She nodded, finally looking at him again. "I'm sorry you end up taking care of me all of the time."

"We take care of each other."

"Doesn't seem that way sometimes," she murmured then continued before he could contradict her. "You didn't happen to grab a shift, did you?"

"Oh, no. Sorry. I should have thought—"

"I should have said." She crossed her arms again. "Women's clothing isn't exactly your area."

"I can get you one." He motioned to the door.

"It's fine. I'll make it back to my room without one." She turned her back to him as she began to unbutton his shirt.

Palmer watched, frozen in place, for a long moment before he forced himself to angle his body and study the wall. Fabric rustled, the silence ungodly heavy around the sound. Palmer finally spoke. "I ran into Adessi in the hall."

The rustling stopped for a split second then returned. "Nico?"

Right, there were two Adessis around. "Yes. Sorry."

The silence stretched on long enough that Palmer began to wonder if Brier would continue at all. She finally asked, "Did he say anything?"

"Only that you talked at some point last night." Palmer went with a vague version of the truth, as that was what Nico had *said,* then added, "And you weren't acting like you used to while drunk."

Fabric brushed against the floor, and the bedframe squeaked. "I should probably talk to him. See if I can piece together some of what happened."

"I can, if you like," Palmer said a little too quickly. He winced internally. They wouldn't need any special connection for that to sound suspicious.

Brier asked after a beat, "Because he likes speaking with you so much?"

"You just... had a hard night." Palmer fought to recover. "If you think it's going to turn into another argument..."

Brier remained silent for another moment before speaking. "I am dressed again, if you want to stop talking to the wall."

Taking a final calming breath, Palmer turned. The dress definitely covered her more than his shirt had, but it obviously hadn't been made to be worn without something under it. The square neckline hung too low, and her arms showed through open patches along the sleeves. He should have realized it went with something else.

Brier waited until her dark eyes caught his. She frowned. "What do you know?"

"What?"

"You know something else you aren't telling me."

He shook his head, doing his best to keep his face blank. Palmer wasn't quite as skilled at it as others in the palace were. "He just said you'd talked and worked some things out after your argument."

Brier continued to watch him. The pressure of her trying to push into his head started to build. The odd disconnect was a blessing for the moment. He was easy enough to read without Brier slipping into his mind. She finally stood, letting the topic drop. "I should probably go get my underthings before I start wandering around *looking* like I've gone mad."

"You look fine."

She stopped in front of him and kissed his cheek lightly before turning for the door. "You'll handle Cerise? That one I don't think I could do right now."

Palmer nodded and watched her slip out the door. He pressed his lips together. He couldn't shake the feeling that he would need to understand what had happened last night in order to understand any of it. And, ideally, he would figure it all out before Brier found out herself.

CHAPTER NINE

CERISE HAD DISAPPEARED. BRIER HAD to assume that was at Palmer's request. He hadn't slowed down enough for her to ask since she'd left his room yesterday. And Nico gave her nothing more than a few bizarrely evasive answers about them having talked at some point before she'd ended up on the roof. So she was left with very little to do but sit and hope avoiding alcohol would stave off another mental break.

"Why is everyone upset?"

Brier looked up to see Rosette had once again seemingly appeared out of thin air. Or she would have if thin air hadn't included the seam running up and down the wall behind her. That passageway was still intact, apparently. "What makes you think everyone's upset?"

"Because they are," Rosette said, entirely matter-of-factly. "And you and Palmer stopped head-talking."

Brier paused. "You can hear us when we do that?"

"Not what you're saying." Rosette shrugged. "But I know when you're doing it."

The girl was always full of surprises.

Rosette took Brier's hand. "You can come play with me. That way you won't be sad."

Brier smiled. As world-wizened as the girl seemed sometimes after all she had gone through, she was still just a child. "What should we play?"

"Come on." Rosette tugged Brier's hand quickly before she dropped it in favor of finding the hold in the seam in the wall. Rosette pulled it open much more easily than Brier would have expected—Brier had struggled with it at Rosette's age—but Brier followed along, letting Rosette happily lead her to the gallery above the throne room.

Brier looked at the little shrine that had been erected on one end—two of her old dolls sitting in the middle of bits of colored tile, glass, and gold. "What have you done here?"

"It's my secret place." Rosette picked up the two dolls, offering the blond one to Brier. "You can have Marie, if you want. She's my favorite."

"Why, thank you." Brier made sure the ground looked generally clear before she sat.

Rosette flopped to the ground, entirely unconcerned, and set to rearranging the rest of her play area. Despite being left alone so much lately, Rosette seemed perfectly happy with all the little toys and trinkets she had found. Still, she would need other children to play with sooner or later. Being left to herself as much as she was likely wasn't healthy.

Perhaps things wouldn't have gotten so messed up if Brier had actually been raised somewhere children belonged rather than being left to run around the Augarian. She wouldn't have even had Nico to play with if Orris Adessi hadn't been attempting to spite his wife. She should have expected Orris to be entirely ruthless, just knowing that he'd been willing to hurt his seven-year-old son to punish his wife for her sins.

Rosette lined up a few more pieces of colored glass—and a ring.

Brier frowned and snatched it up. A thick gold setting cradled a faceted green stone as large as one of her knuckles. "Where did you get this?"

Rosette pulled her heels under her. "I found it."

Brier turned it to the side to look at the crest engraved on the bottom of the stone's setting: a pair of wings around a round bezant. The di Serafin. *Speaking of Nico's mother...* She looked back up, eyebrow raised. "You wouldn't have happened to have 'found' this in Nico's room?"

Rosette's lower lip went out into a pout. "He's a boy. It's a girl ring."

"It's still stealing." Brier curled her hand around it. "What have I told you about—"

Voices echoed up from the room below them, sounding angry enough to stop Brier dead. She frowned, glancing at the railing. Using the distraction to slip away from the coming lecture, Rosette crept forward.

Her own curiosity piqued, Brier slipped the ring onto her finger for safekeeping until she could return it—ideally before Nico realized it had been taken—and followed suit.

"He's back," Rosette whispered, leaning in close to Brier's side.

Brier furrowed her eyebrows and looked at the room below them. Leone stood near the wall, speaking in a low voice to the two largest men who had followed Palmer's friend in from Latysia. Those two were the last men Brier would have wanted to speak to alone in a room. She took it all in, trying to determine if Leone was in trouble, but they were discussing something. The exchange was heated, but a discussion nonetheless. Brier fought to make sense of it, adding the situation to the growing list of things she couldn't begin to understand around the palace over the past two days. Recovering as best she could, she kept her voice low to ask Rosette, "This has happened before?"

"Lion's been here." Rosette pointed, using the nickname Cerise had so graciously bestowed upon Leone. "But alone. He gets letters he rips up."

Brier frowned, trying to hear what the men were saying. Even as Leone gestured violently enough to suggest he was trying to convince the other men of something, his voice remained too low to make out words. Brier leaned closer to Rosette. "Can you hear what they're saying?"

Rosette shook her head. "Do you want me to go listen?"

The men seemed to come to an agreement. The taller one—Jacopo?— nodded and moved off with his friend, leaving Leone in the throne room, looking pale.

Brier pursed her lips and slipped back from the edge. "Wait here. I'm going to go talk to him."

Watching Leone through the railing, Rosette frowned, but she didn't argue.

Back in the passageway, Brier took the second turn, the one that hopefully still led to the staircase just outside the throne room rather than the hall entrance she and Rosette had used. The small tunnel had survived. She caught Leone just as he reached the door to the hall.

"Brier!"

She lifted her eyebrows. Something certainly had to be wrong for him to use her given name unprovoked. She forced a smile. "Hi, Leo."

He started to speak then cut off, leaning against the doorframe in a way that was undoubtedly meant to be casual. "Haven't seen you in a couple days. What have you been up to?"

"Wandering around." Brier shrugged, keeping him pinned with her eyes. "You?"

"I..." he began then seemed to try to read her face. He sighed. "Look, I'm sorry that I went to Nico rather than you. I was just, you know, working things out."

Brier hesitated. Obviously, she'd missed something else. "What?"

"Ah..." Leone stammered. "He didn't... uh, nothing, then."

Brier tilted her head, studying him. "Leo, what's going on?"

"Nothing."

She released a calming breath. "I *really* need people to stop saying that to me right now, Leone."

"Just..." He shifted his weight and glanced over her shoulder. "I was going to head back out to the country this week. I offered to take you with me. Get you out of the city if Nico didn't want to go for some reason. It really does seem for the best, you have to admit. This isn't the place for a woman right now."

Brier shook her head. The pressure behind her skull began to build as things refused to make sense. "You wanted us to leave the Augarian?"

"You at least." Leone looked as if he were debating stepping forward but remained where he was. "I'm worried about you, Chas."

"Going away isn't going to help me any."

"You're sure?"

"Entirely."

Leone bit the inside of his cheek. He finally stepped forward and placed a hand at her hip. "Brier, please listen—"

She shifted back. "What are you doing?"

"Please." He caught her wrist to stop her retreat. "I care about you. More than my cousin would be pleased with."

The pressure grew. Something dangerous bubbled through Brier's veins as her heart rate spiked. She pulled at his hold on her wrist. "Leo, let go of me."

"Just hear me out." He tugged her forward again, oblivious. "I know it's always been Nico and you, and I couldn't exactly compete with that, but things have changed now."

"Let me go," she repeated, the pressure turning to flashes of dark and light as her palms began to tingle.

"Come with me," he continued, his voice starting to flicker in and out as new voices tried to work their ways into her mind. "I couldn't leave unless I at least tried..."

Her vision tried to give out. The voices all talked over one another, converging at once to blot out her other senses. She tried to blink but couldn't fully manage.

Leone was standing much too close to her for whatever was happening. She fought to speak. "Leo..."

Something concussed, the light blinding. Pain shot through Brier's limbs. The burst of energy felt as though it would pull her body apart, scattering her. It snapped back in, knocking the wind out of her. And she fell into Nothing.

Palmer ran through his options. Cerise was already well on her way to Ruhegipfel—at least if she hadn't decided she suddenly had something better to do. And it seemed Nico didn't intend to tell Brier anything more than Palmer had about the night she'd ended up on the roof. If both he and Nico apparently agreed where things should stand with that, they could certainly wait until Goebel worked everything out all at once. Perhaps Goebel had seen something similar before. His family had trained Kosmos's and Chaos's reincarnations for generations. This couldn't be the first time something odd had happened.

With Palmer lost in his thoughts, the low buzz of energy took a moment to register. He tensed. An odd pressure in the air made the hair along his arms stand on end. Looking down, he tried to judge where the energy was coming from. An explosion rocked the floor, knocking the breath from him before sucking it away. He doubled slightly, gasping in the vacuum as he tried to recover.

Nico appeared in a doorway down the hall and looked at Palmer. "What was that?"

Breathing again, Palmer shook his head. "Nothing good."

Nico took off for the stairs without waiting for Palmer to catch up.

Placing a hand under his breastbone as he took a deep breath, Palmer followed, tracking the lingering energy in the air. The trail led him to the old throne room. The open door at the end of the hall reminded him just a little too much of the night he'd found Brier in the library. He stepped up to the threshold.

Despite the explosion's intensity, the room looked remarkably intact—no missing walls, no cracked floors, not even a broken window. His eyes fell to the woman on the floor—Brier. Nico knelt next to her, already trying to rouse her.

"Brier." Palmer moved to her other side and touched her arm. She didn't stir, her skin cold.

"She's breathing," Nico reported.

Palmer nodded, trying to force some sort of healing into her, though he didn't know what was wrong. The energy scattered as soon as it touched her skin, glancing off her as if she wore some invisible armor. Palmer frowned. A groan from behind him made him turn before he could consider it. Hidden amid the scaffolding along the far wall, Leone lay curled on his side. Rosette stood a few yards away from him.

She pointed at Leone the second Palmer caught her eyes. "He was hurting her."

So that explained Leone's state. Palmer touched Brier's face. It was just as cold as the rest of her, but her chest continued to rise and fall.

Leaving Nico to continue trying to rouse Brier, Palmer turned back to Rosette and got a better look at the man on the floor. No longer groaning, the man continued to rock, angry red pox covering his exposed skin. Palmer asked Rosette, "What did you do to him?"

"He was hurting Brier," Rosette repeated, face hard. "I made him stop."

"Hurting Brier how?"

"He grabbed her and said she had to go with him. She told him to let go." Rosette looked back at Brier, her bottom lip trembling. "Then that."

Leone whimpered as the energy around Rosette began to swirl again.

"He's not hurting her now." Palmer held out a hand, not trying to stop Rosette with his own powers. "Stop so we can figure this out."

"He deserves it." Rosette's fists tightened.

"Rosette." Palmer's voice turned stern.

The girl continued to frown, but the energy died down, leaving only the lingering buzz.

Nico finally looked up from Brier and stared at Leone. "What did she do to him?"

"Looks like pox of some kind," Palmer answered.

"And to her?" Nico stood, gesturing down at Brier.

"I was helping." Rosette's voice started to tremble again.

Nico's voice rose. "By blasting them both with whatever—"

"I didn't—" Rosette started.

Palmer cut them both off. "We don't know what happened yet. Let's stop yelling."

Nico shook his head. "All I know is that none of this was ever a problem before you and that brat showed up."

Rosette's energy began to swirl again. "He was hurting—"

Palmer chanced touching her back, forcing the threatening energy to dissipate as he pulled Rosette closer to him. She buried her face against his leg. He rubbed her back lightly, eyes still on Nico. "We aren't what caused this. If she says your cousin was—"

"You think he's magic, too, now?" Nico motioned back at Brier. "How exactly would *he* do that to her?"

"Take him upstairs." Palmer's tone left no room for argument. "You take care of your family. I'll take care of mine."

Nico's jaw worked as his fists clenched. He stepped forward, and Rosette's energy started back up.

"Rosie." Palmer glanced at her, keeping his voice low but stern.

The energy died off, but apparently it was enough to get the danger across. Nico stopped where he was. He looked at Leone then Brier and then back at Palmer. "I'm getting help."

Palmer didn't bother to answer, keeping his own body stiff until Nico had disappeared out the doorway. After a final glance at the now-silent man on the floor, Palmer turned and held Rosette back a few inches so he could crouch to her level.

"I... I... I..." Tears started as Rosette tried to speak through gasps. "I didn't... I didn't do..."

"Rosie." Palmer rubbed her shoulders. "You aren't in trouble, all right? You aren't. You just need to tell me what happened."

"I... I..."

He released a breath, trying to fight down his own annoyance as he calmed Rosette. "Rosie, look at me."

She blinked and took a shuddering breath.

"You're not in trouble. We just need to fix this. And we can only do that if you tell me what happened."

She swallowed. Her breathing was still a little too quick as she tried to talk, but she was at least coherent. "We were... playing. Because... because Brier's been sad. Then we saw him. And he was talking to the scary man. And then Brier went to talk to him. He wanted Brier to... to go. Said that she should go with h-him."

Palmer furrowed his eyebrows. "Go where?"

Rosette shook her head. "He just said he was l-leaving, and she should go. Not stay with N-Nico."

Palmer frowned. Whatever he had been expecting Rosette to tell him, that wasn't it. And it muddied the situation even more.

"I didn't hurt her." Rosette continued shaking her head, fervently enough Palmer half worried she would hurt herself. "He grabbed her when she didn't want to leave. Wouldn't let her go. I was trying to help—"

"I know, Rosie. I know." Palmer pulled her into a hug and rubbed her back as he looked at Brier over Rosette's shoulder. Perhaps he hadn't seen the full scope of Rosette's powers, but from everything he had seen, he knew she wouldn't have done that. He pulled back and met Rosette's big blue eyes. "All right. I need you to do something for me. Can you do that?"

She nodded.

"Go out and get some water and then bring it up to my room. I'm going to bring Brier there and try to get her to wake up. All right?"

Rosette nodded again and took a step back as he released her shoulders. "How much water?"

"Just a bowl." He straightened then watched her run off, her skirts bunched up in her hands. Closing his eyes, he released his own unsteady breath, trying to focus on what he could do rather than the five thousand things he couldn't make sense of—not without his missing visions. Glancing at Leone, Palmer gathered Brier in his arms. Nico could deal with his cousin—assuming he wanted to after hearing the man had possibly attempted to run away with the woman he thought was still Nico's fiancée. Palmer and Rosette had more than enough trouble on their hands without any of that.

Palmer sat on a chair next to the bed, doing his best to ignore the man pacing along the footboard. For hours, they'd waited for Brier to wake, and nothing Palmer did seemed to make the least bit of difference. She just lay there, as cold as death but breathing, protected by some invisible armor that kept Palmer's slowly weakening powers from penetrating.

"You can't... magic her awake like last time?" Nico spoke for the first time since he'd arrived, resting his hands on one of the posts at the foot of the bed as he stopped moving.

"Oh, why didn't I think of trying that over the past six hours?" Palmer didn't bother to curb his sarcasm.

Nico's jaw worked, but he kept his eyes on Brier. "What did the girl say happened?"

Palmer took his time. He felt just as tense as Nico looked, but at least the man had managed to bring his anger in check. He wasn't yet trying to burn Rosette as a witch, unlike some people who had seen Rosette's powers. "From what she saw, your cousin was trying to get Brier to leave with him. Specifically without you."

Nico hesitated, his head turning toward Palmer. "He what?"

"That's what Rosette heard." Palmer held Nico's gaze. "He wanted her to go, she said no, and he grabbed her wrist. Maybe she got upset, maybe something else, but something happened to her, Leone got thrown across the room, and Rosette got angry."

Nico frowned, seeming to struggle just as much to make sense of it as Palmer was. "Why the hell would he try to get her to go with him?"

"You'll have to ask him."

Nico shook his head. "He came to talk to me two days ago, asking if she really was... what she is. He must have finally heard it around here. He was acting worried enough about it that I figured that was why he was planning on going again. Why the hell would he try to bring her with him?"

Palmer's fists tightened. "You knew he knew that and still thought this was Rosette's fault?"

"Leo couldn't have made *that* happen." Nico motioned at the bed. "No matter what he knew."

Palmer ground his teeth as he kept his eyes on Nico. "I assume you've considered who might have sent him?"

Nico didn't answer.

"Since the last Adessi who knew what she was and was trying to drag her off places was—"

"My father," Nico completed, his words clipped short. "Believe me, I'm more than aware."

"Is there any way he could be in contact with your father?"

"We don't even know if my father's alive."

Palmer shook his head, wishing for something, anything, to come to him, but his mind remained persistently empty. "Has your cousin woken up yet?"

"Awake but incoherent," Nico said, beginning to pace again. "That kid of yours did a number on him."

"And you wouldn't have if you saw what Rosette says happened?"

The twitch of Nico's jaw said Palmer had a point. "So what do we do now?"

Palmer hesitated. At some point in the last six hours, Nico had gone from blaming Palmer and Rosette for the incident in the throne room to placing Palmer in charge. No wonder he and Brier had been cycling through fights for weeks on end.

"Well?" Nico asked.

Palmer shook his head. "I already sent Cerise to get Goebel. If anyone will know about this, it's him."

"And until then?"

Palmer looked down at Brier, rubbing his thumb along the side of her hand. "We wait."

CHAPTER TEN

PALMER'S EYES DRIFTED CLOSED, his head falling toward his chest before he started back awake. He looked around the dark room and frowned. He was falling asleep. He hadn't fallen asleep in months. Hadn't gotten close since... Lantello, he supposed. That had been after Sage Visentin's death, when they'd been left alone in the little country church. The village hadn't yet begun whispering that Rosette was a witch, and he and Brier had been fighting. He glanced at the woman lying silently in bed next to him. He had never functioned properly out of sync with her. Now he was failing altogether.

The door opened slightly, revealing a little shape standing in the doorway. "Palmer?"

He forced his mind back to alert. "Rosette?"

"I can't sleep."

Apparently none of them were functioning properly. He shifted an inch closer to Brier on the mattress and patted the place next to him. "Then you can sit up with me."

Silently, she slipped through the door without pushing it any farther open and climbed into bed next to him. She rested her head on his arm, entire body suggesting exhaustion no matter what she had said. "You'll make her better, won't you?"

Palmer tried to think of something reassuring to say but came up entirely lacking. "I'm going to do my best."

"Because you love her?"

Palmer froze. The words caught him off guard after he'd ignored the feelings for so long. Rosette tilted her head up to look at him, little face entirely innocent with her question. Palmer gave her a small smile and rubbed her arm lightly. "Because we both do."

Rosette offered him a smile in return and curled into his side as she fell silent once again. Palmer let her lie there, his other hand going to find Brier's on the mattress. Even if he couldn't heal her this time, she was still alive. Rosette's breathing slowed as the girl drifted to sleep. Palmer felt his own eyes trying to close once again.

Some sound snapped him back awake. He listened, trying to determine what it might have been. Indistinct shuffling came from somewhere down the hall. Carefully, he slid Rosette off him then maneuvered to stand without hitting either woman on the bed. The palace seemed quiet outside the door. Palmer stepped into the hallway, looking either way for anyone who might be up.

A shadow disappeared around the corner. Palmer frowned and took a few steps after it. By the time he looked again, it was gone. He followed it a little farther, peering into the dark hallway. Intuition told him something was wrong, visions or not. He turned back toward his room. Footsteps pounded up the opposite way. Palmer spun.

"Leone's gone," Nico announced before he'd stopped running.

Palmer's eyebrows furrowed. "What? How?"

"Someone helped. There's no possible way he could have gone anywhere himself right—"

A scream cut Nico off. Palmer sprinted down the hall to Brier's room. The bed sat empty, a squirming blanket at the end of it. Crouching, Palmer found a break in the fabric and helped Rosette get her head out. "What happened?"

"A man..." She continued to squirm, getting an arm free. "He threw me off the bed..."

"Where's Brier?" Palmer didn't give her time to gather her thoughts.

"I..." Rosette looked at the bed, obviously at a loss.

"Dammit." Nico turned for the door.

"Stay here. Lock the door." Palmer pointed at Rosette sharply before following.

Nico headed for the end of the hall as Palmer ran to catch up. He turned into an alcove and opened a small door Palmer had never looked twice at. It led to another dark passageway. Palmer didn't bother to ask if

Nico knew where he was going. Only Nico, and perhaps Rosette, matched Brier's experience navigating the palace.

"We need to find her before they get past Gully's men." Nico made a sharp left. "If they get into the city, they could go anywhere."

Palmer nodded, feeling the blast of cold air as Nico pulled open another door to step out onto the piazza. The energy flickered as a lingering memory of Palmer's powers attempted to flare to life. He didn't question it. "The north gate."

Nico nodded and turned for it without hesitation. "Alert the camps. I'll try to head them off."

Palmer opened his mouth to argue, but then again, he wasn't much good in a fight, with or without powers. After a short nod, he ran for the quiet camps. A horse whinnied, and another wave of energy hit Palmer as he looked across the camps. A shadowy horse spurred off, rushing the gate.

"Stop them!" Palmer shouted, not sure at whom, as the men stirred awake. More shouts and a loud crash told him the horse had made it through. Gritting his teeth, Palmer turned for the gate himself.

Rosette fought her way out of the mess of blankets, tripping as she finally got her feet free. She'd barely gotten a glance before being smothered in blankets and hurled out of the bed, but it had been a man in the room. A big one. Her limbs tingled as her anger simmered close to the surface. Not bothering to go after her shoes, she rushed into the hallway and looked for the way Palmer had gone.

The door to the passageway at the end of the hall stood open. Pulling her shift up to her knees, Rosette ran down toward the piazza. Something crashed. Soldiers shouted, running about as they gathered their weapons. Rosette followed her instincts and slipped past it all out into the dark city. Palmer shouted somewhere down the street. Nico's voice answered. Rosette started after them both, ducking through the maze of streets. The farther Rosette got from the walls, the smaller and more closely packed the buildings became. Streets turned into little more than alleys as the large stone houses became boxy shops and then tilted wooden shacks—much like the house Palmer had brought her and Brier to when they'd first arrived in the city.

She came to a dead end where lopsided buildings closed in the alley on three sides. Rosette spun, trying to get her bearings. Palmer had come this way. *He must have.* She just had to find the way he had gone.

"Now, what do we have here?" A man crept out of the shadows of one of the buildings, a few more following him.

Rosette looked at them. A street gang, her memory supplied. She'd seen more than a few of them while in Tetii.

"You're a far way from home, aren't you?" The first man moved closer.

The tingling in her arms came back at full force. She flexed her hands, feeling the power flow through her body. Palmer certainly couldn't get mad at her for using that here.

"You mute?" The man grabbed her right arm.

She spun, her left elbow hitting his stomach before she pushed back, sending a blast of energy that knocked him off his feet. He hit the ground, foaming at the mouth as he jerked. Fear peaked at the end of the alley. Rosette breathed it in. The panicked buzz felt good. Two of the six men turned and ran. The other four seemed ready to do the same. Rosette just smiled and let energy crackle down to her fingers.

Palmer tried to catch his breath, staring out at the inky black ribbon that was the Rumano. Only three bridges crossed the river on this side of the city, but wherever the horseman had gone, he had made it to the other side, out to the open countryside. Of that, Palmer was sure.

"Is he...?" Nico finally spoke, standing just a few feet back.

"We lost him," Palmer agreed.

Nico's jaw worked, but neither man said anything as they looked out across the silent countryside. Nico shook his head. "This had to be planned. He couldn't have gone himself and couldn't have spoken to anyone in the state he was in all evening."

Palmer clenched his jaw, having to agree. His mind caught something.

"Rosette said he was talking to a 'scary man' before Brier went to talk to him. There was someone else in the palace already."

They stood still another moment, letting that fact soak in, then finally, Nico turned back toward the Augarian. "We should get supplies."

Palmer looked at him. "What?"

"To go after her."

It wasn't a question. Whether or not Palmer had been put in charge earlier, following the kidnappers wasn't up for debate. Palmer entirely understood. Turning to follow, he started to speak, but a sudden blast of energy made the words catch in his throat.

Nico glanced back at him. "What is it?"

"Something." Palmer took off running again, trying to track the buzz in the air. Grunts and shouts grew louder as he turned for another part of the slums. Some sort of fight was taking place. Nico's longer legs easily outpaced Palmer as they ran. Palmer tried to catch up, all the same. A hand came out of one of the little shacks and caught Palmer's sleeve. He turned as his momentum jerked the rest of the woman through the doorway. He squinted in the darkness as she caught herself, half-kneeling. "Peony?"

Peony looked up at him, eyes wide.

"What are you doing here?" Palmer helped her up then glanced toward the hidden fighting.

"This is Mortano territory. They'll as soon kill you as look at you with those clothes on."

A man screamed, and Palmer started toward the alley. "Stay here," he called back at her.

The sight at the corner froze Palmer in place. Three men lay on the ground—two convulsing, another foaming at the mouth. A fourth, Nico had on the defensive, fighting more deftly than Palmer knew the man could barehanded.

Then his eyes fell on Rosette. Two large men faced her, backed into a corner as she shot short blasts of energy at them every time they moved—like a cat toying with its prey.

"Rosie!" Palmer exclaimed.

She started then looked over her shoulder at him. One of the two men took the second's distraction, grabbing Rosette's arm. She swung slightly as he attempted to toss the little girl out of the way, but she curled back. She landed an elbow to his stomach then kneed him in the groin for good measure before sending him to the ground with a blast of energy so hot, it glowed red. The man fell to the ground, deathly still. Apparently tired of her games, she dropped the second man as he ran for the open end of the alley. Then she turned toward Nico, laying her hands on the back of the man facing him. With nothing more than a touch, she left him jerking on the ground. Nico's fist sailed over her head, through the empty space where the man had stood.

Rosette stepped back, hands still glowing, and Palmer finally ran forward. He caught her wrist, and a zap of energy zipped up his arm. He hissed, but the glow abated. "That's enough."

Rosette blinked innocently, even as she panted. Then she seemed to register his presence and pouted. "They started it."

And she'd more than ended it, if the six men strewn around the alley were any indication.

Breathing just as heavily as Rosette, Nico recovered from the sudden loss of his opponent. Taking a few steps away, he rubbed his knuckles. "Was she about to hit me?"

"I don't think she recognized you," Palmer said quickly, hoping that was true. He turned back to Rosette. "What are you doing here?"

"I'm helping." Rosette continued to pout.

"Big help," Nico mumbled.

Palmer tightened his grip on Rosette's wrist in warning as she tensed. His palm began to buzz. He glanced at it just long enough to see a pale-gold light working its way to Rosette's hands. Whatever she'd used to fight the men had hurt her, as well.

"Did you do that?" Peony came out from behind the corner, looking at the men on the ground. "To all of them?"

"They started it," Rosette repeated, grumbling as she pulled her wrist away from Palmer. She looked up at him. "Where's Brier?"

Palmer clenched his jaw but forced himself to speak. "We're going after her."

"Now?" Rosette pushed her ripped shift back up her thin arm.

"We're not carting your kid along." Nico sent Palmer a dark look.

Rosette's energy began to build again, starting to leach toward Nico.

"Rosie," Palmer said sternly.

She huffed and crossed her arms.

"We need supplies." Palmer placed his hand between Rosette's shoulder blades to push her forward. Everyone needed to think rationally, and that wasn't going to happen standing in that alley. "We'll talk back there."

Palmer pinched the bridge of his nose, hoping that standing close to the fire in General Gully's study would be enough to keep him awake. More and more, the fact that he hadn't slept in months seemed to be crushing down on him—and he didn't want to think what that meant for the powers he had left. If Rosette continued to use her powers to the point of hurting herself, and he continued to grow weaker... Nico's insistence on leaving her behind was making an increasing amount of sense. She would be better off behind a wall and soldiers, where she didn't need to use her powers at all, than she would be in a fight without him able to help.

Nico finally seemed to have worn himself out with pacing. For the first time all night, he was standing still, leaning against the wall near the door.

Gully had taken up the habit, however, and his large form moved back and forth along his long desk. "How long had she been unconscious?"

"Just since this morning," Palmer answered.

"And why wasn't I told?"

Palmer had to admit that he hadn't so much as considered telling Gully. The general had taken over the daily tasks of running the Augarian since the battle, but beyond coming up against the soldiers every now and again, Palmer avoided getting involved with whatever governance arguments Brier and Nico had with the man. Palmer tried to think of an answer. "I sent for Dominik Goebel to help. He just hasn't arrived yet."

"All of this should have been cleared with me." Gully finally went still, staring down at Palmer.

"General, if I couldn't figure out what was wrong with her, I doubt you could," Palmer responded, the mix of exhaustion and annoyance making him bold.

Any sign of the good-natured general disappeared. The large man seemed to swell as his mood soured. "But I could have prepared a guard. Unless you don't think you could have used that, either."

"If I may?" Nico saved Palmer from having to answer. Nico waited for the general to look at him. "The longer we stand here arguing, the farther she will get from the city. Right now, we have a chance to track them down within a day or two if we plan smartly. That window is quickly closing."

Gully released a breath, stroking his beard as he turned to one of the soldiers behind him. "How many troops are in the city?"

"Do you believe it wise to send a force out after her?" Nico straightened, adopting a formal stance, mirroring Gully's men. He was back to the soldier Nico had been when Palmer and Brier had first returned to the Augarian. "It's no secret what state the city's in. Half the reason we haven't been attacked is for fear of what she might do to an enemy army. If word got out that she's gone..." He trailed off, implication heavy in his tone.

Gully faced Nico head on. "What do you suggest then, Mr. Adessi?"

Nico tilted his head back, somehow managing to look commanding against the looming man. "I have already volunteered to go, as has Signore Tash. The two of us could move more quickly than any sort of company. And we wouldn't gather the same notice from anyone who might be watching the city."

Gully looked between Palmer and Nico then finally settled his gaze on Palmer. "You wish to go?"

"I imagine I have a better chance than anyone to find her," Palmer answered. At least he did if his powers held out.

His eyes caught a flash of movement by the doorway, and he sighed. He'd known when he'd put Rosette back in her room that there wasn't much chance she would stay put—even with her hands still wrapped to cover the rash over her tiny palms. Whatever she'd managed to do to herself, it was proving difficult for Palmer to heal. Palmer tapped his fingers on the side of his leg. If they wanted to leave her behind, they would have to plan exceedingly well.

"Where are they headed?" Gully asked.

"What?" Palmer looked back at the general.

"Where are they headed, since you can sense her?" General Gully pinned Palmer with his gaze.

"Northeast," Palmer said, his answer far too close to a guess for comfort. He could only hope what lingering sense he had of her was more than wishful thinking.

Gully's nostrils flared as he released a breath, but he nodded. "You'll be given two horses and two days' supplies." He looked at one of the soldiers standing off to the side of the room.

"I'll alert the supply wagons, sir." The man gave a shallow bow.

Palmer glanced back at the door. The little face was already gone. No doubt she would reappear soon enough.

"Thank you, General." Nico lowered his head just enough to be respectful before turning for the door, his body stiff and measured. With as quickly as Nico seemed to be switching personalities, who knew which version Palmer would be dealing with as they headed north. He could only hope the soldier standing in the room right then would make it through the trip, as well.

CHAPTER ELEVEN

"**G**OOD GOING, CLOVE. I TOLD you to stay out of it."

"Because you've been minding your own business so well."

The voices forced Brier awake. Her eyelids fluttered. The voices continued arguing between themselves as Brier finally managed to open her eyes. The bright-blue sky nearly blinded her. Wincing, she tried to focus as she turned her head toward the voices. The unfortunately familiar women sat a little ways off, looking entirely the same as they had the last time she'd seen them. Of course, she had also been slowly suffocating to death then. Brier groaned. "Not you again."

"Nice to see you too." Marina sat back on her hands, legs crossed out in front of her on the impossibly green grass.

"Hi, *cara*." Clover gave a small smile.

Brier didn't bother to answer the specter of her twenty-year-old mother and instead focused on Marina, the incarnation of Chaos from before Brier was born. "It's just every time I see you both, I seem to be about to die."

"Well, you don't seem to be dying yet." Marina dropped her head back as though she couldn't bother looking at Brier as she answered. "Your darling mother just got it in her head that she needed to try forcing another vision to you—since that has been working so well—and amazingly enough, her powers didn't do so well when pressed up against ours."

Brier's eyes finally shifted back to Clover. "You've been causing those voices?"

"And what's been causing Palmer's power problems, I imagine," Marina answered before Clover could speak. "We would have been just fine if you'd had just me sharing headspace, but no, of *course* she had to come along and mess everything up."

"You've both been in my head." Brier looked between them as things slowly started to make sense.

"You thought you were just going to leave us in that nether space when you got to come back?" Marina finally looked back at Brier, her dark-brown, nearly black eyes pinning Brier in place. "Do you know how long I had to put up with floating there with nobody but Clover for company?"

"I tried to stop her from following," Clover said.

"Because you'd rather be stuck floating powerless for the rest of eternity than *not* be noble." Marina scoffed. "I don't know how you Kosmoses manage to function in real life with all your selfless morality getting in the way. Then again, I guess 'real life' was never your forte, what with throwing yourself off a bridge..."

Less than eager to hear about her mother's suicide once again, of all things, Brier tuned Marina and Clover out as they started squabbling again. She looked around, taking in the grass, the sky, and the trees off in the distance. They certainly weren't in the wispy cloud world where she'd encountered Marina and Clover last, or even in the dream that had led her up to the roof. This world seemed too bright and so saturated with such deep jewel tones that it felt unreal. "Do either of you have any clue where we are?"

"It's your head," Marina answered, cutting off the rest of her diatribe. "You tell us."

Brier frowned but tried to look past all the color to the landscape. For all the places she, Palmer, and Rosette had walked between Ruhegipfel and Latysia—from mountains to plains, with everything in between— this bright world didn't seem the least bit like any of it. She shook her head. "I take it neither of you know how we might get out of here, either, then?"

"I imagine you have to wake up." Marina studied her nail beds.

"And any suggestions on how I might do that?"

Marina shrugged and looked up at Clover.

Clover offered Brier a tense smile. "It really is your mind. I imagine we need to find some way for you to figure it out."

Palmer shifted uncomfortably in the saddle, earning an unhappy snort from the horse under him. They were barely an hour outside of Latysia, and Palmer's body was already protesting the ride.

About ten yards ahead, Nico twisted to look and then shook his head. "Keep up, Tash."

"First time riding a horse," Palmer answered sharply. "Not all of us were born into it."

"They already have half a night's head start."

"Hopefully they aren't moving too well, either, if they have an unconscious woman and a man recovering from pox with them."

Nico's shoulders rose and fell as he released a breath, but he reined in, bringing his horse back beside Palmer's. "If you could just figure out where they were going, I could ride ahead."

"You think I'm not trying?" Palmer fixed his eyes on the blond man.

Nico started to answer, then his eyes darted over Palmer's shoulder. Palmer twisted to look and almost slid straight off his saddle. The horse whinnied and stamped until Nico grabbed the back of Palmer's collar and pulled him steady.

"Gods, Tash. Try not to be completely useless." Nico released Palmer's jacket a little too roughly. He motioned to the south. "Cart. Looks like a trader of some sort."

Palmer spotted the man on a road he and Nico had left not too long ago, making his way along the packed dirt in the middle of brown winter grass. Palmer assumed the patch of short, scraggly trees at the top of the rise they had been riding across all morning had hidden the man from their view so long. Or Palmer had slowed them more than he'd realized, and the man with a cart had managed to catch up from much farther back than Palmer wanted to imagine.

"We should keep moving," Nico said, apparently deciding that a single man wasn't any kind of threat.

Palmer released a breath but nodded, silently willing his mount to cooperate. Suddenly, an odd tingle hit the back of his mind, and he twisted—this time, staying firmly in the saddle.

"What is it?" Nico's hand went toward the menacing crossbow strapped to his back, and Palmer realized just how tense Nico's body language had become.

Palmer shook his head—more surprised by feeling a jolt of premonition at all over getting any sense of danger. "Do you know how to use that thing?"

"No, I'm carrying it for my health."

A flicker of motion drew Palmer's attention down a hill toward the little crop of trees, and he sighed. "Well, I don't think you need it right now."

Nico sent Palmer a questioning look, but Palmer was already dismounting—less than gracefully, of course.

"Rosette, I know you're there."

"You have to be kidding me..." Nico mumbled as the little blond head appeared up the side of the hill.

"Rosette—"

Two darker heads appeared behind Rosette. Peony and Egidio. His brow furrowed as he looked at the three.

Rosette made sense. He'd done his best to make sure that she would stay put after her display in the alley—hopefully, the soldier he'd tasked with watching her room hadn't come down with anything too awful—but Rosette had a reason to want to help. However, Palmer didn't understand why Egidio and Peony would have followed.

"Dear gods," Nico mumbled, his horse stamping unhappily from how the man moved.

Palmer turned back to Rosette. "I told you to stay in the Augarian."

"Brier needs us." Rosette crossed her arms. "I'm helping."

"Tash..." Nico's voice was a low warning.

Palmer ignored him, still looking down at Rosette. "How did you even get here?"

Rosette's face scrunched up.

"We met Signore Tosto on the road," Peony whispered. "He let us ride with him."

"Signore Tosto?" Palmer frowned as he looked at the woman.

She pointed at the man with the cart.

"Tash, we need to move," Nico said, his voice tense.

Palmer pieced together yet another plan as he looked between Peony and Egidio. "And you both want to help Brier too?"

"Everyone else already left," Peony said.

Palmer frowned, but Egidio explained before Palmer could ask, "Jacopo and the others. They slipped out and never came back last night."

Palmer's eyes flicked to Rosette then Nico. They might have found the "scary man" Rosette had seen before. Though how Leone would have gotten involved with the street gang... Palmer clenched his fists. He should have spent more time watching them all—he'd said they were his responsibility. Instead, he'd been busy trying to solve what was happening with Brier. And he hadn't even been able to fix that. He turned back to Nico. "The longer we argue, the longer we're standing here."

His face hard, Nico said, "I'm not traveling with the brat and her street urchins."

"They're not likely to turn around just because I say so right now." Palmer dropped his voice. "Cittamuarta's not far up the road. We can work this out there."

Nico's jaw twitched, and he leaned forward. "If I knew where they were going, I'd leave you all right here."

"Work on developing your own powers, then."

Nico glared for another moment, but he turned his horse and trotted toward the main road.

Palmer released a breath and ran a hand through his hair before he looked back at Egidio. "Do you know how to ride?"

Egidio frowned. "What?"

"Can you ride?" Palmer tried to keep his own annoyance from coming through his voice. He could try working out a new plan when they weren't standing in the middle of the countryside. Nico might have been able to ride the kidnappers down, but that plan had died not long after Palmer got in the saddle. Maybe he had to revisit bringing at least Rosette with them.

Egidio glanced at the horse. "A little. I haven't in years."

"You're still likely better than me, even in that case." Palmer offered the reins. "Catch up with Adessi and head for Cittamuarta. We can regroup when we get there."

78

"Palm." Egidio stepped forward. "The soldiers said they had kidnapped... I didn't know when I brought them—"

"Go." Palmer didn't want to hear it. The last thing he needed was to start blaming Egidio. "Don't lose track of Adessi. We'll meet you there."

Egidio continued to look uncertain, but he didn't argue. He slipped his foot into the stirrup and pulled himself on top of the horse, not quite as easily as Nico always seemed to manage but with far more skill than Palmer had. Releasing a breath, Palmer watched Egidio take off, then he turned to the girls.

"I can do whatever you need to help," Peony volunteered quickly as his eyes hit her. "I'm really good at—"

He held up a hand and looked back down at Rosette. "Before everything happened, you said Leone was speaking to a 'scary man.' Did you mean one of the men Egidio and Peony came with?"

Rosette nodded. "The one Brier didn't like."

Palmer gritted his teeth and looked at Peony. "Did you know—"

"No!" Peony blinked too quickly, shaking her head. "I didn't... they... no one told me anything! Not ever!"

Palmer tried to discern if she was telling the truth. From what little he could feel, she didn't seem to be lying. He didn't have time to weigh her loyalties any further at the moment. He nudged Rosette between the shoulder blades to start her back toward the road. "Come on. We need to get moving."

The rolling hills flattened out as they approached Cittamuarta. The small walled town rose out of the stretch of plain, its reddish-brown brick a stark contrast to the large tan blocks surrounding the Augarian. Still, the guards along the top, watching the countryside with suspicious eyes, looked a little too familiar for Palmer's liking. The entire world seemed wary of newcomers these days. With the news that had to have come from Latysia, though, Palmer could hardly blame anyone.

The guard beside the large arched gate stiffened at their approach, scanning them quickly. His eyes finally settled on Palmer. "Welcome to Cittamuarta, signore. If you would please state your business."

So his clothing was convincing enough here, as well. Studying the grim faces atop the wall, Palmer supposed it was the best of several possible scenarios.

A boy popped up before Palmer could decide on a response. "Signore Tash?"

Palmer hesitated—hearing his own name had thrown him off. "Excuse me?"

"Are you Signore Tash?" The boy continued before Palmer could answer, "Signore Adessi said you'd be coming with a little girl and her nurse. Paid me to keep watch."

Palmer snorted at the boy's eager face. Though Nico had nothing preternatural to help him, name and money worked just as well, maybe better considering how everything sorcerous was working at the moment. Palmer offered the boy a quick smile. "You've found me, then."

The smile grew as the boy bounced on the balls of his feet, waiting for the guard to let them pass. Just as cheerful, he leaned in close to Palmer's side as he led them into town. "Signore Adessi said he'd give me *another* piece of silver when I brought you."

Palmer lifted his eyebrows. No wonder the boy looked so excited. His clothes were clean, if worn, and he didn't seem to be an urchin, but Palmer imagined that had to be more money than the boy had come close to making in a single day. That also meant a good portion of the town would hear about it seconds after the boy left him and the girls wherever Nico had holed up. Even if Cittamuarta had always catered to wealthy tourists coming to take in the waters of the city's baths, few likely threw around money that liberally. Keeping a low profile had obviously not been high on Nico Adessi's agenda.

Moving expertly through the tightly packed buildings, which were made of the same-colored brick as the city walls, the boy brought them to a three-story triangular building situated in the center of a fork in the road. He looked up at Palmer. "Relais delle Acque. The city's best inn."

"Of course." He should have expected nothing less at the moment. Palmer followed the boy inside. The smell of roasting meat wafted through the front room, making Palmer's stomach rumble.

Peony sniffed then looked at Palmer. "Bistecca Fiorentina. They have actual steak."

A heavyset man looked up from a table in the front room and smiled at the four standing in the doorway. "Signore Tash, so good that you finally made it. Signore Adessi told us you would be joining him."

The boy who had met them dashed forward and took a coin the heavy man offered him, before heading back for the door, his smile wide.

The man looked back at Palmer. "They're waiting for you in the dining room, if you'd care to join? Unless you'd rather get settled in your rooms first?"

"We could eat," Palmer spoke as few words as possible. Saying too much seemed dangerous until he found out exactly what Nico had been telling people about their trip. If Peony had been dubbed a nursemaid, Nico at least had the good sense not to come too close to the truth.

The man lowered his head as if he were bowing then moved across the room. "I am Ernesto Corte, the humble proprietor of this establishment. If there is anything you need during your stay in Cittamuarta, please do not hesitate to ask. Your comfort is our utmost priority."

Palmer nodded, catching Rosette's arm as she started toward something shiny along a far wall. She pouted as he sent her a dark look, but she continued moving forward with them.

Corte opened a door into a wood-paneled room and lowered his head once again. "Signore Adessi, the rest of your group has arrived."

Nico looked up. He and Egidio took up the only occupied table in the room. Setting his wine glass down, he twisted to better face the door. "Tash. Glad you finally made it." He flicked his eyes to Corte. "Bring out a plate for Signore and Signorina Tash if you would."

"Of course, signore." Corte quickly moved back out of the room.

Nico picked up his glass once again and sat back in his chair. "Sorry we started without you. We weren't sure how much longer we would be waiting."

"We couldn't have been that far behind." Palmer crossed his arms as his eyes drifted to the food on the table—the half-dozen plates looked obscene after months of rations. "Though apparently you've already made yourself at home."

"We're obviously not making it back to Latysia within two days. I figured we'd at least be delayed long enough to buy more supplies," Nico returned, picking up a roll. "Might as well make the most of it."

Rosette pressed herself against Palmer's leg, looking at the food, just barely refraining from going after it. Palmer nodded permission before looking back at Nico. "And Signorina Tash?"

"Your daughter," Nico said dryly as he motioned with his eyes to where Rosette was digging in to what food was still on the table. "She suffers terrible headaches. Why we're here to take in the waters."

"I see," Palmer answered.

"And you, of course, brought her nurse." Nico glanced at Peony. "Convenient she was already dressed as one."

"What?" Palmer frowned.

"One Brier's old nurse left behind, I believe." Nico motioned dismissively at the plain black dress. "And works well enough. She doesn't exactly look like that girl's mother. And she's certainly not dressed well enough to be family to either of you."

Peony crossed her arms tightly across her middle.

"I'm supposed to be a valet or something, if it makes you feel better, Pea," Egidio murmured then fell silent once again as Corte brought in more food and empty pleasantries.

Time running short or not, Palmer couldn't pass up the surplus and sat to eat. He looked at Nico. "We can pay for all this?"

Nico snorted, clearly unconcerned as he went back to his wine. "I rented us a room upstairs if we need to spend the night, but the market is just up the street. They actually have supplies here, obviously. I'm sure we can get what we need."

Palmer just nodded, digging into the rich food, courtesy of the Adessi estate.

CHAPTER TWELVE

A FTER SO LONG RATIONING, PALMER felt sick from having a full
meal. He placed a hand on his distended stomach and looked
around the circular market for the supplies they would need
to travel for perhaps days. The task served as a distraction from the
lingering nausea.

Compared to the rest of town, where buildings were packed three
or four stories high along tight streets, the gaping piazza in the center
of the city came as a shock. The domed city temple sat off to one end,
beautifully decorated to honor Heke, God of Healing, with the tall town
hall facing it. What Palmer could only assume was the Cittamuarta baths
completed the circle—its long row of columns followed the perfect curve
directly across from the main market entrance. Smaller than the Augarian
piazza and decorated with the ubiquitous red-brown brick rather than
marble, the space still sent a pang through Palmer's chest. The packed
market seemed so... normal.

Something brushed his leg, and he looked down just in time to see
Rosette slip behind one of the booths. He shook his head but didn't
bother to chase after her. As long as he didn't hear an uproar somewhere,
he would assume she wasn't getting in too much trouble. She had been
behaving herself while at the inn, more or less.

Palmer glanced at Peony and Egidio; both were standing near a cart
holding some sort of red root vegetable Palmer didn't recognize. Then he
took a spot next to Nico at a small stall selling packs. "We need to have
some sort of plan."

Nico kept his eyes on the wares, taking a moment before he answered, voice low, "I'm not traveling with them. We're not going to catch up with three on foot."

Palmer made sure the others were out of earshot. "We could leave Egidio and Peony here. Leave after they go to sleep tonight." The city was certainly in better shape than the Augarian, and Palmer couldn't imagine they especially would care about going after Brier. Not if they *didn't* have something to do with the kidnappers. "Rosette—"

"I told you I'm not traveling with her," Nico hissed.

Palmer shook his head. "She's travelled farther before. She knows how to keep up, and her abilities—"

"Could end up with us dead where we stand." Nico finally looked back. "Or, I'm sorry, *me* dead where *I* stand, since I don't happen to share your 'abilities.'"

"She doesn't just hit anyone."

"She very nearly did me last night." Nico's teeth clenched. "The girl's dangerous—and a brat—and not all of us have the luxury of ignoring that."

Palmer glanced around for wherever Rosette had gone. She was still out of sight, but no one seemed to have come down with any sudden illnesses. He shook his head. "You want me to just leave her here?"

"She can stay with her new nurse." Nico motioned dismissively toward Peony. "Unless you care more about those three than finding Brier. In which case, point me in the right direction, and I'll find her myself."

Palmer tightened his fist, half tempted to tell the man to take off, then. Gods knew Rosette had never taken a single order Palmer had given, but he had traveled hundreds of miles with her before. He had no doubt Rosette could make it to wherever the men had taken Brier. Still, the thought of Rosette's glowing red hands and the burns he hadn't been able to heal...

He had left her behind in the first place for a reason—only partially because Brier would kill him if he let anything happen to the girl. If her powers grew while his weakened, who knew what would happen. And if her powers weakened as well... whether Nico or Rosette, Palmer needed someone who could fight better than he could. Without powers, a seven-year-old girl wouldn't last long up against grown men.

Palmer forced his hands to unclench, even if he didn't feel any less tense. "How long can you keep the room at the inn paid out?"

Nico frowned. "How long do you think we'll need?"

"They'll need a place to stay while we're gone."

Nico looked at him for a beat before it seemed to register that Palmer had agreed to leave the others behind. He nodded. "I'll pay it through the week. If we aren't back by then, I imagine we'll have bigger issues."

That was certainly true. Palmer glanced around once again for Rosette before dropping his voice lower, in case she was nearby. "We'll have to go after everyone's asleep. Rosette's not going to stay put unless we're long gone by the time she wakes up."

Nico clapped Palmer's shoulder quickly as his only sign of agreement. Then he picked up one of the packs and went to the front of the stall to purchase it. Releasing a breath, Palmer turned to the next stall, trying not to think too much about it. Any of it. Leaving Rosette. Brier being unconscious. Brier waking up alone and leaving a crater where a village had once been.

Something caught his wrist. An old woman looked up at him, a small vial in one hand as she held onto him with the other. "For you."

"Oh." Palmer looked at it, trying to pull away from her unusually firm grip. "No. Thank you."

"No," she insisted. "For you."

"I... don't have any money," Palmer lied as he glanced around for Nico, Egidio, or Peony even. None of them seemed to be paying any attention.

"Not to buy." She forced the vial into the hand she had by the wrist. "You need. Will save everything."

Palmer's eyebrows furrowed, but the woman turned away, disappearing back into the crowd before he could gather himself. Palmer studied the clear liquid inside the vial before surveying the crowd. *Save everything.* He was growing a little tired of needing to save things. Still, he slipped the vial into his pocket. Friend or foe, he couldn't always tell with the unexplainable. He would just have to try to work it out back at the inn.

Despite being a product of Brier's mind, the bizarrely still world didn't seem in the least bit familiar, no matter how far Brier walked. She scanned the horizon in front of her, where the trees thinned, searching for any memory she might have linked to the wide, flat plain—anything that might tell her where she was—but she came up empty. And without being able to figure out where they possibly could be, Brier wasn't likely to be able to lead anyone back out again.

"Is your plan really just to keep walking?" Marina broke the blissful silence they had been maintaining for what had to be the past hour. Brier couldn't tell with the way the sun hadn't moved.

"Do you have a better plan?" Brier didn't bother to look at her, trying to find anything that could at all resemble a familiar landmark.

"You could always just die for good and give me your body."

"Marina," Clover chided.

"I'd have much more fun with it, I'm certain," Marina returned. "I mean, what did you ever do besides almost throwing her off the roof, Clove?"

Brier's body went rigid, then she forced herself to turn. "What?"

"I'm sure you remember 'waking up' on the roof?" Marina arched an eyebrow. "Clove tried to take over and nearly had you acting out her suicide."

"I was trying to help." Clover met Brier's eyes, face looking pained from the amount of contrition etched on it. "Marina had—"

A clap of thunder cut Clover off dead. The crash sounded unnaturally loud in the silent world. Brier spun back toward the expanse of plains— the dark clouds had suddenly appeared on the horizon.

"Now that's different," Marina murmured then raised her voice over the thunder. "I think you upset her, Clove."

Not stopping to ask her possessors their opinions, Brier started forward, the clouds drawing her in. Suddenly the ground blurred, and the plain she had been studying flew under her feet before she stopped with a jerk at the storm front. She blinked, trying to regain her balance.

"What do you think that is?" Marina's voice made Brier start. Both other women were still standing directly behind her, even after the blur of travel.

Brier released a breath and tried to stop her stomach from constricting into knots as she turned back to the storm. She had spent so much time looking for something familiar, but the stone stairs that had appeared in the middle of the otherwise-empty plain made her wish she'd never found it. She hadn't seen those descending stairs since the Augarian had come down. They had been destroyed, as far as she knew. Then again, even if they hadn't been, they certainly didn't belong in the middle of nowhere under a threatening storm cloud.

"Is that...?" Clover asked.

"The stairs to the Augarian catacombs," Brier said. Another clap of thunder sounded, though no lightning had flashed. Brier clenched her jaw, less than enthusiastic about the prospect of going underground in this odd world. Still, something told her she had to. She took a few careful steps forward, making sure the same jarring jump didn't happen again. When the ground remained solid, she moved to the top of the stairs.

"You sure you want to do that?" Marina remained where she was.

Brier made her way down the gray stone steps into the far-too-familiar tunnel.

"I'm not going in there," Marina called after her.

"Nobody asked you to," Brier mumbled, running her hand along the rough walls as Clover followed her into the catacombs.

The steps went on for longer than Brier remembered. A pressure began in her chest, slowly turning into a dull ache that radiated through her body. She took a deep breath, and the suddenly icy air pricked her lungs. Looking familiar or not, they certainly were not the catacombs she knew.

"Are you sure we should be going this way?" Clover asked as the ground evened out. Her voice sounded slightly garbled, as though coming through water.

Brier glanced back at her, just to make sure she hadn't started dripping again—the way she had the first time Brier had seen her—but Clover looked entirely dry, even in the eerie blue light that seeped into the tunnel along with the icy chill. Brier looked away. Young, pale, and sad, Clover's face looked far too similar to the one Brier had been seeing in the mirror over the past weeks. Her father certainly hadn't been lying when he'd said Brier took after her mother.

The thought registered, and Brier suddenly knew where they were headed. As if her realization was all the old tunnel had been waiting for, the fresh grave sitting on an upper recess illuminated. Brier frowned, trying to see where the beam of sunlight had originated, but all the other walls remained just as solid as before. She released a breath and turned back to the recess in the wall. She'd visited her father's grave only once—the day she, Palmer, and Rosette had returned to the Augarian. It likely didn't even exist now—who knew where her father's body had ended up in the aftermath of the battle—but there, in the impossible beam of light, the fresh grave looked as if it had been lifted inch by inch from Brier's memory, down to the roughly engraved name and seal carved into the rock on either end. She traced one of the old library crests. As if she had walked straight into a memory, the stone felt the same as it had the last time she had stood there. Though it certainly hadn't been Clover behind her that time. And it hadn't been so cold.

Clover stepped forward and sucked in a breath as she saw the name herself. Of course. Clover might have been dead nearly two decades, but Citron Chastain-Bochard had been her husband.

Brier let her hand drop as the dull ache turned sharper, speaking in an attempt to fill the silence. "He died while I was gone. Was killed, I suppose. I wasn't even at the funeral."

"Killed?" Clover asked, her voice sounding more and more garbled—as if she were drowning on dry land.

"Poisoned," Brier said, her voice shaky. She took a breath, fighting the wave of grief washing over her. The last time she'd seen it, the grave had solidified her resolve and left her knowing she had no choice but to fight what the Augarian had become in her absence. This time, all she felt was sorrow. He was gone, and she had never gotten to say goodbye. As far as she knew, he thought she was dead herself when he was lying there, dying. That was what everyone had been saying about her disappearance, after all—that she had been killed. What could it possibly have been like for him? Sick, dying, believing his entire family had died before him...

Crossing her arms tightly against her stomach, Brier looked at the woman who looked far too young to be her mother. "He was a good father, if you wanted to know. Nearly slept in that library of his, but I do believe he loved me. And you, I imagine, or he wouldn't have always been so sad."

Clover looked straight ahead, her lips pressed into a thin line.

Another pang of grief pierced Brier's chest. She fought to breathe as memories invaded her mind—the sadness she'd always seen in her father's face and the distance that had grown between them as she'd gotten older and spent less and less time in the library they'd loved so much. She squeezed her eyes shut as thunder crashed somewhere above her, echoing down into the stone passageway.

"It'll drown you," Clover said, barely audible at that point. "That sadness. You can't let it."

Brier opened her eyes, glancing back at her mother. The woman was still staring blankly at the wall with the same grim expression.

Her voice continued to quiver in Brier's head. "I couldn't fight it. You can still find a way out of the darkness."

"What?"

Clover started and looked at Brier questioningly.

"What did you say?" Brier asked.

"I didn't say anything." Clover shook her head, the motion blurry.

Forcing herself to step back from the grave, Brier turned for the stairs. She left her arms wrapped tightly around her middle as she fought off the chill settling into her bones. "Come on. We need to get out of here."

Clover didn't seem to be listening.

"Come on," Brier repeated, grabbing the woman's wrist. She started forward as the downward spiral began to spin through her mind.

Sitting in the corner of the dark room, Palmer fought to stay awake. Egidio had gone to sleep the minute he had lain down. Peony hadn't been far behind him when she'd taken a spot on the bed. However, Rosette, lying next to her, remained awake, as if she knew something was going to happen. Maybe she actually did. Though he had been careful to make sure she hadn't overheard, Palmer wouldn't put it past her. He considered bringing her along after all, but he'd already made his choice. They didn't have time to work out a new plan.

Eventually, Rosette drifted off with the other two. Unable to remain seated much longer without falling asleep himself, Palmer grabbed his pack and nudged Nico on his way toward the door. The man was upright before Palmer could blink. Meeting eyes for a beat, they both nodded and moved silently out into the hallway. Nico turned for the stairs.

Palmer shook his head, whispering, "Our humble proprietor will be downstairs. We should go out the back."

"We need someone to bring our horses," Nico returned.

"You think that will help?"

"To carry our packs, at the very least." Nico glanced back at the room door, which remained closed. "And even an idiot should be able to ride on a road, if we get the chance to stop going cross-country."

Palmer acquiesced and followed Nico downstairs, letting the man handle Corte with the same entitled ease Brier had always seemed able to call on in such situations. Stepping out into the cool night, Palmer looked back at the triangular inn. No lights had come on. He didn't spot Rosette lingering in the shadows anywhere. Perhaps they would actually make it out of the city without company.

Nico knocked his knuckles against Palmer's and handed over a set of reins. "They'll be fine."

Palmer nodded, then without bothering to mount the horses, they moved out onto the dark, deserted street.

"If we travel an hour or so—off road—we'll be far enough to lose anyone who might still decide to come after us." Nico all but said the name *Rosette*. "Then we'll have to rest. After last night, I don't think riding through is an option."

Palmer couldn't argue. They slowed as the closed town gate came into view. Releasing a breath, Palmer looked at Nico. "Should I talk to them, or are you going to let your purse do that for us?"

Nico passed off his reins and left Palmer with the pair of horses. Just how much money Nico had brought with him, Palmer didn't know. He could only hope it held out as long as they needed it.

Rosette slid through the empty streets, mumbling mean things about Palmer under her breath. She had fallen asleep for half an hour at most, and he had left. Again. She understood leaving the other two behind— she'd expected him to when he said they were going to stay the night. But leaving *her*? He was lucky he was out of range for her to blast him with... something. Even if it wouldn't do anything to him.

The edge of her skirt caught a crate. She ducked against a wall as the box shifted, hoping the movement wasn't enough to attract attention. She would have to switch into something simpler if she wanted to catch up. For the moment, she made her way through the shadows, straight toward the gates of the city. She counted the guards at the front gate and on top of the city wall then pursed her lips. There were enough of them to be bothersome but not enough to make slipping out impossible. She'd gotten past more. Rosette studied the gate itself. With it locked and being watched closely, there was no way to go through without convincing someone to open it. And that wasn't likely to happen for her. She looked at the rough walls. They wouldn't be too difficult to climb, not more so than the scaffolding in the throne room of the Augarian.

"Psst."

Rosette jumped. Her body tightened, ready to fight.

A boy moved out of the deeper shadows. "It's just me."

Rosette didn't react.

The boy tilted his hat back, and the light revealed a woman's face.

Frowning, Rosette took a few steps forward. "Peony?"

Peony nodded and dropped the hat back down to shield her face. "You're going after Palmer?"

Rosette hesitated but then nodded.

"I want to come."

Rosette scanned the boy clothes. They were convincing in the dark. She could do that too if she left her beautiful dress behind entirely—not that she wanted to do that. She frowned and swished the skirts slightly. Pulling her shoulders back, Rosette placed her hands on her hips in a way she hoped looked commanding. "It's going to be dangerous."

"No more than anything else these days."

Rosette pursed her lips.

"I have more clothes for you if you want." Peony motioned back into the alleyway. "Nicked them from a clothesline."

So the frail woman knew how to take care of herself. Sort of. *I could have done that. Better than her.* She just hadn't wanted to. Rosette shrugged but nodded. "What do you have?"

Peony grabbed a bag sitting not far away in a dark corner. She pulled out a dark pair of breeches. "These should fit you."

Rosette took them, slipped them on under her skirt, and tucked her short shift into the top before pulling off her dress.

Peony offered a jacket and let Rosette pull it on before speaking again. "So what are you thinking? We go up and over?"

Rosette leaned back toward the edge of the alley and looked up the wall. She turned back to Peony. "You think you can make it?"

"I can try."

"Well, if you can keep up, you can come." Rosette lifted her nose haughtily. Folding her dress before setting it behind a crate, she grumbled about Palmer in her head once again for making her leave it behind. Then she slung her small pack in place. Without waiting for Peony, Rosette crept to the end of the alleyway and watched the men stationed at the gate. Her eyes fell on a jagged piece of wall, leading up to just behind one of the watchtowers. Hopefully, as long as the guard was looking outside the walls rather into them, she and Peony would be able to skirt around the shadows there. She sprinted until she hit stone.

Sticking her foot into the jag of rock, Rosette hoisted herself up—spending less than a second to make sure the bandages around her hands didn't cause a problem. With her fingers entirely free, she could still scamper up the cracks without a problem. A quick look down as she neared the top told her Peony was following, not quickly, but managing her way up all the same.

Rosette gripped the top of the wall, listening for signs of movement. Soldiers down the way. Peony breathing heavily behind her. Nothing directly in front of her. Giving a final push with her legs, Rosette levered herself over the wall and got her feet under her again with a quiet grunt.

A guard stood at the front of his watch, looking out over the moonlit countryside.

Rosette gathered energy in her hands, hissing as it stung her palms.

She sent it out a little too soon. It still hit. The guard's hand went to his stomach, and the sound of a suppressed gag carried in the night. He moved off to the side and vomited.

"Did you do that?" Peony whispered as she pulled herself the rest of the way up.

Rosette sent her a dark look. If Peony had thought to say more, the words dried up in her throat. She snapped her jaw shut and followed in silence as Rosette looked for a way down opposite the sick guard. The walls were smoother on the outside. Climbing would be difficult. And the stairways would just lead them back down inside the city.

Somewhere behind them, voices gathered as the sick guard drew attention.

Peony's eyes widened. "What do we do?"

Rosette kept moving, her eyes scanning the ground below them. A patch of bushes caught her attention. She judged the distance.

"You aren't thinking of jumping?" Peony followed at Rosette's heels.

Rosette pulled herself up onto the ledge.

"You'll get yourself killed," Peony hissed.

Rosette shrugged, not bothering to consider if Peony was right. After a step forward, she was in the air, slightly curled, ready for impact. The balls of her feet hit first. The bush held her just enough to keep her from rolling. Shaking off the adrenaline, Rosette poked her head out.

A shout went up, followed by confused voices. Rosette crawled out of the bush and bounced on her legs to work off the jolt. Peony looked at the bush then at the men down the wall. As she climbed up and jumped, her grimace was visible from the ground. She hit the bush bottom first, letting a small whine escape.

Rosette tilted her head. "You jumped."

"Didn't have much choice." Peony rubbed her tailbone, looking up at the wall.

Rosette shrugged again as she glanced up then started away as quickly as she dared.

CHAPTER THIRTEEN

PALMER LEANED AGAINST THE TREE they had hitched the horses to, yawning as he tried to judge how late it was. If he woke Nico too soon, neither of them would be functioning come morning, but if he waited too long, he would fall asleep where he sat. He wouldn't be much use as a watch that way. Forcing his eyes to remain open, he shifted his weight. The round vial rolled in his pocket. His breath caught in his chest. He certainly hadn't been thinking about the *glass* vial he'd slipped into his pocket half a day ago. Suddenly worried he'd broken it, he pulled it out slowly. The stopper remained in place; whatever was inside looked exactly the same as it had before. He tilted it back and forth as he studied the clear liquid in the moonlight.

He had to assume the old woman had known something about who he was. Why else accost a stranger in the market to give him... a mysterious vial? But was she trying to help him or hurt him?

You need. Will save everything. The words floated around his mind. He pulled out the stopper and sniffed the liquid. Odorless, colorless, it truly seemed to be just water. And the lingering intuition he'd been relying on didn't tell him anything else about it. It didn't feel dangerous, but then it didn't necessarily feel safe. What was the worst that could happen? His powers already weren't working. And if it was poison, well, he seemed to be healing quickly enough to fight off a small dose. Or, if worse came to worst, part of him would reincarnate.

Trying not to think too long on that last thought, he took a sip, perhaps a quarter of the small vial. He grimaced at the slightly metallic aftertaste that stuck to his tongue. The vision hit him before he could recover—full color, more vivid than any he'd experienced in months.

Leone grimaced as he slid off the horse. He hit the ground too hard as his legs seemed unable to catch him. The angry pocks that had covered his face had dulled slightly since Rosette had attacked him, but the man was clearly still ill.

The dark-haired man in front of him looked back, pulling Brier's limp form off the equally dark horse. "All right there?"

"I will be." Leone tried to take a step forward but ended up sitting where he was as his legs shook. "I would have told them to grab the brat too if I'd had the chance. I'm starting to think that old Seer has a point. Monsters in the Augarian."

The man nodded and glanced at Jacopo and Bruno, who were squabbling over a loaf of bread. "The sooner we make it to Venchia, the sooner this is all over."

The vision snapped away, day fading back into night roughly enough that it left Palmer's head spinning. He stared wide-eyed at the open vial before he capped it and stuffed it into his pocket. He stood then nudged Nico with his foot. The man shot upright, hand going to the crossbow by his side.

Palmer spoke before Nico had a chance to lift it. "Venchia."

Nico blinked, seeming to take a moment to place himself before he rested back on his elbows. "What?"

"They're taking her to Venchia."

He still took a moment. "You're sure?"

Palmer nodded, doing his best not to question a vision that felt so solid.

"What's in Venchia?" Nico lay the rest of the way back on his pallet, rubbing his eyes. "It's just old ruins."

"I don't know," Palmer said. "But it's where they're headed."

"I suppose it's at least a destination." Nico sighed. His eyes remained closed for a moment before he sat up once again. "Go ahead and get some sleep. Must be time to trade off anyway."

Unable to bring himself to argue, Palmer switched spots with Nico to lie down. He closed his eyes, and for the first time in what felt like lifetimes, he slept.

Morning came sooner than appreciated as the sun peeked out from behind a thin layer of clouds. Pushing himself up, Palmer released a breath then rolled the pallet, erasing any sign of their little camp, save the bent grass where he'd slept. Nico didn't seem in a mood to talk, and Palmer saw no reason to force it. So they ate quickly before starting off in silence.

The flat stretch of plain tapered off as they continued north. Tall hills that were almost mountains sprouted from the landscape seemingly at random around otherwise-gently rolling hills. Palmer spotted little villages perched here and there along the top of the mountains. Otherwise, they didn't meet a soul as they walked.

As the sun once again began to dip low in the sky, they encountered a stream.

Nico finally broke his daylong silence. "We might as well stop here. We're going to start getting more mountains the farther we go. They'll be easier to navigate in the light."

Palmer nodded, patting his horse's neck. The beast seemed much more pleasant now that Palmer wasn't trying to ride it. After finding a place to hitch the horses while giving them enough room to graze, Palmer and Nico set up camp and tried to make some sort of meal.

Nico popped a handful of nuts into his mouth, watching Palmer over the little fire they'd risked making.

Palmer finally looked up and raised an eyebrow. "What?"

Nico took his time chewing before he spoke. "Is this what it was like for you all, trying to get back to Latysia?"

A legitimate question. Palmer frowned. He wasn't sure what he'd been expecting, but it hadn't been an invitation to an actual conversation. He looked down at the dried fruit in his hand. "Like this, but with fewer supplies. We were scavenging most the trip."

"And that was enough?"

Palmer took a bite and shook his head. "If Brier's dresses suddenly grew three sizes on her return, sure. Plenty."

Nico's jaw locked.

"The last stretch was the worst of it," Palmer continued, softening his tone enough to sound congenial. "We weren't going to travel over winter, but we didn't have much choice. By then, there wasn't a lot to eat between Lantello and Latysia. Before that, we could pick things from farms."

Nico frowned. "Lantello?"

"We stayed there awhile. She didn't tell you that?"

Nico dropped his eyes to his hands, looking a little too interested in the dirt under his nails. "She never wanted to talk about it. The whole 'kidnapping.'"

"We were actually kidnapped. She didn't lie about that."

The corner of Nico's lips twitched as if he didn't quite believe it, but he didn't argue.

Palmer pressed his lips together, taking a moment before he continued, "After we ran, we ended up in Lantello. Stayed with a Seer there in this little country parish. We were considering staying there before he died."

Nico lifted his eyes without moving his head.

They'd even talked about getting married and living there, them and Rosette. Palmer figured he'd better not share that part. "But Rosette could sense when the Seer was dying, somehow. I guess Brier could, too, but she was a little less dramatic about it. The town started whispering Rosette was a witch, so we figured we'd outstayed our welcome. Had to leave."

Nico took his time before speaking. "You'd still be there otherwise?"

"Maybe. Though, who knows? There were enough people looking for us. We might have been found out either way." He paused, watching the man across the fire. "And she was worried about you."

Nico's brow furrowed. "Me?"

Palmer nodded. While in Lantello with Brier, he'd seen odd visions about Nico caught in a dark room somewhere, but he didn't bother to elaborate on them—or how upset they had made Brier.

"What was she worried about me for?" He looked back down at his hands.

Palmer shrugged, saying the only thing he could think to. "She cares about you."

Nico released a breath through his nose, his jaw locking. He started to speak but cut himself off. He began again. "You..."

Palmer waited for Nico to continue. He finally shook his head. "I...?"

Nico released another tense breath before meeting Palmer's eyes. "While you were gone. You both..."

Even without powers, Palmer knew what the man was trying to ask. He waited to see if Nico would actually say it.

Nico grimaced but said it: "Did you have sex with her?"

Palmer's eyebrows rose at the sudden brashness, but he shook his head. "No."

Nico's entire face reacted—more emotions than Palmer had perhaps ever seen the man express flashed over his face in the same second. He recovered. "No?"

"Being on the run and taking care of a six-year-old doesn't well lend itself to... any of that."

"Since you've been back, then?"

Palmer shook his head then continued at Nico's disbelieving look. "Do you need me to swear on my mother's grave or something?"

Nico leaned forward over his knees and ran his fingers through his hair before interlacing them at the back of his skull. So it seemed guilt, more than jealousy, had prompted him to ask.

"Any reason you needed to know?" Palmer tested him.

Nico didn't answer.

"You'd feel less guilty about her not remembering if she'd been with me first?"

Nico's head snapped back up.

"That vision I got, of all things." Palmer sat back and looked up at the swath of stars above them.

After a beat, Nico asked carefully, "What... vision?"

Palmer brought his eyes back down, silently wondering if that was a serious question.

"How long have you known?"

He shrugged.

"What did you tell her?"

Palmer swallowed but shook his head. "I didn't."

Nico's eyebrows furrowed, but he didn't ask any more questions. He looked back at his hands. "She wasn't acting like herself. I knew... I should have known..."

The thought died off as Palmer finally let the memory of the vision flood back, focusing on the odd flickering over Brier that made it look as if two women were standing there. He was missing something—of that, he was certain—but what, he couldn't pinpoint.

Cerise. He'd never seen her copy another person in her shapeshifting, but from what he'd seen, it would be possible. Posing as Brier like that was low, even for Cerise—but Cerise did thrive on conflict. And she and Brier had just had a fight. Placing his hand over his pocket, he felt the vial. He pressed his lips together, debating if he should try using it again with an eye on what Cerise had done that night before he'd found Brier. He wouldn't entirely put it past her—

"We should try to get some sleep," Nico said, voice stoic once again as he stood and kicked dirt to snuff out the fire. "I can take first watch."

Palmer just nodded as the fire died, casting their camp into shadows. Still, even as he lay down, he couldn't get his mind to stop turning, trying to find the missing pieces to the puzzle.

How Brier hadn't missed walking. They weren't hungry this time—at least she wasn't—but traversing hill after hill brought back one too many memories of slogging her way back to Latysia in the dead of winter. And the chill that had followed her out of the odd memory version of the Augarian catacombs wasn't helping. Half wanting to simply go to sleep and see if she eventually woke up, Brier forced her legs forward. She didn't bother trying to talk to either woman behind her as they moved past hill after hill.

A bright flash made her miss a step. The crash of thunder followed the lightning—as it was supposed to.

"Do we think that's a good or a bad change?" Marina asked.

Brier shook her head, furrowing her eyebrows, as the next flash lit up another building in the distance. She moved a little farther up the hill to get a better look.

"What's that?" Marina continued, as if it barely mattered no one had answered her first question.

"I think it's Lantello." The image grew clearer the more Brier looked. "The church there, at least."

"What does that mean?" Clover asked softly as another flash of lightning streaked past the church.

"If we're in some version of my memory," Brier said, "we're headed backward."

If either of the other women had more questions, they didn't bother to ask them. Just as well, Brier supposed, since she wouldn't have been able to answer any of them anyway. At least Lantello had a few memories happier than her father's grave. That had to be a step in the right direction.

She didn't bother to consider it strange when two blurred steps left her directly in front of the little church. The firelight flickering in the windows made the church look inviting. Still, Brier hesitated as she placed her hand on the front latch. As dark as the last memory had left her feeling, she wasn't entirely sure she wanted to see another.

"Well?" Marina asked, an edge in her voice.

Brier pushed open the wooden door. Seeing the shape by the fireplace, she froze. The name escaped before she could think. "Palmer?"

He didn't move or so much as register her presence. He simply stared into the fire, knees pulled up to his chest.

"You aren't the only one who's hurting, you know." Brier's own voice floated out of thin air as the memory stirred to life. The shape by the fire jumped when Brier—a past Brier—materialized, face tense as her and Palmer's raised voices carried around the sanctuary.

"Oh, poor little rich girl. Lost her mother and then got to spend the rest of her life being taken care of while doing whatever she wanted. Yes, I think our lives are nearly identical."

"You hated your life," past Brier returned. *"I got that, but don't you dare discount mine just because you're pitying yourself."*

"Ask anyone, Bri, who had it worse off. I don't think they'd say you."

Brier blinked, trying to force the memory back out of her mind.

The past Brier and Palmer faded, leaving only the fire going on the far side of the room. Silence lingered.

"What the hell was that?" Marina stood where the memories had been a few seconds before.

Brier swallowed, the tension in the air pushing down on her. "A stupid fight."

"Sounded like a pretty serious one to me." Marina looked at Brier across the expanse, her dark eyes dangerous.

It had been, Brier had to admit, but their argument had been about so much more than that moment. She hadn't been entirely unhappy living in the Augarian before she'd learned who she was—what she was. Sure, she'd been bored and relatively useless—a pretty face the boys kept around—but she'd been fine. Then things had changed. And nothing had been fine anymore—things were either great or awful. Could anyone really blame her for wanting *fine* just a little while longer?

It always seemed Palmer could.

Brier did her best to think of the good that had been in that place—the warmth Sage Visentin had shown them when they'd arrived, all looking much worse for wear after their trek from Ruhegipfel. The nights she'd spent with Palmer and Rosette, relying on each other to make it through after the old Sage had died. None of those memories made it through the haze of unpleasant emotions surrounding her.

If this was her head, it was a sorry place to be. She clenched her fists. Annoyance was beginning to overtake the sadness that had followed her since her father's grave. The lightning flashed again, and thunder rumbled close after. Clover grunted, her knees buckling. Brier's eyebrows rose. "Clover?"

"I'm fine." She spoke through a grimace. "Just... I don't feel very good."

"We should get out of here," Brier decreed, whether or not Clover's malady was the little church's fault. She helped Clover back up to her feet. Even with the assist, Clover wobbled. Brier turned back to Marina and frowned as the woman remained on the far side of the room, staring at seemingly nothing. "Marina?"

A dangerous energy began to spread around her.

"Marina, we're going." Without waiting to see if the other woman followed, Brier helped Clover toward the door, trying to put as much distance between them and the little church as possible.

CHAPTER FOURTEEN

THE MOUNTAINS GREW ROCKIER AS they continued north, where outcroppings shot up between the larger peaks.

"Perhaps we should find a road." Nico finally spoke as they led their horses around yet another pile of boulders. "We know where we're going. It's just going to slow us down trying to travel cross-country like this."

Palmer nodded. He opened his mouth but cut off before he could speak a word.

"What?" Nico asked.

Palmer slowed to a stop, something tickling at the back of his mind. He tried to follow it, but it squirmed away. He looked forward. "Can you see anyone out there?"

Nico frowned, but he moved up the outcropping and squinted into the distance. "No... wait. There are horses."

A lump formed in Palmer's throat. "I think that's them."

Nico stiffened. "Are you sure?"

"Not at all."

Nico released a breath through his nose then climbed back down before he pulled his crossbow off his back. "Good enough for me. Let's go."

Between the menacing bow and the tension Palmer could feel coming off the man, Palmer wasn't sure he wanted to see what would happen if it was in fact Leone out ahead of them. Nico hitched their horses to a gnarled tree then crept forward, low to the ground. Palmer followed.

Down in one of the little dips between the hills, four men were scattered around. Two sat in the grass as a blond with his back toward them spoke to a dark-haired man standing next to a large black horse. A lump covered in a cloak was draped over the beast's shoulders. The knot in Palmer's stomach said he knew what—or rather whom—that was.

Something clicked next to him, and the sound of wood creaking followed. Palmer frowned as the bolt cranked into place in the bow. "You're going to try shooting them?"

Nico kept his eyes forward. "I have good aim."

"And you think you can shoot all four before they realize where those bolts are coming from?"

Nico's jaw set, but he stopped to consider the question. Palmer tried to work out a plan himself. As menacing as it looked, the bow didn't seem the most practical for shooting more than one person in a reasonable amount of time. And Palmer didn't exactly have many powers that would come in handy incapacitating a group of men, even if those had been working.

Perhaps, if he had been thinking, he would have brought Rosette after all.

Something twanged, and one of the men in the grass grunted, slumping over. Palmer looked at Nico, eyebrows raised.

He already had the bow back down, cranking another bolt into place. "You might want to get to that horse," he said, voice matter-of-fact. "That will draw everyone else this way."

"You could have said that before shooting him," Palmer hissed.

Nico shrugged as well as he could while cranking. With few other options, Palmer skirted the dip in the hills, trying to come up behind the two men by the horse while they were still looking at the injured man in the grass. Face confused, the larger man in the grass—Jacopo, Palmer determined—rose up on his knees, bending over the other. With a grunt, he slumped, as well. Palmer's stomach twisted. "Good aim" had been an understatement, and it didn't entirely sit well with Palmer how comfortable Nico seemed using it.

"Get her out of here!" Leone's sharp voice broke through Palmer's shock.

The dark-haired man vaulted into his saddle, turning the black horse up the next hill before Leone could get his foot into a stirrup. Palmer straightened fully, watching the horse gallop away. Catching up was impossible, especially with their horses tied up over the next hill. Hoping Nico wasn't already taking aim at his cousin, Palmer rushed down the hill. He caught the man's leg just as Leone went to swing his other over the second horse. Leone hit the ground, and his horse whinnied unhappily as it fought to regain its balance.

Leone grimaced. As if the wind had been knocked from him, he gasped for breath. Palmer glanced back at where Nico had to be but saw no sign of the man. Palmer pulled the short sword from his belt.

"Of course it's you," Leone finally managed, his eyes following the blade pointed at his throat. A horse tore past, along the ridge of the hills, following the black one. Leone glanced after it, moving only his eyes. "Should I assume that's my cousin?"

"Would be a safe guess." Palmer adjusted his grip as much as he dared.

The moment of vacillation was enough to give him away. Leone studied Palmer's hold on the hilt, judging it, before meeting Palmer's eyes again. "Have you used a sword before?"

"Yes," Palmer answered, doing his best not to think of the battle he had found himself in the middle of when the Augarian fell.

"Ever stabbed anyone?"

Palmer clenched his teeth.

"Didn't think so." Leone shifted then put both of his hands up when the point of the blade pressed tighter against his throat. "We can keep it that way."

"Who was that?" Palmer nodded in the direction the two horsemen had gone.

"Who?"

"That man." Palmer's grip tightened on the sword, but he couldn't bring himself to move it any farther forward.

Leone studied Palmer's face, and a tense moment passed between them before Leone spoke again. "You might as well let me up. You aren't going to kill me."

"Are you certain of that?"

"Do you think you are?"

Palmer hesitated, unable to bring himself to actually hurt the man but not able to step back, either. The sound of approaching hooves made Palmer glance right. Leone's foot connected with Palmer's shin, throwing Palmer off balance. He took two stumbled steps backward then caught himself, shifting to keep Leone from getting off the ground. Just as Palmer pointed his sword back at Leone's chest, a bolt hit the ground less than a yard from Leone's arm. Palmer looked up, careful to keep his stance strong so the man on the ground couldn't get free. Nico stood next to his horse, already fitting another bolt into his bow. Palmer frowned. "You could have hit me."

"I didn't." Nico kept his eyes on Leone as he started toward them, leaving his horse at the bottom of the hill.

"Nic—" Leone started.

"I'm talking now." Nico clicked the bolt fully into place before moving forward. "And there are two ways this can go. You can answer Tash's question now, or I can step in, and you can answer mine. And for the record, Tash has a few more qualms about getting blood on his hands than I do."

"Nic, you wouldn't..." Leone attempted to shift again. "I'm your—"

The next bolt dug deep into the man's thigh—until it hit bone. Palmer took a startled step back, his body trying to send out some calming energy to ward off the destruction radiating from Nico. But even if Palmer could gather that kind of energy, who knew if it would work with someone other than Brier. Still... "Adessi—"

"Want to keep telling me what I wouldn't do?" Nico spoke over Palmer as another bolt went into the crank. He kept his eyes on Leone. "Because I have a feeling you'll get it wrong. Now, you can start talking and tell us something that's worth keeping you alive for, or we can look at the bolt over there and compare how far this one goes into the ground once it's gone through your skull. Tash and I, at least. You won't likely be in much shape to look after that."

Palmer started again, "Adessi, we don't—"

"Family matter, Tash. Stay out of it." Nico never looked away from the injured man on the ground. "So, Leo. Who was that, and where is he going?"

Leone whimpered. "Cosimo de Santis. He works for your father."

Palmer tensed, half certain Nico was going to shoot Leone.

Though his finger remained on the trigger, Nico didn't move. "And where's my father?" Nico asked, the words low, dangerous. He kicked Leone's injured leg when the man didn't answer. "Where is he?"

"Venchia." Leone's already-pox-scarred face twisted up in pain. "There's a doomsday cult there. He's working with the Seer there."

Things went silent for another moment before Nico finally lowered the bow. Without another word, he turned and grabbed the bolt sticking out of the ground. "Come on, Tash," he said, heading for his horse.

Palmer blinked, looking between Nico and the man bleeding on the ground. "You're just going to leave him like that?"

"Prefer I kill him now?" Nico glanced at Palmer over his shoulder.

Palmer swallowed, not doubting Nico's sincerity for a second. Nico pulled himself up on his horse and nodded at Leone's mount. "Take that one. Looks better rested than yours anyway."

Glancing at the man on the ground, curled around his injured leg, Palmer pulled himself onto the horse as best he could. Nico didn't so much as hesitate, spurring off northward. Palmer pressed his lips together, not entirely comfortable leaving a man in Leone's state lying in the middle of the countryside—no matter what he'd done. Already at the top of the hill again, Nico didn't seem to be planning to stop for anything short of the end of the world. And because Leone had proved the name of a town, Nico had no real reason to wait for Palmer, outside the eventual need to sleep, assuming he wanted some sort of watch. Grimacing, Palmer sent a final look at Leone. He was an Adessi. Someone would have to come back for him. Maybe if one of Leone's friends had to circle all the way back, it would give Palmer and Nico the chance to get Brier before anyone made it to Venchia. Doing his best to convince himself he was doing the right thing, Palmer started off after Nico. He only hoped the knot forming in his stomach wouldn't stay for as long as it felt it would.

"Are you certain we're going the right—"

"Ask one more time, I'll give you warts." Rosette narrowed her eyes at Peony. The woman snapped her mouth shut and looked forward. Rosette puffed out her cheeks then released a breath. Peony was doing a fair job of keeping up, but she insisted on constantly asking if Rosette knew where they were going. She, Palmer, and Brier had walked for a million times as long as she and Peony had, but they had all been together, how they were supposed to be. Now Rosette was stuck with some woman who wasn't like them at all, trying to—

The smell of blood snapped Rosette from her thoughts. She slowed, breathing in as she felt the energy shift in the air.

"What is it?" Peony asked.

Rosette ran the last few yards up the hill as she held onto the straps of her pack to keep it from bouncing on her shoulders.

"Rosette?" Peony called after her.

Rosette pursed her lips, taking everything in. Two bodies lay in the grass, one over the other. Shafts of some sort of sticks were poking out of them. Flies already flocked around the wounds in the warm sun. Peony gave a short yelp as she reached the top of the hill, her hand flying over her mouth. Rosette barely glanced at the woman before going to inspect the bodies. The charge of energy lingering in the air made her skin tingle happily. It made her hands feel better. She tilted her head, kicking one of the bodies over to look at it. Peony squeaked as her eyes went wide. Rosette looked at her questioningly.

After a shaky breath, Peony whispered, "That's Jacopo. And Bruno."

Rosette studied the men's glassy, open eyes for another moment before starting farther across the space. The tall grass had been trampled at the base of the dip. Dried blood streaked the ground as though an injured person had crested the next hill. Rosette looked back to Peony. "Someone else was hurt. No body, though." She began walking back, following the faint trail until it stopped, hoofprints taking over. "They had a horse, maybe?"

Peony seemed to be barely listening as she stood silently by the two bodies.

Rosette looked around for other signs of the injured man but saw nothing. She returned to Peony and looked down at the men. "They were your friends?"

She looked up at Rosette, tears hiding just behind her eyes. "It's hard to explain. I didn't even know them before the city came down, but..."

"You took care of each other," Rosette supplied with a nod.

"I would have died without them."

Rosette understood the realities of life on the street. She swung the pack off her back and fumbled for the purse hidden in a pocket. Pulling out four coins, she pushed the pack back and placed the coins over the bodies' eyes.

Peony looked at her, sad face questioning.

Rosette shrugged. "It's what they did when someone died back home. For their ghosts to not have to stay."

Peony nodded again and whispered a soft prayer before finally turning away. "There's no sign of where anyone else went?"

Rosette pointed. "Same way we're going, I think."

CHAPTER FIFTEEN

B Y THE TIME THE SUN had sunk close to the mountains, Palmer's entire body was sore—and he couldn't imagine the horse under him was much happier, having a man bounce awkwardly on its back every time Nico forced them into a trot. As the last of the light fell dangerously low, Palmer finally broke the silence. "We can't ride through the dark. We're going to have to make camp."

Nico didn't answer for so long that Palmer wondered if he'd heard at all, but he finally reined in and released a heavy breath. "We'll eat something then see if there's enough moonlight to keep going."

There wouldn't be, not based on the night before, so Palmer didn't bother arguing. They set up silently and made a meal from what was in Nico's pack and the ones on Leone's former horse, which was, in all honesty, more than they'd had in Palmer's.

Palmer took a long drink from the wine they'd found then passed it off to Nico. The man took it and drank quickly. Sighing, Palmer finally broke the silence. "Are you all right?"

Nico looked up, just a shadow in the growing darkness. "What?"

"Not really my business, but with everything that happened..." Palmer didn't especially want to think of that afternoon, let alone speak about it.

"I'm fine." Nico let his head drop again. "Why wouldn't I be?"

"You were just..." Palmer wasn't sure how to explain the energy Nico had been throwing off. "Have you been feeling strange at all? Since you and Brier..."

Nico shifted back to looking at Palmer but didn't answer.

"How you felt during all of that. Your energy. I was just wondering if maybe she could have had something to do with that. If all of that was new."

"Your visions really are crap if you think that was new," Nico mumbled. Palmer frowned, but Nico continued before Palmer could think of something to say. "If it's this dark, we might as well try to get a couple hours of sleep. Do you want to go first?"

"I'll watch first." Palmer shook his head, fingers going to the vial still safely in his pocket.

Nico began to make a pallet while Palmer just watched him and listened as everything went quiet once again. After waiting just another moment to be safe, Palmer pulled the vial free. He held it between his fingers, trying to work out just what answer he should try to see in the short burst he expected the liquid to give him. He made a face. Palmer knew what he had to do to figure out what had been wrong with Brier and what possibly was still wrong with Nico. Sighing, he popped out the stopper and took a small drink, focusing on the night he had found Brier on the roof.

The hall of the palace came into focus. A flickering Brier stumbled as she turned the corner. Closing her eyes, she rested against the wall. The flickering ceased for a moment as she gathered herself.

"Dear gods, did you fall into a barrel of wine?" Cerise's voice cut in as she moved down the hall.

Brier groaned and put her back against the wall. "Leave me alone."

"Just was wondering." Cerise stopped in front of Brier. "I think I'm getting drunk off the fumes."

"You really can't leave well enough alone, can you?" Brier snapped. "You just have to keep poking and prodding and messing about until you break something."

Cerise lifted an eyebrow, looking Brier over. "Are we talking about something specific?"

"Just..." Brier flickered again then recovered. "Leave us all alone. We don't need you here. We all have enough to figure out without you trying to cause trouble."

"Ah." Cerise smirked. "We're talking about your little love triangle?"

110

"Leave well enough alone." Brier poked at Cerise's shoulder, nearly missing.

"You're calling it well enough?" Cerise looked down at Brier's finger then back up. "Though I suppose it's working for you. A little less fun for Nicolas, what with you stringing him along and all."

"I'm not 'stringing him along.'"

"Really? You mean you and Kos aren't entirely wrapped up in each other anymore?"

The flickering came more quickly. Brier seemed ready to pass out. She turned down the hall, her words becoming slurred. "Just leave us alone."

Cerise let Brier wander off. Brier turned a corner, and suddenly another woman was there.

Palmer frowned, nearly thrown out of the vision. Focusing, he coaxed it back, studying the new woman. Some lingering familiarity hid under the odd dark glow she gave off. He pressed his eyes closed more tightly, watching.

Though the woman was about Brier's size, the similarities ended there. With dark curly hair and dark eyes, she looked more like Peony than anyone else in the palace. And suddenly, she didn't seem the least bit drunk as she made her way to another room. She smiled, looking at Nico sitting on the end of a bare bed, with his own bottle of wine. "Drinking alone?"

Nico looked up then made a face. "Smells like you're one to talk."

"I'm fine." The woman shook her head, sitting next to him.

"Bri..." He pinched the bridge of his nose. "I can't be around you if you're drunk right now."

"Why's that?" The woman rested back on her hands, not seeming the least bit thrown by being called Brier's name.

"Because I'm well on the way there myself, and nothing good will come from both of us being here and drunk right now."

"That's debatable." The woman leaned closer to him, the sheet-less mattress shifting under her. She dropped her voice playfully. "Anyway, I'm not drunk."

"Bri—"

111

The woman kissed him as he turned to face her. He paused, letting her kiss him for a moment before he pulled back.

"Brier. Don't do this just to—"

"I wouldn't be here if I didn't want to be." She kissed him again, reaching for the buttons of his jacket.

He pulled back when her fingers went to undo his shirt. "Brier—"

"You want me," the woman said, letting her fingers trail up his chest. "Tell me you don't."

"You're drunk."

She laughed and leaned forward to kiss his neck. "Do you want me to walk a straight line or something? I'm not." Her hand slipped under his shirt, and her voice dropped as she put her lips by his ear. "You want me. Here I am. Right now. You just have to take me."

Whatever sense had held Nico back seemed to snap. His hands went to the laces of her dress as she slid his jacket and shirt over his head in one movement.

Palmer's eyes shot open, the room dissolving into the dark outside. He looked toward the lump that was Nico as he tried to place the woman in the vision—certainly not Cerise. It suddenly clicked. Marina. The previous incarnation of Chaos. He had seen her with Goebel in the vision he'd had last summer at Ruhegipfel. And that left nothing but more questions. Had she been there, or had he seen her in place of Brier? Maybe it had been Brier's body but not *Brier*.

Palmer bit the inside of his cheek, letting the thoughts circle. No matter what the answer was, it wasn't good.

Brier pushed through the odd storm, trying to keep an eye on both of the other women as Marina charged forward with a frightening fervor and Clover dropped farther and farther back. Even as the thunder faded off into nothing, lightning still streaked the sky, making the hairs on the back of Brier's arms stand on end. The odd charge in the air couldn't be helping whatever new afflictions their last stop had caused.

Marina suddenly stopped dead. Her eyebrow cocked as she looked back at Brier, nearly smirking. "What do we think that is?"

Brier looked straight again, squinting as another flash of lightning split the gray sky. The lightning passed, and Brier saw a new set of stairs directly in front of them, leading upward alongside a set of jagged mountains. Brier had to fight down the urge to attempt burning them to the ground after the past two stops.

"Ruhegipfel, do we think?" Marina's voice was an unsettling mix of angry and upbeat.

Brier kept her eyes forward. The mountains certainly looked a good deal like the range she, Palmer, and Rosette had traversed leaving the Goebels. The stairs, however, those looked as though they'd been lifted straight from the Augarian. The juxtaposition compounded the tension building inside her.

A thump and a grunt behind them made Brier turn. Her eyes widened. "Clover?"

"I'm all right." Clover held up a hand, the rest of her body doubled over her knees where she sat on the ground. "I just... need to sit."

"Now this is interesting." Marina's voice carried back down the stairs from where she stood near the top.

"Go ahead." Clover nodded Brier forward. "I'll be fine."

Still frowning, Brier shook her head. "I don't need to go."

"Is there another way out?"

Brier couldn't even say if the memories were doing anything but tormenting her. Without knowing what had brought her into this world in the first place, she sincerely doubted awful, awful memories were the way out. She glanced over her shoulder at the stairs. But what chance did she truly have if she didn't keep going... somewhere? Anywhere. She gave Clover a tense smile. "We'll be right back."

Clover didn't so much as look up to acknowledge Brier had spoken.

Releasing a breath, Brier turned for the stairs, trying to place where she had seen them before. The sky grew brighter the higher she climbed, and the lightning flashed against pale blue as a warm wind brushed over her.

"Are you going to try to jump again?" Marina taunted, stepping forward as Brier stopped where the stairs flattened out.

Brier furrowed her eyebrows then looked around. They were back on the roof of the palace—during the day, though. With the temple dome still standing to one side and the bustle of Latysia floating over the walls, it was nothing like the night she had woken naked on the roof. The scene had to have come from before she'd been kidnapped in the first place. How long before, though, she had no idea. She searched for anything bad locked back in her memory, but things almost felt... happy.

The door that had formed in front of the stairs behind her flew open. Images of her and Nico passed straight through her side, aiming for the far side of the roof. Stepping farther back, she watched him catch younger her around the waist, spinning them back toward the wall of the old stairwell as she laughed.

"Not fair!" Younger Brier's back hit the wall as she seemed to stay up only by catching herself on Nico's arms. "That's cheating."

"Maybe I'm just trying to make sure you don't go off the side." He boxed her in.

"I'm not that drunk." She giggled.

"I think that's up for debate."

"You're just sore you were losing."

The memory clicked, somewhere in the back of Brier's mind. The beginning of Nico's first year attending the university—he wore black academic robes haphazardly over his clothes. The man was already skipping class, not even a week in, to get drunk with a newly seventeen-year-old her. She flicked her eyes to Marina, suddenly a little too aware where the memory was headed. Marina just watched, head tilted, with that same odd smirk.

"I don't know about losing." He remained where he was, a little too close, with her still pinned.

Brier feigned innocence, playing with the edge of Nico's robe where it hung open. "I was clearly ahead."

"Maybe. But I'm the one standing here with a beautiful woman pressed up against a wall."

"Is that all I am? Just some 'beautiful woman'?" Brier giggled again, her fingers disappearing under the robe as she slid her hand along his waist. The memory settled in so deeply, current Brier could feel the thin cloth of his shirt under her palm and hear her heart beating a little too quickly, even past the alcoholic haze that had made her bold.

"No." He watched her. "But keep doing what you're doing, and it's going to be a little hard to remember that."

Brier smiled, eyes dropping from his as she traced a finger along his lower back. "Is that so?"

He leaned into her, dropping his voice. "Think very carefully about what you're doing, Bri."

"I don't want to think." Past Brier flicked her eyes up to him.

Reality blurred as Brier could nearly feel his lips come down on hers, the rush of heat flooding her head as much from the sensation as from knowing Marina was still watching, as well. But the mix of alcohol and the years of treading that dangerous line made past her and Nico reckless. Her skirts bunched at the side as his hands went to her hips, sliding her farther up the wall.

"You had that and still were debating between him and Palmer?" Marina's voice broke into the rush pulsing through Brier's body.

Brier opened her mouth to respond, certain her face was flushed bright red, as the memory continued to play out in the background. The university bells pealed, cutting present Brier off as much as it made past Brier and Nico jerk apart, both panting.

Brier glanced down as the bells counted off the hour, as if suddenly realizing how dangerously high her skirts had been pulled, her legs bare to mid-thigh where they stood on the middle of the roof. Still, she didn't untangle herself. Looking back at Nico, she continued to breathe a little too quickly. "Everyone else will be getting out of class?"

Nico nodded and took another moment himself before he slowly let her slide back down. Her skirts dropped as her feet touched the ground. "I told Rush and Leo I'd meet them."

She nodded.

"I could stay?" he said, the weight of the question underneath the statement settling over them.

Brier wet her lips. The earlier recklessness had dwindled as her buzz wore off and reality settled back in. She shook her head, trying to keep her voice light. "It's fine. Tell them 'hi' for me."

The memory faded as Nico moved back to the door downstairs. Marina's scoff broke through the silence. "Life is truly wasted on the living, isn't it?"

"Excuse me?" Brier looked at her, finding herself at the top of the stairs, surrounded by the mountains once again as the roof faded away.

"Thirty minutes with that body of yours, and I lived more than you have your entire life."

"What?"

"And with the number of men just standing around in that city the past few months..." Marina shook her head. "Nico's my choice, obviously, but I would have taken any of the men over there you liked. Palmer, one of the soldiers... anything other than sitting around, moping day after day after day. We're goddesses. *Divine.* People should bend to our will. We should not bend ours to theirs."

Brier tried to answer, but Marina's words were flying out so quickly, they were difficult to follow.

"And you just sit there!" Marina turned to face Brier head on. "*You* got to live, and all you did was sit there like some prim little doll. How can you even call yourself a—"

"Brier?" Clover's voice carried up the stairs, cutting off Marina's tirade.

Brier glanced behind her and saw the woman slowly climbing the stairs as water gradually flooded the plain and began to overtake each stair, one at a time.

"Great, she's going to start dripping again," Marina murmured, rolling her eyes as the rise of anger slowed back to a low burn. "Guess we're going to be waiting up here together, huh?"

Brier stared down at the flooded plain, her mind churning as quickly as the water below.

A bird chirped. Palmer stirred, his neck smarting from how he'd fallen asleep against his knees. Wiping the sleep from his eyes, he looked around. A low mist had settled into the dips in the landscape overnight, looking golden as the sun peeked over one of the mountains. Nico remained on his little pallet, as if he hadn't moved at all since falling asleep. Another bird answered the first. Palmer yawned, nudging Nico with his foot.

Nico started awake, halfway up to sitting before he looked around. His eyes settled on the slowly lightening sky before he looked at Palmer. "You didn't wake me."

"Fell asleep," Palmer admitted.

Nico released a breath, pulling his knees up as he rested his arms across them. "You wouldn't survive day one as a soldier, would you?"

"Was obviously more my father's calling than mine."

Nico glanced at him.

"He *was* a soldier," Palmer clarified, standing. "Though he died in battle, so maybe he wasn't a very good one, either."

Brier would have latched on to the derisiveness in his tone and asked more. In the months he had spent with her, Palmer had avoided saying anything meaningful about his father. He certainly wouldn't have managed to evade the topic, saying something like that to her. But Nico merely nodded and rolled up his pallet.

The first bird chirped again, this time fully catching Palmer's attention. He frowned, looking around.

"What is it?" Nico glanced at him.

Both birds had gone deathly silent. If they even were birds. Palmer scanned the hills around them, then the mist in the dip. "Do you feel like we're being watched?"

Nico grabbed his crossbow and straightened fully. "Do you?"

A whistle rang out, and a line of horses appeared along the top of the hill as men on foot marched up from the valley. Nico's bow leveled, but in the face of a row of harquebuses, Palmer couldn't imagine it would do much good. The organization also said the men weren't thieves of any sort. As the men closed in, Palmer put his own hands up, speaking as they came to a halt, only a few yards away. "We're just traveling through."

The man at the center, who seemed to be the leader, looked Palmer and Nico over quickly, his eyes pausing on the bow.

"You're not going to shoot all of them," Palmer hissed.

Looking as though he were considering trying, Nico lowered the bow until it pointed toward the ground.

The leader looked back at Palmer. "How old are you?"

Palmer frowned. "What?"

"How old are you?" he repeated.

After sharing a confused look with Nico, Palmer turned back to the man. "Twenty."

The leader looked at Nico and only got a short nod as Nico agreed for himself. Considering both of them for another moment, he turned to the man next to him. "Take them back to Our Lady."

"What?" Palmer looked at the circle closing around them.

Two of the foot soldiers grabbed Palmer's and Nico's tethered horses as another jerked the crossbow away from Nico, earning himself a deadly glare but no real protest. As the three men moved back into line, Nico shot Palmer a hard look, but even he didn't speak as they were slowly shuffled west—decidedly off course.

CHAPTER SIXTEEN

T HE TOWN TO THE WEST seemed to rise from nowhere. Built along the far side of a hill, the stone walls remained entirely out of sight until they swung out wide, coming up through a protected valley. Palmer glanced next to him. Nico didn't look back, his eyes watching the circle of men escorting them. Palmer studied the group. Not particularly menacing, they still seemed dead serious, walking with their harquebuses shouldered but ready as they climbed the winding path to the city walls.

Moving up to the gate into the town, Palmer tried to think of something to say, but nothing came to him. Whatever these soldiers were interested in Palmer and Nico for, they didn't seem interested in an argument. The man at the front of their escort strode up to a man just past the entrance—the only person in sight in what appeared to be an otherwise-empty town. "We found these half a league east. We are bringing them to Our Lady."

The man looked Nico and Palmer over quickly before nodding. "She's still asleep. Put them in the waiting room."

Palmer and Nico let themselves be shuffled the rest of the way into town and up to a midsized circular building that looked to be the city temple. They were summarily shoved through the curved door before it slammed and locked behind them. Finally alone, they abandoned their silent understanding to keep quiet.

"Our Lady?" Nico glanced at Palmer before looking around the room, taking in every seam in the wall and each of the stained-glass windows.

Palmer moved more slowly. Something about the room seemed odd. Much smaller than the one in the Augarian, the building was no doubt a temple. Several of the symbols that had been carved under the windowsills had been chipped away and replaced with crude renditions of symbols that looked only vaguely familiar from his time as an acolyte. Palmer searched for the information, somewhere in the lesser-used part of his mind. His eyes fell on one of the better-rendered symbols—a star within a circle between a pair of hands—and it came to him. Astarte. The conflicted feminine. Love, beauty, and when needed, war. He turned back to where Nico was studying the door. "I think they're a cult."

Nico frowned, looking over his shoulder.

Palmer pointed at the symbol. "Following Astarte, I'd think."

"So... they're planning on introducing us to a goddess?"

Someone stirred in the adjoining room, the energy just enough to reach Palmer's senses. He released a breath. "Yes, if you're also calling Rosette and Brier goddesses."

Nico blinked then groaned. "So one of your people."

"I don't know about 'my people.'"

"Well, someone like you, whatever you want to call it. It seems every damned person we meet these days is one." Nico tried the knob. The latch caught. "Can't you walk through walls or something?"

Palmer shook his head. "That's Cerise."

"And if we had Brier, we could just blast our way out," Nico mumbled.

"Or have her open the door." Palmer barely kept himself from rolling his eyes. "She didn't get out of that room you had her in by picking locks."

Nico's cheek twitched. "It seems more and more like just about anyone else would have been more useful to have along on this trip than you."

"Including Rosette?" Palmer said, a little snidely. Even she might not have been able to take on all the men who'd found them, but between her and Nico, they would have had a fighting chance. "If we'd taken *her* with us—"

"I'd about—"

The far door clicked open before Nico could finish whatever rant he'd planned. A woman now stood in the doorway. A vague sense of recognition hit him.

The name came out of Nico's mouth. "Carmella?"

"Nico Adessi-Guillroy." The woman walked into the room, her gauzy dress floating behind her. "I have to say, of all the possible people I thought might find their way to Elatita, you were never one of them."

The name clicked into place. In the thin, clinging dress, Carmella Huerta—Huerta-Rey under the old conventions—looked older, more womanly than she had done up in the full pink dress at Brier's birthday party last summer. The pretty, smooth face, honey-brown eyes, and dark ringlets, however, made up the same woman Palmer had seen almost a year ago, the same woman Egidio had been so taken with that he'd insisted on sneaking out to attempt speaking with her. Palmer wondered if Egidio had ever actually sent that letter he was going to write her.

"Of all the possible people I thought might come through that door," Nico returned, "you weren't one of them. What are you doing here?"

Carmella held out her arms, motioning to the old temple around them. "It seems the people here think I'm a goddess."

"Not so different than normal, then?" Nico said.

Carmella smiled, revealing a line of pretty, white teeth. "Perhaps. Though if I recall correctly, you were never one to say so."

Nico didn't answer, but the corner of his mouth actually tipped up into something like a smile.

Carmella's eyes flicked to Palmer, and she looked him over quickly. "And who's your friend, Nic?"

"We've actually met," Palmer said.

Carmella's eyebrows arched.

"At Brier's birthday last summer." Palmer crossed his arms across his chest awkwardly as he introduced himself. "Palmer Tash."

Carmella offered him a mirror of his own quick smile, though even the name didn't seem to register in her memory. She looked back at Nico. "What are you doing out this way? I heard you were in Etrusa."

Nico frowned. "Where did you hear that?"

"When you left after... the unfortunateness with Brier Chastain-Bochard," Carmella said delicately. "I was told you went to Etrusa."

Any hint of a smile disappeared. Nico's face turned hard once again. "No. I didn't."

Carmella blinked, her brown eyes wide and innocent as the energy in the room started to shift. "I was sorry to hear about her, Nic. Really."

"What are you doing?" Palmer frowned.

Carmella's wide eyes shifted back to him.

"You're manipulating the energy in the room," Palmer said. "To do what?"

Her eyes narrowed slightly, and the wave rushed at Palmer. His hands came up on instinct, but it glanced off him, scattering harmlessly into the walls. She paused then cocked her head, diverting the energy to Nico. It seemed to float around him, not soaking in. She looked between Nico and Palmer, eyes finally settling on the latter. "Are you protecting him?"

Palmer shook his head.

"So what are *you*?" she asked.

"I asked first."

She held his eyes for a long moment before shrugging. "They think I'm Astarte."

"And you can affect men like she does?"

"People in general," she said, glancing back at Nico. "Most of the time, especially men." She looked back at Palmer. "And you?"

"Kosmos," he said, without further explanation, even if the name wouldn't match up exactly to the Augarian pantheon. "Though most of my powers aren't working so well with Brier unconscious."

Her eyebrows furrowed. "Brier Chastain-Bochard?"

"Chastain," Palmer agreed. "With the Augarian mostly gone—"

"I heard she was dead," Carmella said.

"Not yet," Nico finally answered. "But she might be soon if we don't keep going."

Carmella looked at him for a long moment, her eyes running over him. "And you, Nico just-Adessi? What are you?"

"I'm just me," he said, continuing quickly. "But we do have to go."

She frowned but didn't argue. With another shrug, she leaned back against the wall, her body curved enticingly. "They aren't going to let you go."

Nico stiffened. "They?"

"The guards out there." Carmella motioned to the far door. "You're both young, healthy... they aren't going to just let you leave again."

"They'd keep us captive?" Palmer asked.

"If you tried to go. A plague broke out here not too long ago. Came in from the coast and wiped out most of the town. Between that and the news of 'old gods' destroying Latysia, they started gathering anyone they could find in the countryside to prepare for the end of the world. That's how they found me. One of the girls here apparently knew I was 'special.' Now, when they find men around, they bring them to me. If they pass inspection, they're put into the guard to supposedly protect the city when the dead walk and the sky rains blood or whatever it is they're saying. Personally, I think they're just looking for healthy men to help repopulate the town. The women made it through the plague much better, for whatever reason."

"They think you're a goddess." Nico apparently was willing to ignore the rest of her explanation. "You can't order them to let us go?"

"I can scramble their senses to a point." Carmella sighed, studying her nails. "Make people especially... pliant. But other strong emotions keep me from entirely overriding some decisions. Fear, in this case." She looked up again, studying Nico through her lashes. "But you don't seem afraid. If you're not special, why don't I affect you?"

"Carmella." Nico met her eyes, unamused. "With all due respect, if you are the only reason I don't get to Brier before she does actually die, there will be hell to pay, goddess or not."

"Ah, of course." Carmella sighed dramatically, dropping her hand as she straightened from the wall once again. "It always does seem to be her, doesn't it? You realize you're the only man to ever choose her when he could have me."

"I am *deadly* serious, Ella." Nico held her eyes, face unchanged.

"You were always so infuriating, Nic." She released a breath, finally looking away. "I suppose I'll see what I can do, for old times' sake. But I warn you, you're both probably in better shape than ninety percent of the men in town. They'll be loath to let you go."

"Then you'll just have to convince them," Nico said. "I have full faith in you."

Brier pressed her eyes shut, her head feeling about ready to split open as the women behind her continued to squabble. Marina's arguments were growing grander and grander as her anger intensified; Clover's voice was soft but annoyed when she did respond. Brier ignored them both, feeling their little platform tilt as the water around them churned.

"It wasn't your choice to make." Clover's voice broke back through Brier's thoughts. "If she didn't want—"

"We're the *same person*," Marina cut her off. "Chaos, Chaos. *You're* the one who shouldn't be here. And at least *I* realize what we are. Gods shouldn't mope. We can do whatever we damn well decid—"

"Will you both just shut up?" Brier held her hands out sharply, and a clap of thunder finally joined the lightning flashing over them.

Marina waited for it to pass before continuing, "You know I'm right. Really, which of us would you want to be? The one who drowned herself from moping? Or the one who actually went out and did things?"

"And got herself burned alive," Clover snapped.

"That wasn't—"

"I said enough!" Brier looked at them, eyes flicking back and forth sternly before they settled on Marina. "And if you actually want to know, neither of you. You're an idiot who got herself killed by charging into a battle you thought would be fun. And you"—her eyes shifted to Clover—"gave up before you even understood what you were."

Clover's face contorted. "Brier..."

"You did." Brier kept her eyes on her mother, taking a shaky breath. "You gave up. And I won't. Because I'm not you. I'm not either of you. And no matter how broken I become, I will *never* be either of you. I'll be me. And whatever damn me I want to be. So you can both shut up and let me think, or you can keep bickering until I find a way to blast you both into oblivion."

Marina's face contorted. "You can't—"

"Just try me." Brier set her jaw. For the first time since Brier had arrived, both Clover and Marina had been struck speechless. *Finally.* Brier released a breath. "Now, if both of you will remain quiet for two minutes, I'm trying to figure out what to do. All right?"

Clover shrank back into herself, and Marina spun to the side in a huff, but neither spoke. And Brier supposed she would take that for the moment.

CHAPTER SEVENTEEN

PLACED IN A SMALL WOODEN house filled with cots, blankets, and gaunt men dressed in worn homespun clothes, Palmer couldn't say if actually having a roof over his head was any better than sleeping outdoors while the tension of time ticking down kept him awake. And his mood only soured further as he and Nico were rallied in the morning to be put through whatever training the town had developed for their kidnapped soldiers. Drilling, sword work, target practice... how harquebuses would help stop the end of the world, Palmer didn't know, but it seemed the Elatitans were set on them learning. They were set on everyone learning, judging from the training grounds that seemed to have taken over what had once been a small market square. Wooden piles that had once been buildings were still visible behind the straw targets and dueling rings. Only the arched temple and tall stone clock tower with its broken clock sitting at one end of the training grounds had apparently escaped destruction in the name of martial utility.

While Palmer managed to muddle through, Nico continued to make things look much too simple whenever given a new task. Even if the man hadn't been endlessly annoying in the university classes they had shared—coming in late, spending entire classes talking with his friends in the back—he would have been rather simple to loathe. Nico was attractive, rich, and seemingly immeasurably talented at anything he tried. If his powers didn't return, Palmer would never hold a candle to him.

Palmer shook his head, watching one of the older men show Nico how to load the matchlock of his gun—whether that was wise or not, getting a weapon that close to a man who looked ready to snap more than a few necks barehanded. Palmer knew it would do no good to start sizing himself up against any of the other men around him. He had far more important things to worry about than jealousy—like making sure Nico Adessi *didn't* snap and get them both killed. After the day before, that seemed more likely than Palmer especially cared for.

"You." A northern-accented voice broke into Palmer's thoughts as a man stomped forward.

Palmer looked over, eyebrows raised.

"Our Lady has requested you." The man stepped in front of Palmer, his feet hitting the ground with more force than seemed possible with his frail body and blotched skin that he shared with many of the survivors of the plague Carmella had mentioned. When Palmer didn't answer, the man frowned. He grabbed Palmer's arm. "We do not keep Our Lady waiting."

Palmer didn't fight it, sending one glance back to where Nico was standing. The added tension in Nico's jaw was the only apparent sign of alarm. Palmer gave as much of a shrug as he dared then turned for the converted temple at the center of town.

Carmella stood at the door, waiting for him.

"My Lady—" The man beside Palmer cut off as Carmella lifted a hand.

"We need a moment, if you don't mind." Carmella offered him a smile.

The man looked between Carmella and Palmer. "My Lady, are you sure that's..."

Warm energy swelled in the room, and the man drifted off before he finished his thought.

Carmella continued to smile sweetly. "We'll be just fine. Thank you for your help."

The man nodded silently as he stepped back outside.

Palmer watched, waiting for the door to close before he spoke. "That does seem like it would come in handy."

Carmella shrugged and took a seat on one of the cushioned couches along the curve of the wall. "It was stronger last fall. Been having some problems with it, in all honesty, lately. Though I'd like to believe that isn't Brier Chastain's doing."

"It's likely it is connected." Palmer glanced behind him and sat so he was directly across from her. "Ever since something went wrong with Brier, something's been wrong with me."

Carmella studied him, absentmindedly playing with the tassel of a pillow next to her. "And that's why you need to save her?"

Palmer hesitated just for a moment. "One of the many reasons."

Carmella watched him for another beat, then her hand stilled as she glanced toward the door then back to Palmer. "Does Nico know you're in love with her?"

Palmer frowned. "What?"

"That *is* my area, if you believe all this goddess stuff." Carmella sat back against the wall. "You aren't going to say you aren't?"

Palmer swallowed but didn't bother denying it. "Nico and I have a working relationship, for now."

"And when you find her? The Nico I knew was never very good at sharing his toys."

"Are you saying she's a toy?"

"No." Carmella sighed, pursing her lips slightly. "She would have been immeasurably less annoying that way."

Palmer gave her a questioning look.

"Only man to ever consistently turn me down, and it was all because of her." Carmella shook her head, returning to playing with the tassel. "It's rather upsetting when you're thirteen. Especially when everyone else always told me I was prettier."

Palmer kept his eyebrows furrowed. "Were things really that shallow over on your end of the Augarian?"

Her eyes flashed angrily at him. "Are you aware how few other things women are judged upon? Appearance and breeding are what find women husbands, and I would have been better than her in both if the Adessis hadn't thrown all their money after Signorina Chastain-Bochard for whatever reason. Do you really think she could have afforded all those dresses of hers on her father's income? To a girl, believe me, it feels like a grave injustice."

Palmer made a face. "If it makes you feel any better, Orris Adessi just tried to kill her a couple months ago. And he likely still is."

Carmella frowned, her smooth forehead furrowing. "What? Orris Adessi-Guillroy always *loved* Brier. She was basically his pet."

"And he tried to burn her alive. Part of what brought down the Augarian."

Carmella's brow remained furrowed, as if she couldn't fully grasp what he was saying. "If that's true, why is Nico here with you?"

"Half to save Brier, half to shoot his father, I'm pretty sure."

"I can't imagine the Adessis would be much approving of patricide."

"Well, he already shot a crossbow bolt through his cousin's leg, so I'm not sure he cares much what his family thinks at this point."

Carmella blinked. "What cousin?"

"The one that helped kidnap Brier." Palmer did his best not to think too much about it.

Carmella sat back, eyes searching Palmer's as if she expected him to announce he was joking. "I always knew he was attached to her. You would have been blind not to. I didn't know he would kill people for her."

Palmer shrugged, not entirely sure Nico's slowly building body count was connected solely to Brier.

"And you're all right with that?" she asked.

Not entirely. Palmer shrugged again. "The end justifying the means at the moment, I suppose. Plenty more have the possibility of dying if we don't reach Brier in time."

"And you're *most* worried about that." She scanned him knowingly then continued, "If not the killing, doesn't his connection to her bother you? They have a long history that doesn't involve you."

Palmer hesitated but let it go. "If it does or doesn't, I'm not going to chance letting her die because I don't want to deal with Nico Adessi."

Carmella studied him for another moment, her face unreadable, before the corners of her lips curled up into a smile. "I spoke to those in charge. They aren't thrilled with the idea of losing both you and Nico."

Palmer accepted the change in topic. "And you can't 'convince' them?"

"I told you, strong emotions overpower me, especially with me not in top form."

"So we're trapped here?"

"They don't *want* you to go," Carmella said. "I can't change that. But I could give you a distraction if you were inclined to attempt slipping away."

Palmer frowned, considering her words. "What kind of distraction?"

"If you haven't noticed"—she looked away as if her own answer were of no interest to her—"I'm the only woman on this side of town. That is entirely by design. The women in Elatita, as a whole if not all individually, decided that they preferred to live apart from the men, following their plague. With so many men dying and families destroyed, they weren't interested in forming new ones."

Palmer just listened, waiting for her to continue.

"Of course, if they lived with no interaction, it wouldn't matter what guard they developed against the end of the world. Everyone here would eventually die out anyway. That's where the festivals come in."

"So they're... what, exactly?" Palmer frowned. The idea of what she was suggesting already sat oddly with him.

"Fertility festivals, I suppose would be the best description." Carmella's full smile reappeared. "Though they're nothing the Augarian would approve of, I'm certain. The Elatitans refer to them as *notti d'amore*. All held in my honor, of course. The point is, though, people tend to be rather... distracted on those occasions. If someone was to, say, wander off one of those nights, I doubt anyone would notice until morning."

Palmer tried to ignore the fact that the town seemed more bizarre each time he learned something new about it. "How soon could you set one up?"

"I could call one for tonight if you wanted." She shrugged.

The sooner, the better. Palmer nodded in agreement then slowed after a moment. "Would you want to come? You were kidnapped, too."

"I'm fine here. Being regarded as a goddess has its perks."

"Even with these... festivals?"

"Well, I don't have to take part." She twisted a black ringlet around

129

her finger. "Though I would like one thing from you in return for my help."

Of course. "All right?"

"When you're finished with whatever you need to do out there, you'll come back here. Something tells me we aren't finished with whatever there is for all of us." She smiled. "You can even bring Brier, if you must."

With any luck, Palmer would never have to step foot in Carmella's strange town again. Still he nodded, willing to deal with whoever could get him back on the road. And perhaps she would want to escape by the time he made it back. He forced something like a smile onto his face. "All right."

Palmer's stomach twinged. The palpable excitement in the air energized the entire town. Releasing a breath, he ignored the tingle flowing around him as he looked out at the groups of men scattered around. So far, he hadn't felt any interference from Carmella, but the town didn't seem to need it.

"I admit, I'm a bit interested to see what this whole 'festival' is," Nico murmured, eyes double-checking the dark corner where the new pack Carmella had managed to supply was hidden.

Palmer shook his head. "Not why we're here."

"Still, I've never been kidnapped by a sex cult before." Nico turned, doing his best to fade further back toward his wall.

"I would have been perfectly fine never having been." Palmer followed, searching for the best place to break off from the rest of the men.

"Not all of us took a vow of chastity." Nico disappeared before Palmer could respond.

"I was never ordained," Palmer mumbled under his breath. He stood in place another moment then finally moved to his own spot, attempting not to be seen by the men working their ways toward Carmella's temple.

A large hand clasped Palmer's shoulder. The large middle-aged man looked down at him. "Heading the wrong way, lad."

"I... I was just... I don't..."

"Not nervous, are you?"

"I... no... I'm just ..." The word came out of Palmer's mouth before he could think the better of it. "Married."

The man laughed, pushing Palmer forward. "Not in Elatita, you aren't."

Palmer managed to wrench away. "I... I'll be right there."

The man sent Palmer a suspicious look, but he strolled toward the temple without more argument then disappeared into the buzz.

Palmer slipped into the darkness, trying to gather himself once again. He felt Nico watching, hidden in the shadow of another building across the way. Palmer waited as long as he dared before he bent to slip his pack on. A cheer went up, freezing him in place. Nico peeked around the stone to look down at the temple. Palmer felt the warm energy starting. Carmella appeared. Palmer's eyes stayed on Nico. Carmella hadn't affected him before, but as powerful as the energy was growing, Palmer didn't want to test the bounds of Nico's immunity. Not when they had a limited window of opportunity to get away.

Managing to catch Nico's gaze, Palmer nodded and started down the far street toward the gate. Another cheer went up, and faint pipe music started up in the center of town. Footsteps made Palmer pause and hug a wall. But the man running down the street didn't bother to look around in the slightest. Palmer released a breath and kept going.

A single guard stood at the gate, looking toward the temple forlornly. The man had been selected to miss tonight's festival in the name of safety, no doubt. Palmer searched for something to throw. A pebble, maybe, something that would distract the guard long enough for Palmer and Nico to slip by.

After a soft thud, the guard hit the ground with a grunt then lay still. Palmer froze. Nico moved forward and pulled the bolt through the man's neck to free it before looking at Palmer expectantly.

Palmer forced himself forward, not looking at the dead guard as he followed Nico out the gate. "You didn't have to kill him."

"Sorry, I thought we were in a hurry." Nico didn't slow, and what looked like one of the crossbows they had been training with that afternoon was slung over his shoulder. How and when he had managed to steal that, Palmer had no clue. Nico glanced back. "Anyway, they were the ones wanting me to practice my aim this morning, with all that 'training.'"

Palmer bit his tongue as they started for the winding road back down to the rest of the rolling hills. Whatever had made life so cheap to Nico Adessi was likely something Nico either wouldn't want to talk about or Palmer wouldn't want to hear. Or if there hadn't been a moment Nico could point to, what did that mean? Had the man always been willing to kill? Or was it some other side effect from having been too close to Brier? If Carmella had never affected him, it would seem Brier had left some lasting impression beyond their friendship. Palmer forced himself to move on. "I suppose they're obviously going to know we're gone now when they see that guard. How long do you think we have before they come hunting for us?"

"With all their licentiousness to attend to?" Nico cocked an eyebrow, the bloody bolt hanging limply from his hand. "I think we'll be able to put more than enough distance between us before they notice."

The tingle grew into a full buzz the farther Rosette moved north. Since finding the two bodies, Peony had remained silent. Rosette didn't especially mind as long as it meant she asked no more questions about where they were headed. So Rosette continued after the feeling, adjusting every time the tingle changed.

A couple hours later, she reached a group of strange stones. She stopped, looking at the unnaturally perfect lines in them. "What do you think this is?"

Peony seemed to start from her thoughts and looked at Rosette. "It's a stone, isn't it?"

"Someone carved into it." Rosette ran her fingers over the grooves then raced toward the next row of rocks a few feet ahead of the first. Half buried, those remained in a straight row, their tops curved. She looked back at Peony. "It's like a pillar or something."

Peony walked up beside her and frowned at the stones before she looked back at Rosette. "We must be getting close to some ruins."

Rosette nodded, looking into the distance. The energy hit her. Pain, somewhere nearby. More than pain. Agony. Flexing her fingers, she scanned the horizon—a pair of horses crested the hill. One carried a dark-haired man with a bundle over the front; the other was a blond man who looked in pain, as if he might slide off his horse. Rosette dropped lower into the grass, pulling Peony down with her.

"What—" Peony started as she saw the riders.

The buzz intensified with the pain... and another familiar feeling. Rosette stopped herself from darting forward. "They have Brier."

Peony looked at her. "Are you sure?"

Rosette nodded then followed the horses as quickly as she dared, keeping low to the ground as the riders turned, putting Rosette and Peony along their left side. At the crest of the next hill, Rosette nearly tripped. An entire ruined city filled the expanse below them, reaching down toward a thin river at the bottom of the slope. She curled into herself, watching the horses join a bumpy path that led under a mostly standing arch of tan stones. She considered trying to follow the same way, but the path offered no hiding places.

She spotted a line of connected squares that looked as though they had once been houses but were no longer more than a collection of walls—like the Augarian palace would have become if no one had tried rebuilding it for years and years and years. There were always places to hide in the palace. Motioning quickly, Rosette darted forward again.

She reached a crag in one of the walls just as the horses turned down a street that looked like it had sunk a foot below the house walls. They headed for what looked like one of the temples Brier and Palmer had back home—round with a cracked dome roof over it. She followed, ducking from corner to corner, without waiting for Peony. Rosette hoped Peony wouldn't be stupid if she couldn't keep up. Better for her to stay behind than get them caught. Finally, Rosette found a spot at the corner of what had to be an alley. She stopped, watching the horses move toward a line of men outside the temple.

"What happened to you?" a voice reached them as the horses came to a stop.

Rosette's face pinched as she recognized it—the man who had wanted to hurt them back at the Augarian. Orris Adessi.

"Your son." The blond man, Leone, slid off his horse, half collapsing as his foot hit the ground.

Rosette felt the spike of pain and caught a glimpse of the bloody bandage wrapped around his upper thigh.

"My son?" Orris repeated, voice less than sympathetic.

"Came after her." Leone motioned quickly at the bundle before his hand went back to his thigh. "Shot me in the leg with a damned crossbow."

Panting a little too noisily, Peony slipped into to the alley, stopping herself on the wall with a slap. Rosette glared, but the men didn't seem to have heard.

Orris glanced at the bandage on Leone's thigh. "Was he aiming for your leg?"

"Certainly seemed that way."

"Good to know he's still a good shot." Orris turned to the other horseman. "She's alive?"

"Was this morning." The dark-haired man pulled the cloak off the front of his horse, revealing Brier's limp body.

Rosette's chest swelled, her own energy pulsing through her fingers as anger rushed in. The burn in her palms felt good this time. She clenched her fists. She would have to aim one by one or wait until Brier was no longer in the way before she cursed them all.

Orris glanced at another dark-haired man behind him—one dressed in a long brown robe. "Check her."

The man shook his head fervently, fingering a strand of wooden beads, touching each bead one by one.

Orris scoffed. "You can prophesize her coming but can't touch the girl?"

"She is not a girl," the robed man said. "She is the vessel. The vessel of our goddess who shall cleanse our souls—"

"Yes, yes. World ending, burning our excesses—I've heard your sermons." Orris waved the man away and turned to a different man. "Check her."

Hesitantly, the second man moved forward and brushed his fingers against Brier's neck. When he didn't stop breathing, he moved his hand to the side with a more solid touch and waited a second before looking at Orris. "She's alive, but I don't know how much longer she will be."

"We just need a little longer." Orris looked to the dark-haired horseman. "Take her down to the tents. Don't let her die now."

The man nodded once then took his horse's reins as he started deeper into the ruins.

"Wait," Orris snapped as the horse turned. He grabbed Brier's left hand, looking at the green stone in Rosette's ring glinting on her finger, before turning to Leone. "Where did she get this?"

Leone swallowed, face pale enough Rosette was willing to believe he would pass out if he didn't sit soon. "Nico must have given it to her?"

Orris shook his head and wrenched the ring off before shoving it into his pocket. "The boy never did have any sense when it came to this girl." He looked at the horseman. "Take her."

The man nodded and once again started away.

Orris turned back to Leone, a different anger radiating off him. Whatever that ring was, he didn't like it. Glancing down at Leone's leg, Orris shook his head. "Go get yourself looked at before you bleed out."

Leone nodded. The man who'd checked on Brier moved forward to serve as a crutch, then they both moved farther into town. Orris spun, speaking hurriedly to the robed man—his voice too low for Rosette to hear—as his hand went back to the ring in his pocket.

"It's a girl ring..." Rosette mumbled under her breath, narrowing her eyes at him.

"What do we do now?" Peony whispered, looking down at Rosette.

Rosette kept herself from blasting the two men left in the space. If they knew about Brier, they probably knew how to hurt Rosette too. She pulled back around the corner and turned to Peony. "We try to save Brier."

CHAPTER EIGHTEEN

WALKING AS BEST THEY COULD through the night, Palmer and Nico had found some sort of road by the time day broke.

"We can't be far from Venchia at this point." Nico stepped onto the packed dirt, angling north once again.

"Less than a day if we don't overshoot it, I imagine." The word *shoot* conjured less-than-pleasant images after the past few days.

Nico just nodded as silence fell between them once again. The waves of energy made the hairs on the back of Palmer's neck stand on end. Dark anger—it had to be Rosette. He looked off in the distance, trying to see any sign of her. Somehow, the girl had not only followed, but passed them. That seemed about right for the determined little girl.

"What is it?" Nico asked.

Palmer realized he had stopped walking. "Nothing." He shook his head, starting again with a quicker pace.

"Did you... *see* something?"

"No." That was at least the truth.

Nico studied him, face suspicious, but continued forward.

Another set of hills and a stretch of ruins came into view. Palmer slowed once again, studying the crumbled stones that seemed to have once been a grand arching entrance. Palmer clenched his jaw, staring at the overgrown path leading away from the main road. Recent foot traffic seemed to have trampled the long grass back down. He looked back at Nico. "I think we're here."

Nico swung his stolen bow off his shoulder to ready it. He scanned the edge of the ruins. "We should get off the main path. Try to come around the side, maybe."

Palmer nodded, not questioning Nico's tactical instincts. Growing closer to the standing arch, Palmer could make out more of the ruined town. A short domed building sat atop the rise of the hill they were on. Other ruined walls stretched out a short distance away, making up what must have once been little shops or houses. But, in all of the crumbling stone, Palmer didn't see any sign of people. He glanced at Nico. "Do you see anyone?"

Nico frowned, rising onto his toes as he searched the town himself. "Not yet."

Palmer felt for anyone out ahead of them. The low hum of Rosette's energy—and maybe, just perhaps, Brier's—radiated back to him through the emptiness, coming from somewhere across the stretch of the town. He looked back at Nico. "Maybe no one is on this side of town?"

"If my father is here, he wouldn't be that much of an idiot." Nico shook his head, sliding both his crossbow and pack from his shoulders. He left the pack resting along the bottom of the rubble. "The grass isn't very long here. There aren't many places to hide outside the city when these piles of old stone are the tallest things around. You let someone get into the ruins, however, and they suddenly would be able to set up an ambush with the cover. If there's any security whatsoever, they're going to want to stop intruders before they make it into the city."

Palmer just nodded, leaving his pack next to Nico's.

"I'm not sure if there are men farther in, or if there are ones we just can't see standing around here." Nico began to string his bow. "Either way, we'll need to be careful and try to get as far into the city as possible before someone stops us. We're not much of a match for more than a man or two right now, on open ground. Not when I can only get off a couple of shots a minute."

"Should have found a longbow?" Palmer attempted humor.

"Was never trained on one." Nico shook his head. "Crossbows are easier to learn. For most people."

Palmer raised an eyebrow—the last jab sounded more friendly than annoyed for once.

Nico continued before Palmer could speak. The teasing tone

disappeared at once as he returned to issuing orders. "Stay low to the ground as we get closer, if possible, and head for the walls back there. If we're lucky, we'll be able to find cover before anyone passes this way."

Palmer nodded, not bothering to think about what would happen if they weren't lucky. Pointing the bow forward, Nico moved away from the scant shelter. Palmer released a breath, trying to ignore the feeling of trepidation settling deep into his stomach at having to approach without any sense of who might be around—especially after what had happened the last time someone had snuck up on them. He brushed his fingers along the slight bump that was the vial, still safely in his pocket. If only he didn't completely lose where he was when using it, the liquid might have come in handy.

Nico tensed, and Palmer heard footsteps on the soft earth. Seeming to move before he thought, Nico disappeared behind the nearest cover, a low, crumbled wall. Palmer ducked next to Nico a second later, unsure if he'd managed to make it without being seen. Nico didn't comment, keeping his back pressed tightly against the rough wall. But the footsteps continued on, turning away from the wall.

Nico released a slow breath, looking at Palmer.

"We made it into town." Palmer attempted a smile.

Nico didn't answer, lifting himself just enough to see over the crumbling wall. He shook his head and came back down. "Not far enough. There's not much better cover than this until we hit whatever ruins are along the streets farther in. Any clue which way we should aim?"

Without bothering to attempt an explanation, Palmer pointed the way he could feel Rosette.

Nico nodded. He stood back up and scouted the way Palmer had pointed before dropping back down quickly.

"What?" Palmer asked.

"We found the guards," Nico murmured, holding himself stiff once again as another set of footsteps moved toward them.

Palmer clenched his teeth, remaining as motionless as possible next to Nico. If luck was with them, the guards were patrolling the edge of town to keep people out of the ruins—like Nico had said—and would pass by. If luck wasn't with them, the owner of the first set of steps *had* seen Palmer and gone to find friends. Palmer strained his mind, trying to determine anything that might help them, even if it was pointless. Without using the little vial in his pocket, Palmer was as human as the man next to him.

"You all heard the signore." A voice carried from a little ways off. "Take your posts."

The feet began moving again, spreading out. A long moment passed, then Nico pressed up once again, eyes barely rising over the top of the wall before he dropped again. He reported, nearly too low to be heard, "They've set up a proper guard along the perimeter. Too many to fight off."

"So what do we do?"

"Barring divine intervention..." Nico glanced at Palmer then continued when Palmer could only grimace. "We hope they don't come this way and spot us before we find a way to move, or we try to run it and hope they don't spot us that way."

"And?" Palmer didn't try to pretend he had anything to offer.

"Both make us more likely than not to be spotted. One, we'll just be more pinned down when they do see us."

"So we make a run for it?"

Nico shifted to the balls of his feet, looking ready to sprint even as he continued to crouch. "I get caught, you keep going. I plan to do the same thing, situation reversed."

Palmer nodded, knowing that if one of them got caught, it wouldn't be Nico.

Nico took one last breath then mouthed a silent countdown, shooting off as he hit *one*. Palmer swore under his breath and got to his feet, already behind as they ran for cover.

A shout went up somewhere behind them. Palmer couldn't make out the words past the blood pounding in his ears. Nico cut to the right. Unsure if he was supposed to follow or veer off, Palmer turned after the man and ducked into a row of boxy ruins. A gun fired. More shouts came but no more bullets.

"Alley." Nico pointed, barely getting the word out before he darted down an alley in the opposite direction.

So that answered that. Palmer went where directed, weaving his way, alone, through the increasingly smaller streets, headed in Rosette's general direction. The roads turned rougher—some buried under piles of dirt, others uneven stone sunken in the street. Palmer's legs began to burn as he tried to keep his balance over the dips and rises. Around another corner, the alley opened up into a large, open square—larger than even the market in Latysia had been—with nothing but sporadic columns offering cover. He hesitated, debating whether to backtrack or risk another open expanse. He turned and froze.

A tall, dark-haired woman in a limp dress that looked as though it had been made of sackcloth rounded the corner. The beads in her hand stilled as their eyes met silently. Her gaze finally dropped to his clothes, her hand bunching the beads tightly. "Unbeliever!"

Palmer's eyebrows furrowed. His confusion over what she'd said battled his need to get away before her shouting garnered more attention. Something rustled behind him, then a sharp blow took his knee out from under him. Landing with a grunt, Palmer looked back at the woman just in time for her foot to come down, pinning him. A group of guards came around the corner, killing any reason to try to shake loose.

"Hands up." The man at the front motioned with his harquebus. "You're coming with us."

Rosette slowed as she passed the last row of the connected cubed houses. Rows of canvas tents came into view, and small groups of people dressed in matching tan clothing walked along the river. They all seemed to be working, though none of them were looking at each other. Rosette frowned. The clothes Peony had stolen were plain, but compared to the tan sacks everyone down there wore, Rosette might as well have still been in one of Brier's old dresses. The women barely looked different from the men.

"There must be a hundred of them," Peony murmured, looking across the camp.

Rosette's eyes fell on a group of women doing wash at the bank. She copied Palmer's tone to say, "Wait here," before scurrying forward. After making it into the line of tents, Rosette paused and crouched low to the ground, waiting to be sure no one had noticed her.

Everyone continued with their chores. Rosette might as well have been invisible. She dashed out and grabbed part of the stack next to the washerwomen then disappeared before anyone noticed she'd been there. She frowned at the scratchy fabric as she paused back behind the tents. There had to be *no* good fabric in the village if everyone was wearing the sacks. She'd worn better while living on the street. She returned to Peony all the same and sorted through the pile for something that would fit them.

Peony took one Rosette shoved at her. "Why did you do that?"

Rosette rolled her eyes. "So we fit in, of *course*."

Peony frowned, but she changed without complaint.

Having found the smallest scratchy dress in the stack, Rosette stripped out of the boy clothes and pulled on the new outfit. Though the hem stopped at about her ankles, the sleeves swallowed her up, hanging far past her fingertips. *Maybe it was meant to be a shirt?* She made a face and ripped the sleeves as best she could to bring them up to her wrists.

The rough cloth left her fingers red and raw. Rosette scrunched up her nose. *It's like the tent people are* trying *to be uncomfortable.* She didn't try to make it feel any better. The sooner they could find Brier and get home, the sooner everything would go back to how it had been—them together, with nice dresses.

After checking that Peony had changed, Rosette peeked out over their hiding spot to make sure the rest of the scratchy-dress people were still occupied. An odd scraping sound made her drop back down. She pressed herself close to the stone, moving as much as she dared in order to look around.

"Signore," a voice called out before Rosette could figure out where the sound was coming from.

The scraping stopped, and Rosette saw half of Leone's body beside one of the tents. Anger began to bubble up once again at the sight of him standing there, leaning against a crutch. She clenched her fists.

He answered the other man. "I'm headed to my quarters to rest, if you don't mind."

"They said you'd want to be told," the other voice continued. "Your cousin was captured."

Leone hesitated, hopping slightly as he redistributed his weight on the crutch. "Nicodemo? That cousin?"

"He and his companion," the voice agreed. "They've been locked up at the caves."

"Has my uncle said what to do with them?"

"Just that they should stay there until he has the time to deal with them."

"Thank you." Leone sounded a little too pleased as he headed the opposite way, with his shuffle-scrape.

Rosette slid back down and turned to Peony. "That's Palmer."

Peony nodded with more conviction than Rosette had seen from her, ever. "We need to help him."

She frowned. "We need to help Brier."

Peony hesitated just a moment then straightened her shoulders. "He has powers too, doesn't he? We could use his help."

Though it sounded like a stupid excuse, Rosette admitted that was true. Making people sick would keep them away from Brier, but none of Rosette's other powers would help the way Palmer could. And he would actually be able to carry Brier if she was still asleep. Rosette finally nodded, scratching her arm under the awful fabric. "We need to find the caves."

CHAPTER NINETEEN

PALMER LOOKED UP AS THE door to the cell swung open and a new set of guards shoved Nico in quickly before the bars clanged shut again. Nico met Palmer's eyes, breathing a little too quickly, though, for a man who looked in fairly good shape. Perhaps he'd been smart enough not to fight long enough to get himself injured. They remained silent as the guards left, moving past the mouth of the little cave the prison had been built into. Once they were alone, Palmer finally spoke. "You made it longer than I did."

"They turned the whole damned town against us somehow." The stillness broke as Nico began to pace, studying their new cage. "A bunch of damned cultists jumped me."

So it hadn't just been that one odd woman. Palmer didn't bother to stand from where he was resting against the far wall. "They call you an unbeliever too?"

Nico paused and looked back at Palmer.

"The... people that got me started shouting I was an unbeliever."

Nico's eyes flicked to the side as he considered the information. "It has to be how they're protecting the town. Turn the cultists on any newcomers. Keep everyone else out."

Palmer nodded. The theory seemed as likely as anything else.

Nico continued to mumble under his breath—something along the lines of cursing and repeating the word *cultist*—as he began moving once again, shaking each of the bars along the row as if looking for a loose one. Even if they managed to slip through the bars, though, Palmer wasn't sure where they would go from there. Though the three walls surrounding them in the little cell seemed to have been natural to the cave the prison was built into, there had certainly been work done. The ceiling sloped up away from where the bars had been put in place. Wooden beams supported where they must have dug—beams that looked just slightly too easy to knock out of place if someone wanted to bring the cave down around the prisoners. Palmer's theory felt a little too credible, especially when the guard that had been left behind seemed perfectly happy to stand just outside rather than under those beams himself. Maybe, since fire hadn't worked the last time, the new plan was to try to get rid of anyone with powers by smothering them with earth.

Palmer forced his mind off those less-than-cheery thoughts. "How far did you make it?"

"Not far enough." Nico finished with the last bar in the row and returned to pacing. Silence began to drag on before Nico snapped, "Are you even sure we were going the right way? Can you actually 'feel' Brier or whatever it is you used to do?"

Palmer weighed the energy he felt in the air, trying to determine how much was Rosette and how much might be Brier. "I think so."

"Anything more than 'think' you can give me?"

Palmer felt for the half-empty vial in his pocket and debated pulling it out. Well, if there was any time to use it... "Perhaps."

Nico glanced at the vial as Palmer took it out. He frowned. "What's that?"

"I don't know." Palmer shook his head, looking at the vial between his fingers. "But it's the only thing that's giving me any sort of visions right now."

Nico stopped mid-step. "You've had a way to see things this entire time?"

"How do you think I knew to head for Venchia?" Palmer returned, twisting out the stopper. "Warn me if someone comes."

Nico continued to give the same half-confused frown, half-angry glare in Palmer's direction, but he didn't argue. Taking a sip, Palmer closed his eyes, trying to focus on the town, waiting for anything that would help pinpoint Brier. The day shifted to night as an old amphitheater took shape in his mind.

"The end of the world draws near." A man stood on the flat expanse

that had once been a stage for the ancient Venchians. His arms rose as his voice echoed up the theater. "The wars of men have stirred the wrath of the gods. The old gods. The gods of death and destruction. The gods of conquest, war, and famine. It is these gods who shall rule. Who shall burn the world."

The congregation seated on the old cracked steps buzzed with the man's words.

"The excesses, the greed long fostered in the Red City has brought our destruction," the man continued. "They attempt to rebuild, forever ignoring that they will bring our doom. We must all cleanse ourselves if we do not wish to share their fate. Purge yourself of corruption—your greed, your venality, your vanity—as we purge this city of our sins. Let them burn so our souls may not..."

The scene shifted with a jerk and took on the grainy quality that signified a vision of the future—the difference was shocking.

The same amphitheater, once again at night, but there was no crowd, no sermon. Men moved around in the moonlight, setting up a row of boxes and something that looked like a mix between a table and a stone pedestal in the middle of the flat stage. A new man moved out of the space, a limp Brier in his arms. Carelessly, he shoved her onto the pedestal.

"Careful," the man from before snapped as he moved forward, his brown robes sweeping the ground. "Do you not know who you hold?"

"We have this handled, Sage." Orris Adessi stepped forward, into the vision. "There is no need for you here."

"This is Persaea, signore." The man, the Seer, puffed up. "Her vessel. It would be wise to treat her with some respect if you do not wish your end to be eternal torment."

Orris looked less than concerned for his soul, turning back to the men with the boxes as the Seer pulled a row of beads from the pocket of his robe and ran them through his fingers.

Palmer tried to shift the vision away from the man to see Brier, or even Orris, but it lingered as the Seer mumbled an End of Days prayer Palmer vaguely remembered from his time at the temple. Whether or not the man was instructing caution, he thought the world was ending. The vision began to sputter. Palmer attempted to call it back, willing it to not force him out just yet, but he only ended up sitting in the cave with his eyes closed. Whatever the vial held had worn off. And his own proper visions hadn't returned.

Releasing a breath, Palmer recorked the vial and looked at Nico. "She's here. Or will be, if she isn't already. The cult thinks she's Persaea."

"The Goddess of Destruction?" Nico apparently hadn't given up his glare-frown.

"They heard what happened in the Augarian. Seems like an easy enough mistake to make. 'Chaos' isn't in our pantheon."

"But they're *worshipping* destruction?"

Palmer pictured the odd sackcloth dress the woman had been wearing. "Penitents would be my guess."

"I think I'd have chosen the sex cult," Nico mumbled under his breath.

"I'm sure Carmella would be thrilled."

Nico shook his head, not bothering to dignify the comment with a response. "So they want her to what? End the world?"

"Would be my guess," Palmer agreed. "And your father's figured out how to use that to his advantage, I'd bet, as well."

An odd scraping shuffle stopped Nico before he replied. Leone limped past the guard posted at the mouth of the cave, leaning heavily on a crutch. Nico's body went so tense, Palmer half expected something to snap.

"I said you had to be somewhere around here." Leone looked at his cousin, eyes narrowed. He motioned to his wounded leg. "Didn't think we could have beaten you with this."

"I'm surprised you made it at all," Nico returned, his mouth barely moving.

"Since you left me for dead," Leone spat.

"If I'd wanted you dead, you would be."

Silence slid into the room as Leone's eyes dropped over his cousin. The tension cracked in the air. "Tell me, cousin, did Chas know what you'd turned into before she agreed to put that ring on? I'm just wondering if I should be even more worried about her."

"Don't call her that," Nico growled.

"You're the one who started that nickname."

"And you've lost all right to use it."

"*I'm* the one trying to help her." Leone jabbed at his chest, nearly throwing himself off balance.

"*Help* her?" Nico's voice rose dangerously as cracks started to show in his carefully controlled demeanor. "How? By getting her killed?"

"You'd prefer to ignore what's happened to her and get *everybody* killed?" Leone's scarred face twisted. "Uncle Orris's alchemists have found a way to get that *thing* out of her. It's why she needed to come. Once it's out, we'll have the old Chas back."

"My father told you that?" Nico shook his head when Leone paused. "You *believed* him?"

"You let him try anything with her, and he will end up killing her," Palmer finally spoke from his spot on the floor, his voice far more level than either Adessi's. The tone brought both sets of eyes to him, so he continued, "Brier has been that *thing* as long as you've known her. He won't 'fix' her."

Leone shifted uncomfortably. "The girl I knew wouldn't have destroyed the Augarian."

"She wouldn't have, either, if your uncle hadn't attacked her the first time." Palmer finally stood. "If anyone's to blame for that, it's him."

Leone looked at Palmer for a moment. Something unsure passed through his eyes before he snorted. "If that's what you need to tell yourself."

"You're kidding yourself if you think my father is trying to help her." Nico's hands curled around the bars of the prison. "Have you ever met him?"

"He's always loved Chas," Leone argued.

"I doubt he's ever loved anyone as much as himself. Do you think he moved us to Latysia because he wanted to help rebuild the Augarian out of the good of his heart? He has been chasing power since I could barely talk."

"And I'd heard he went because your mother was an adulteress."

Nico's jaw locked, and his fingers seemed to lose all blood flow as they clamped around the bars.

"Her parents had to pay him off to recognize Gisella as his, right?" Leone cocked an eyebrow.

Nico remained silent, though Palmer could almost see on Nico's face all the ways he was thinking of finishing off his cousin. Palmer cut in before either Adessi could continue. "You're sentencing her to death, you realize, if you let him do this."

Leone looked at Palmer, that hint of doubt—or perhaps conscience—passing through his eyes once again, before he shook his head. "Even that would have to be better than living with that thing in her."

"Who says that's your choice?" Palmer returned, but Leone was already limping away from the prison as quickly as it seemed possible for him at the moment.

"Next time I see him, I am going to kill him." Nico mumbled to himself as he released the bars and flexed his fingers.

Palmer didn't bother to consider just how real that threat likely was. "Well, we first need to get out of here."

CHAPTER TWENTY

WITH THE ODDLY SUNKEN ROADS through the middle of town and uneven stones that seemed too widely spaced to be proper cobblestones, walking through the ruins tired Rosette's legs more quickly than the days of walking to get to the town. Dodging a particularly deep dip in the road, Rosette turned for what she hoped was the part of the hill most likely to have caves.

A flood of energy made her eyes cross. Her foot caught in one of the dips, nearly making her fall. She steadied herself and looked around.

"What?" Peony asked quietly.

"Palmer," Rosette said. He could use his powers again. She started after the feeling. "This way."

The odd cobblestone disappeared as the roads became more confusing. After a few wrong turns, they'd once again made it to the edge of the broken buildings, this time against the side of a hill—the kind of place there would be a cave. The scrape-shuffle made Rosette stop and duck out of the way. Huffing, she grabbed Peony's arm and tugged the woman to get her out of the way. Leone stormed down the hill, his crutch threatening to go out from under him anytime he took too big a step.

"That must be the cave," Peony whispered, pointing toward a shadow near the end of the path.

Rosette nodded, waiting for Leone to turn down another path before she started up herself. A guard stood outside the cave, looking rather bored. Rosette studied the slight bulge in his pocket. She leaned toward Peony. "What do you want to bet me those are keys?"

"What?"

"In his pocket." Rosette motioned with her eyes. "That looks like keys."

"How can you tell?"

Rosette frowned. "You learned to pickpocket but *not* what keys look like?"

"There weren't a lot of actual *people* around to steal from. I found crates and things."

Rosette rolled her eyes. Apparently, she would have to do *everything*. The energy continued to radiate from the little cave, though not as strongly as before. Still, that had to be him. She studied the guard, debating the best way to grab the keys and get inside. She could pretty easily run by him and grab them out of his pocket, but then getting inside would be an issue. If she made him sick, he wouldn't be able to stop her getting inside, but he might leave—or attract attention.

"So what do we do?" Peony asked.

Rosette glared. The woman wisely snapped her mouth shut, letting Rosette continue to work things out. The anger bubbling in Rosette's stomach made the decision for her. She let the energy she'd been bottling up flow toward the guard in a wave. He hunched slightly, hand going to his head, but he didn't fall over. Rosette frowned. Her powers had gotten weaker. That wasn't fun.

On to her next plan. Glancing at Peony, she directed, "Watch for anyone else coming."

Peony nodded. A little dull or not, she took direction well.

Rosette scanned the expanse next to the cave before dashing forward and accidentally on purpose running into the guard's leg. She looked up innocently as her two small fingers made it into his pocket and pulled out the keys. "I'm sorry, signore."

The guard frowned, placing a hand on her shoulder. "What are you—"

She sent another wave at him, focusing up his arm. He shouted as hives broke out. He fell to his knees, jerking slightly. Maybe that was overdoing it a little. But it had worked. And the burn definitely felt good. Another wave knocked him out, and Rosette motioned to Peony as she headed into the cave.

While she waited for her eyes to adjust to the dark space, she heard Palmer's voice. "Rosette?"

"I guess we know what that was, then," Nico mumbled.

Once again able to see, she spotted the two men—and the bars in front of them—and Rosette hurried forward to look for a lock.

"Why aren't you still in Cittamuarta?" Palmer stepped toward the bars.

Rosette stopped by the lock, her fury starting up again as she glared.

"Don't anger the one with the keys, Tash." Nico reached out to take them. Rosette didn't bother to stop him—though he needed to be brought down with hives too, if she had anything to say about it—keeping her eyes on Palmer as the other man twisted to get the right key into the lock.

"Rosie—" Palmer moved up to her as the bars swung open.

Rosette's foot connected with Palmer's shin. Hard. "You left me!"

Palmer exclaimed, pulling back and catching her shoulder to keep her out of kicking distance as he recovered. "Hey, now."

"You left." Her lip began to tremble even as she fought it off. "You left me."

"We were coming back." He dropped to her level, though he continued to favor the leg she'd kicked. "I promise. We knew you'd be all right there for a few days."

Rosette sniffled, and Palmer tugged her forward, wrapping his arms around her the way he did when she was upset. She continued sniffling, so she let him hold her, even as her fists remained clenched.

"Touching as this is," Nico broke in, "we're in a bit of a rush."

Rosette narrowed her eyes at him over Palmer's shoulder. He'd been trying to ruin everything since ever, but he was right. She pulled back to look at Palmer. "They took Brier down the hill. There's tents there."

Palmer nodded, glancing outside the cave before he looked back at Rosette. "Did you make the guard sick?"

Rosette nodded.

He glanced at the beams above them then stood. "Then let's get out of here before he starts feeling better."

"That might take a while," Peony murmured.

Palmer frowned, eyes flicking to the woman as if he'd just noticed her there. His brow furrowed, and he looked as if he were about to talk, but he just placed a hand between Rosette's shoulder blades and steered her out as Nico stole the guard's gun.

They ducked around the side of the hill and behind a group of rocks, all of them staying low. When they were as out of sight as they could be, Palmer finally looked back at Peony. "I suppose I shouldn't be surprised about Rosette, but why are you here?"

Peony blinked, mouth opening and closing stupidly.

Rosette rolled her eyes. "She wanted to come. We're helping."

Palmer's dark eyes came back to Rosette. He shook his head but rubbed her hair affectionately. He looked back at Nico as the blond man messed with the gun. "Did they train you enough with one of those?"

"I suppose we'll see." Nico leveled it and looked down the barrel before lowering it again. He turned to Rosette, his jaw tense, but he hadn't sounded as mean as he normally did. Maybe he was trying. "You know where Brier is."

Rosette still frowned at him but supposed she should answer. "They were taking her down to the tents to make sure she didn't..."

"Didn't what?" Nico asked.

"Didn't die again," Rosette said, looking back at Palmer. "They said they need her for something."

Palmer's mouth twitched slightly as he looked across the town.

"Then why are we standing here?" Nico turned toward Palmer, apparently done with anything else Rosette had to say.

Palmer continued to stare at the town, his tense look slowly turning dark. "It's almost sunset."

"So?" Nico asked.

"In my vision, your father was taking Brier to an amphitheater at night."

"At night? Tonight?"

"I'm not sure." Palmer looked back at Rosette. "How many tents are there?"

"A lot," Rosette answered.

Palmer released a breath. "If it is tonight, we don't have time to search tents."

"So we go to the amphitheater?" Nico asked.

"I'm not staying here." Rosette crossed her arms, cutting off what she knew had been coming next.

Chewing the inside of his cheek, Palmer looked at the three of them before settling on Rosette. "You've already been down to these tents?"

Rosette nodded.

Palmer pressed his lips together for a moment then addressed Nico. "Rosette and Peony can go back to the camps. With them dressed like that, the cultists will be less of a problem. We'll go to the amphitheater. That way, we can cover both."

So he wanted them to split up again, but at least he was letting her help. Rosette nodded. "We can do that."

Palmer pointed at her. "Don't take unnecessary risks. If you find trouble, do what you need to escape and find us. Am I understood?"

Rolling her eyes, Rosette nodded.

"Go on, then." Palmer motioned.

Rosette offered a quick smile and grabbed Peony's wrist to lead the woman back down to the tents.

By the time Palmer had navigated the maze of uneven streets, the entire town was in shadows, the sun lost beyond the mountains. Palmer and Nico reached a rise, with the old temple to one side and the arches marking the edge of the amphitheater to the other. Palmer took a step forward.

Nico caught his wrist and shifted the harquebus. "Guards."

Palmer spotted two shadows standing under one of the arches. He glanced back at Nico. "You shoot that thing, and we'll have half the town running this way."

Nico released a breath through his nose but didn't bother to lift the barrel. "We'll have to get around them."

So they'd finally found a situation where Nico's go-to response wasn't to kill first and *then* sort it out. Palmer's eyes fell on a stretch where the wall between two arches had crumbled. He gestured at it quickly. "That way."

Nico nodded, following silently. Built along what seemed to be a natural incline, the cracked step-seats led down to a flat expanse that appeared to be the stage from Palmer's vision. Crouching, Palmer crept forward to get a better view. His stomach clenched as he saw the setup. Men moved along a row of tall boxes to one side. Another pair circled a pedestal in the center. Mostly blocked from view, the shadow in the center was still unmistakable. Brier's white shift glowed in the moonlight.

"What are they doing?" Nico hissed, the voice making Palmer start.

Palmer shook his head, fighting the urge to charge forward without a plan, watching as they strapped Brier down and ran some sort of wires between her and the boxes. "Whatever it is, it isn't good."

"Really," Nico muttered, his body tensing and then relaxing as if he couldn't decide whether to start forward or not.

"Are we ready?" Orris Adessi's voice echoed upward as if amplified. Palmer's hand went out to keep Nico in place, just in case.

"It'd be worth it," Nico murmured. "Shooting him."

"You'd be as likely to hit Brier as him at this distance." Palmer glanced away just long enough to look at the harquebus. "That isn't your bow."

Nico's jaw locked, but he didn't argue.

Another man answered Orris down on the stage, and a soft whir started as a pair of men turned a crank on the boxes to the side. Palmer furrowed his brow, unsure at this point if he was feeling Nico's tension or his own. The whir continued, but other than Brier's body jerking slightly, nothing happened.

A minute later, the cranking men stopped, wiping their brows as they looked at the men standing around a smaller box.

"Did it work?" Orris's voice carried once again.

"It seems so, signore." A man by the smaller box straightened. "And it seems to be holding for now."

"We should finish before that isn't the case, then." Orris motioned to the men standing around, his smile audible.

"Signore." A man by the pedestal looked up.

Orris waved him away and left with the smaller box. The man by the pedestal touched Brier's neck then started away himself.

"They're all leaving." Nico straightened slightly. "They're just leaving her there?"

Palmer bit the inside of his cheek, the knot in his stomach pulling tight. The world hadn't started breaking apart as it had the last time Brier died, but then the tall boxes were nothing like what they had found under the Augarian library when they had saved her. The men had to have done something to her—Orris Adessi sounded far too pleased for them not to have—but there was no fire, no raining blood... Palmer couldn't make sense of it. When the amphitheater was nearly empty, he forced himself upright again and looked at Nico. "Let's go."

CHAPTER TWENTY-ONE

THE CHILLED AIR SMELLED DAMP. But that was right, wasn't it? There'd been a storm. Or a flood... Brier slowly opened her eyes, trying to place where she was. Something had happened—something important, with dark clouds and howling winds. But the more she tried to remember, the more quickly it slipped away. Like trying to recall a dream.

Her eyes scanned the dark sky and the jagged columns. She smelled the lingering smoke caught behind the damp in the air. This certainly wasn't anyplace familiar. Still, any sense of trepidation was buried under a serene lightness. She tried to push herself up to sitting. Her arms caught where they were above her head.

She pulled again, looking up to see the leather restraints keeping her on the marble table. Simple leather buckles, they didn't seem especially menacing. Being restrained should have been an unsettling development, all things considered. But fear didn't register. Flexing her hands, she stared at the leather. The buzzing started before she could fully note it. Slowly, the restraints frayed as they dissolved into nothing. Wrists free, she pushed herself up. And her ankles caught. She sighed and dissolved those with a wave of her hand before swinging her legs off to the side of the table as she looked around. She rubbed her wrists, trying to understand the new landscape. It looked familiar, and yet she couldn't make sense of it. Mountains, there had certainly been mountains. And someone... a woman...

"Brier."

The voice snapped the thought away and made her turn. Seeing Nico crouched a yard or so away, she blinked. Palmer's head appeared over a piece of fallen stone. She looked between them. "What...?"

Leaning forward, Nico grabbed her wrist and pulled her toward their hiding spot.

She followed without complaint and looked down at the two crouching men, taking in their dirty, strained faces. She just tilted her head. "Anyone care to fill me in on what exactly has happened?"

A pebble scuttled over the ground nearby, causing Nico to jerk her down. He picked up a harquebus that had been lying on the ground next to him and readied it.

Brier frowned, studying the gun. "Please don't tell me I've woken up in the middle of another battle."

"Not yet." Nico scanned the area around them.

"This way." Palmer motioned with his head and started for a far set of crumbling stairs leading out of the unfamiliar ruins. Someone shouted. An explosion followed. A bullet ricocheted off the ground, luckily nowhere near them. Nico turned, lit the match cord, and pulled the lock.

Brier's hands flew to her ears as the bang reverberated through her. Even if the shot hadn't struck whoever had fired at them, at least the smoke provided cover. Palmer and Nico began running, and Nico pushed her forward as he pulled a pouch from his pocket. If he'd planned to reload, he quickly abandoned that idea as they rushed up the steps toward a row of decaying arches, gun bouncing too much to be of any use.

"About this not being a battle..." Brier pulled her shift out of her way to keep up, imagining she looked a fair deal like Rosette.

"It hopefully won't be." Palmer panted. "If we get out of here."

Another shot, this one a little closer, pinged off a stone to their left. Swinging her in front of him, Nico half pushed Brier off her feet, shepherding her forward as Palmer led the way. Brier barely registered the town around them, trying to keep her balance as the ground rose and dipped, until they finally slowed and ducked into a little square room with cracked walls. Brier looked up and saw the clear night sky next to the jagged edge where half of the roof had come down. This was certainly not the Augarian. And not really the mountains. But the serenity lingered. Things were feeling *right* for the first time in months.

Nico stood in the doorway, scanning the street, even though things had gone silent. Palmer rested his elbows on his knees as he caught his breath. He glanced up and met Brier's eyes, with mixture of exhaustion, disbelief, and elation.

Brier just looked back at the odd room. Her knee tried to give. Tipping sharply, she caught herself on the rough wall. A piece of chipped plaster scraped her hand.

"Bri." Palmer straightened, his arms going out, preparing to catch her if she tipped again.

She bent her leg back and forth as she tried to get it to behave, feeling both men's eyes on her. Their heavy breathing filled the room, and it hit her. She wasn't out of breath. She brought her hand up to her mouth, testing it. No air hit her palm. She wasn't breathing at all.

"Are you all right?" Nico stepped forward.

Brier paused, trying to feel out her body. Everything felt... still. She met Nico's eyes. "I think I might have died again."

Nico's brow furrowed as he moved closer. "What?"

Palmer straightened and beat Nico to her. He brought his hand to her neck. A jolt shot through his fingers into her skin, and a thud echoed through her chest. He wrenched back.

Nico froze, looking between them. "What is it?"

Brier winced, rubbing her chest. "I think he's trying to restart my heart."

Palmer gritted his teeth but slipped his hand under hers and pressed it to the middle of her chest. The shocks pulsed through her painfully—her entire body seemed to reject them. She convulsed, half trying to jerk away, even as her hand pressed down to hold his in place. Finally, her heart started and began to keep time on its own. She gasped, the air in her lungs feeling stale. Coughing, she stumbled into the wall as her leg gave out. Nico's hands found her waist, and he pulled her against him to keep her upright.

"Dear gods," she panted, trying to get the words out.

Palmer grimaced and doubled over as he clutched his hand to his chest. "Let's... not do that again anytime soon."

Brier shook her head, her legs trying to find a place under her. "I'll do my best to keep from dying again in the near future."

"I don't know." Palmer looked up. "You're making a habit of it at this rate."

"Are you all right?" Nico shifted her slightly to allow her legs to straighten.

She managed to catch herself enough to hold some of her own weight. "I don't think my body's very happy with me."

Nico looked at Palmer, careful not to release Brier. "Can you help with that?"

"My arm's still burning." Palmer shook his head with a wince. "I don't think I can touch her right now."

"I need to sit." Brier's legs gave out once again. Nico's arm tightened around her, but he helped her down to the ground. Lightheaded, barely breathing properly, Brier sat against the stone wall, trying to get her body to obey her orders. She hadn't been this weak since she'd suffered a bout of ague as a child. Dropping her head back to rest against the wall, she finally asked, "Would one of you please tell me what's happening?"

"We're in Venchia," Palmer supplied. "You were kidnapped. Again."

"I'm making a habit of all manner of unpleasant things." Brier shook her head as much as she could manage. Some memories were starting to filter back at the very least—the Augarian throne room, the pressure building in her head... "Who kidnapped me this time? Not Goebel?"

"Leone and two of those thugs Tash let into the city." Nico rocked where he was, seemingly torn between remaining next to her and checking the street again.

"You weren't petitioning to keep your cousin out," Palmer returned.

Something eerily dark passed over Nico's face, but he didn't respond as he moved to the doorway.

Palmer offered her a weak smile, reaching out as if to touch her before he caught himself and pulled back. "Orris Adessi is here."

Brier's stomach bottomed out, the rush of adrenaline at his name making her feel as though she were completely healed for a split second.

"He had you hooked up to some sort of machine," Palmer continued. "I imagine it's what killed you this time."

"He does have a talent for that," Brier murmured, glancing at Nico. If he had any thoughts about his father's presence, they were locked away behind one of his stoic masks. She looked back at Palmer. "So what's our plan?"

"Kill him," Nico answered matter-of-factly.

"Get out of here," Palmer amended. "Once you can."

Nico leaned a little farther out the door before looking back at Palmer. "Our packs might still be outside town. Those are our best chance for food or water right now."

Palmer shifted his attention, leaving Brier to watch whatever new dynamic had formed between the men while she'd been lost in the blackness that filled her head. "People are going to be swarming from the gunfire if not looking for us. With both the guards and the cultists—"

"I can handle myself, Tash," Nico cut Palmer off, though there was no malice in his tone. "Anyway, you can't heal her if you collapse yourself. None of us have eaten."

Palmer frowned but nodded. "See if you can pick up Rosette at the same time. She likely heard the gunfire, as well."

Brier's brow furrowed as Nico gave a rather sarcastic salute and slipped out into the night. "Rosette's here?"

"I tried to leave her behind." Palmer finally took a seat next to her, careful to leave a large gap so that they weren't in danger of touching. "She's a stubborn little girl when she sets her mind to it."

There was no denying that. Brier nodded, trying to piece together a memory flickering at the edges of her consciousness. "She was there, wasn't she? When whatever happened with Leone happened?"

"She gave him a nice case of pox for his trouble." Palmer nodded, offering a weak smile. "Do you not remember?"

"Everything's a little scrambled at the moment. Like I can't tell what was real and what was a dream." She looked back up at the clear sky through the roof as the strange mix of images fought for her headspace.

"Were you dreaming?" His hand slid slightly closer to her before he seemed to catch himself.

She tried to remember. A face flashed through her mind—a mix of two faces, perhaps?—but it was gone before anything made sense. "I think so." She let the hint of a memory go as she looked back at him. "How long was I unconscious?"

"Better part of a week." Palmer made a face. "We had a few problems getting up here."

"We... meaning you and Nico?"

He paused. "Is that surprising?"

"Just that you two managed to spend a week together and didn't maim one another."

"We both had a very good reason to deal with each other," Palmer said, sliding his hand back away from her.

Brier watched him for another moment before she let her head drop against the rough wall once again. Her eyes began to drift closed. Her entire body was as tired as it had been when she, Palmer, and Rosette had spent days on end walking through the mountains.

"I wish I could touch you."

She let her head loll toward him, the statement hanging between them heavily, before she managed a nod. She looked back up at the patch of sky. "Are your powers still weak?"

"They don't feel especially good at the moment. Took a lot to heal you. They weren't working at all while you were unconscious. Maybe they're coming back slowly?"

Brier blinked. "They weren't working at all? Why?"

He paused, brow furrowing slightly, as if he were waiting to see if it came to him. He finally made a face and shook his head. "I never work right when you aren't."

That would have sounded sweet if dire implications weren't hovering over them: without Palmer's powers to balance out Brier's, the destruction could get away from her. "You found your way all the way here without your powers."

He fished something out of his pocket. "Well, I had this."

Brier tried to force her eyes to focus. They fought against her. "What is it?"

"I'm not sure." He tilted the glass vial and watched the clear liquid at the bottom slosh back and forth. "An old woman gave it to me while we were on our way here. If I drink it, I can get my visions back, at least for a couple minutes. It's how I found out..."

Her eyes moved up to his face. "Found out what?"

He started to answer then cut off, studying her. "How are you feeling?"

"Exhausted," Brier said, voice dry. He continued to watch her. Brier released a breath. "I've been too tired to be upset so far, Palmer, but you're starting to try my patience."

"Do you feel like *you*?" he asked.

"I suppose?"

"I think you're possessed." The words seemed to tumble out of him all at once. "Or *were* possessed."

Brier frowned. "Well, if you count being incarnations—"

"No. Not like that. When I drank some of this"—he motioned weakly with the vial—"I had a vision about you from when you blacked out. Only it wasn't you doing things. It was the *last* you. Marina."

The mixed face popped into Brier's mind once again. The haze from the first—well, the second—time she had died. Some cyclone she'd been caught in before she'd woken up on the marble table. Marina taunting her—being sucked away into the oddly whirring wind. The rush of memories made her lurch forward. Her body unable to keep momentum beyond the first jerk, she began to tip.

"Bri!" Palmer's arm went out.

She waved him off before he could hurt himself by touching her. Releasing a breath, she let herself slump to the side. Though dirty, the floor was smoother than the wall, and she truly needed to lie down. "She was there. When I passed out."

"What?" Palmer didn't fully pull back but didn't seem about to touch her anymore.

"Both times," Brier continued. "When I was in that tube and this. Marina and..."

"And?" Palmer asked.

The blond woman clicked into place in Brier's memory. "My mother."

Palmer hesitated. "Your mother?"

"The last you," Brier said, her mind trying to fit the rest of the pieces into place. They'd been in some clouds. Or in some mountains. Or... encircled by water. It all blurred together, outside the odd whirring sound that had surrounded them and the darkness it had brought.

Brier blinked to clear her head. "Before, when I was frozen in that smoke in the Augarian battle, I saw Marina and Clover. The last us. Marina said they'd been stuck with each other ever since Clover died."

"Clover, your mother," Palmer clarified, slipping the vial into a pocket of his pack.

"That's what I just said," she said, watching him pause as if he were debating putting the vial somewhere else—or perhaps just digesting the information—before turning back to her.

"She was the... last me?"

Brier started to nod then gave a short laugh. "How did I...? Do you know what her maiden name was?"

"Brier, wha—"

"De Palme," she continued. "How did I miss that? I'm forgetting... I just can't remember..."

"Brier," he said sharply.

"She was there, with Marina." Brier went back to trying to explain, the odd cloud world from her former death overriding the watery mountains. "My mother. She drowned herself after I was born because she'd started having visions, bad ones, and she didn't know what they were. I bet she died not far from where *you* drowned when you were younger."

Palmer's face contorted. "I'm... your mother?"

"Oh no." Brier shook her head. Just that motion felt as though it took too much energy. "She's nothing like you. I don't think. It's all such a mess in my head. Half of it doesn't make sense."

Palmer released a short breath. "But you saw this all when the Augarian fell? Why didn't you tell me? I could have helped. Maybe we would have actually known—"

"I'd just *died,* Palmer." If she counted the number of times he had kept information from her in the name of protecting her... he was no one to judge people for keeping things to themselves. "What do you really want from me? They—" She thought of the pressure she'd felt in her head since the battle, as if it were too full. That feeling that had been conspicuously absent since she'd woken. "What did Orris do this time?"

Palmer looked at her, his face saying he was still caught on her earlier train of thought. "What?"

"This time when he killed me," Brier specified. "What was I doing on that table?"

163

"I don't know," Palmer admitted. "But—"

"What did it look like, then?" Brier asked, continuing when he looked ready to argue. "Please."

Palmer pressed his lips together, his eyebrows furrowed. "There were two men turning a crank around a large box. Orris walked off with a smaller box when they stopped. Leone said his uncle was going to cure you. Take Chaos out of you."

Brier felt the power trying to tingle in her fingertips. Even if her body was too tired to consider attempting to test it, she knew it was there. He hadn't gotten that, but in the cyclone she'd felt in her head... "I think it almost worked." She met Palmer's eyes. "He just got Clover and Marina instead."

It had to be nearing midnight by the time Nico reappeared at the door, but Palmer didn't quite feel tired enough to sleep. He could only hope that meant his abilities were returning. He motioned for quiet, glancing at Brier on the ground. She'd been so still since she'd drifted off, Palmer had to keep himself from checking to make sure she hadn't died yet again.

"She should eat something." Nico kept his voice low as he dropped the packs in the corner.

"She could probably use the sleep more right now." Palmer shook his head. "She was too tired to even truly be upset that your father was here."

Nico made a face and pulled out some of their remaining rations. "I would have been back sooner, but I had to skirt the town twice to get around the guards."

"And you didn't find Rosette?"

"Not while running the perimeter, no."

Palmer nodded. He would have to trust Rosette to make it one more night by herself. After this week especially, she'd proven she could do that. He took a handful of nuts and glanced over to make sure Brier was breathing, before looking back at Nico. "We think we've worked out why your father looked so pleased with that box."

Nico lifted an eyebrow.

Palmer assumed that was the only prompting he would get. "He thinks he has Chaos inside of it."

"But he doesn't?" Nico tore off a bite of the tough dried meat they'd found in Leone's belongings.

"We don't think so."

Nico sat silently for another moment as he chewed, seemingly running all the information over in his mind before speaking again. "Then what does he have?"

"Brier's memory is spotty, but as far as we can tell, two—I'm not sure what you call them—'specters' that had been in her head."

"Specters?"

"The last incarnations of us. Came with her when we brought her back the first time, we'd have to guess."

Nico looked at Palmer for a beat before shaking his head and going back to the meat. "Makes as much sense as anything else with you two."

"It's why she didn't seem drunk but couldn't remember the next morning," Palmer said, letting the words hang heavily in the air. "Best I can figure, the others in her head could take over when she blacked out."

Nico locked his jaw, looking at Brier before back to Palmer. "Does she know?"

"I still haven't told her."

"Why not?"

Palmer wasn't sure he had a good answer for that himself. Saving her from the embarrassment, perhaps. Or just the awkwardness of the situation. Maybe even his own lingering jealousy. He pushed aside the thoughts, settling on: "Same reason you haven't?"

Whether or not that made sense, it seemed to work. Nico's eyes dropped away once again. He cleared his throat, attempting to muffle the sound. "So what does it mean, if my father has the 'specters'?"

"We're not sure." Palmer shook his head. "They could be some sort of memories, maybe. Entirely worthless."

Nico looked less than convinced. "Or?"

Palmer released a breath but had to acknowledge the possibility. "Or there are two polar opposite forces trapped in that box, just waiting to explode."

"Great. So he's ending the world again." Nico offered Palmer the meat and took the nuts in return.

"Possibly," Palmer agreed.

The dark look flashed across Nico's face, though he remained silent.

"You didn't find your crossbow to shoot him?" Palmer guessed.

Nico nodded once. "I'll have to find something else when I get the chance. The harquebus is all but useless without other men to make a line. Just as likely as not to hit its target at any distance and takes too long to reload if it doesn't."

Palmer didn't bother to ask where Nico had managed to work out just how to fight with firearms. The day in Elatita seemed to have been enough for the man to load and shoot with some competence. Who knew what else he had picked up.

"I'd take a long bow, if we could find it," Nico continued. "I'm not quite as trained on those, but it would shoot more quickly than the other two."

"Why train you on a crossbow in the first place, then?" Palmer asked. "Rather than something that shoots faster."

"Takes less time to master," Nico said. "And speed wasn't a necessity with what I was doing."

Palmer considered asking more, but a flicker in the back of his mind distracted him before he could.

"What?" Nico asked.

Slowly, as the block in his head shifted just an inch, his entire body became more aware of Brier. Their connection was starting to function again. He glanced back at where she lay on the dirty floor, before smiling at Nico. "She's getting better."

"You can... sense it?"

Palmer nodded. "I can."

CHAPTER TWENTY-TWO

B RIER STIRRED, MOISTURE HITTING HER face. She forced her eyes open. The light drizzle was falling through the roof where parts were missing. She shifted away from it, looking around. Nico had returned at some point during the night and was slumped in a corner. Palmer sat against a wall, his chin resting against his chest. She frowned. He was breathing slowly enough to be in one of his meditations, but he actually looked asleep.

Palm…? She trailed off as she remembered how he hadn't been able to hear her before.

He stirred all the same, blinking a few times as he focused on her.

She pushed herself upright. Her entire body ached, but it at least seemed functional. *Can you hear me?*

It's faint, he answered, the voice a whisper. *But things seem to be starting to work again.*

Brier glanced around then picked up a clod of dirt and studied it in her palm. The energy came sluggishly and made her hand burn, but the clod began to dissolve, slowly flaking away into nothing. She looked back at Palmer.

Palmer moved closer. Carefully, he touched his hand to hers. Energy sparked again, but it felt more like pinpricks than searing pain. Palmer still winced.

"You're going to wear yourself down," Brier whispered. "I'll be fine."

"The better you get, the better I get, it seems." Palmer's eyes met hers. He took his hand from hers and moved it up to her cheek, grimacing with her as the pinpricks spread from there. "Even if I didn't want to, it seems like it would be in my best interest."

Brier closed her eyes and tried to accept the energy moving into her. When it became too much, she flinched away. "Sorry."

Palmer's hand remained in the air next to her, an unnatural heat radiating off it. She glanced to the side and saw that his palm was bright red before he dropped it to his lap.

She frowned. *I don't want to hurt you.*

"I'm fine," he returned, even as he babied his injured hand. He twisted to look at the corner Nico slept in. "You should eat something. Then we can try to find you a dress or something. Unless you want to try to save the world in your underclothes?"

"At this point, I'm not sure the world would care." Brier placed a hand on her stomach. She knew she should be hungry, but she wasn't. She glanced at Nico then at the doorway. "He didn't find Rosette?"

"I'm sure she's fine." Palmer moved to stand. "She made it all the way here by herself."

"You shouldn't have let her come." Brier frowned.

"You think I had a say? She's as stubborn as you are."

"Or you," Brier returned.

Nico started as their volume rose. He straightened from his slump and looked across the room. "What's happened?"

"Brier's awake." Palmer grabbed one of the packs without further preamble.

"And generally functioning." She gave Nico a weak smile, unnerved by the tension in his body.

Nico nodded once before looking at Palmer. "Are we good to move then?"

Brier frowned, furrowing her eyebrows, as she studied the side of Nico's face—half because of the near snub and half because he'd once again asked Palmer's opinion, or perhaps permission, over hers. Whatever she'd missed, she wasn't sure she liked it.

"My powers still aren't fully working, which means Brier likely isn't entirely healed," Palmer answered easily, clearly at ease with the exchange. "The two are obviously connected."

"You think my father is going to wait to do whatever he's planning to do with that box long enough for both of you to entirely heal?" Nico asked.

Palmer pressed his lips together, shaking his head. "We should find Rosette and find something other than the harquebus, hopefully, in the process. If we have both Brier and Rosette and you armed again—"

"I'm sitting in the room, you realize?" Brier cut into the planning.

Palmer looked at her, eyebrows slightly raised. "Do you not feel up to that?"

"Just prefer not to be talked about like I'm not here." Brier chanced trying to stand. Her head swam, but she kept her legs under her.

"We need to decide what to do." Nico watched her, his face still oddly hard. "Tash and I actually have some idea of what's out there right now if you want to listen to us."

She looked at him, narrowing her eyes as she tried not to sit again. "Watch it, Nic, or you'll start sounding like your cousin with me."

His jaw twitched before he stood sharply and turned back to Palmer. "Get her something to eat. I'll go look for the kid."

Palmer opened his mouth, but Nico had already disappeared outside.

Brier blinked, dizzy after the exertion of standing. She rested against the wall rather than sit again, looking at Palmer. "What's happened to him?"

Palmer took a moment, watching the empty doorway, before he opened one of the packs and pulled out a bag of some kind. "He's been like that since you were kidnapped."

"Is he all right?" she asked, already knowing the answer. Things hadn't been all right since she'd returned to Latysia before the battle, and they certainly weren't now.

Palmer hesitated for a moment. "Can't say I spent much time the last week trying to have deep, meaningful conversations with him." He offered her the bag. "You should try to eat."

Brier took it and finally sat, attempting to make the near collapse look somewhat graceful. "I'm more thirsty than anything."

"We still have some wine, if you want it." Palmer went back to the bag.

She took the skin he offered her, uncorking it. Despite its sweetness, the liquid burned as much as trying to use her powers had, as if her body were trying to reject the intrusion. She forced herself to drink all the same before pulling the little bag open to look at the nuts inside. Releasing a breath, she looked back at Palmer. "But something's happened? With him?"

Palmer wouldn't meet her eyes as he seemed to pick his words carefully. "He hasn't wanted to talk. Wasn't my job to try to get him to. We get along a lot better when we *aren't* talking."

"So, you... what? Decided to come after me and then didn't talk the entire way?"

"More or less," he agreed, then finally offered a smile. "He's much less curious about me than you were."

She choked down a few nuts and chased them with wine. It didn't help. Her stomach revolted, trying to send both right back up.

"Bri." Palmer started forward as she curled into herself.

She held out a hand to stop him from touching her then waited for the nausea to pass before she spoke. "I don't think my body's very happy about being alive right now."

"It's just going to have to get used to it again." Palmer sat next to her.

"The man who has killed me twice is out there with something that could destroy the world, and I'm stuck here, barely able to stand." Brier closed her eyes, resting her head against her knees. She felt the warmth of Palmer's hand on her back the second before the needle pricks started. The nausea came rushing back. She flinched away. "Stop it."

"I can handle it," Palmer said.

"Well, I can't," she snapped, then released a slow breath. Gaining some sort of control once again, she turned her head to look at him. "I don't know if I can face anyone like this."

"You can wait here," Palmer said quickly. "We can do it without you. I'll keep Rosette safe, and she can—"

"I'm not having Rosette fight my battles."

"It isn't your battle." His voice hardened just enough to edge out argument. "It's *our* battle. And if this past week has shown anything, it's that Rosette can handle herself. And I'll be there. I wouldn't let anything happen to her."

"You couldn't stop things from happening to me," Brier said, nearly flinching herself when he did—his expression making it look as though she had struck him. But she couldn't retract it. "You are a protector, but you aren't all-powerful. Especially not right now. We can't expect you to be."

He swallowed, seeming to attempt a demeanor as hard as Nico's had been but not quite managing. "This isn't the same thing. The same battle. It's just us and him."

"And whoever was shooting at us last night."

Palmer shifted, moving slightly in front of her so he could hold her eyes. "Bri, I need you to trust me."

She closed her eyes, the words making tension move up her shoulder blades. "Palmer—"

"Just this last time. Please, trust me."

"She's just a little girl." Brier shook her head.

"Only if you're saying we're just some kids ourselves," he argued.

She opened her eyes and looked into his, knowing she was already losing the battle.

"You know I'd die before I let anything happen to either of you."

"I know," Brier said softly. "But I can't lose you."

"You won't," he promised. "Neither of us."

"Brier!" Rosette burst through the doorway long before Brier could eat enough to constitute anything close to a proper breakfast and threw herself around Brier's shoulders.

Tipping with the momentum, Brier fought to stay seated upright as she smiled, unable not to. "It's good to see you, too, *piccola*."

"Palmer tried to leave me behind." Rosette pulled back, her forehead creased with distress for a split second before she puffed up. "But I wouldn't let him. I helped."

"I'm sure you did." Brier glanced at Palmer before looking back at the little girl, who was caked in dirt and wearing a sack of a dress. Once they were out of danger, she would certainly need a bath. Undoubtedly, all of them would. Her eyes dropped to the dirty bandages wrapped around Rosette's palms. "What's this?"

"She hurt herself, overusing her powers." Palmer crossed his arms.

"They're fine." Rosette tore at the bandages to show Brier. The skin was slightly red, like a rash running laterally across the center of her palm, but it didn't look bad.

"It's why I didn't think she should come," Palmer said.

Rosette pouted and crossed her thin arms. "I was *helping*."

"And now you get to help more." Nico moved into the doorway, a new supply of weapons strapped to him. Brier pressed her lips together, seeing a sword, dagger, and bow and arrows. She had the sneaking suspicion he had more hidden on him. He barely glanced at Rosette and Brier, though, before looking back at Palmer. "We found their stockpiles. Kid of yours is proving to come in handy, I admit." He shot yet another look at Palmer that Brier wasn't sure she understood. "Now if you and she can help with anyone getting down there, I can handle my father, I'm sure."

Brier frowned. "If he still has that box, you don't know what he'll be able to do."

"What box?" Rosette asked.

Brier forced her expression to soften as she looked at the girl. "The man who hurt me before, he has a box that could be very, very dangerous. We don't know what's in it yet."

"I can get it." Rosette nodded eagerly. "I got the guard's keys to get Palmer and Nico out of that cave."

Brier glanced at Palmer, questioning silently. He shook his head, waving as though he would explain later. She looked back at Rosette and rubbed the girl's arms before feeling just how rough the fabric of the dress was. "We're going to let Palmer deal with the box, but if you're careful, you can help him get down to it."

Rosette seemed satisfied with the compromise, nodding happily as she turned back to face the others.

"What should I do?" Peony asked, her head appearing just over Nico's shoulder in the doorway as she stood on tiptoe to see into the house. Nico took a step forward to let the woman inside, looking as if he'd forgotten she was behind him. Brier frowned, trying to count up the things that had obviously happened while she'd been unconscious and she needed to ask about. Nico's eyes slid to Palmer, clearly annoyed.

Palmer cleared his throat. "Oh. Peony. Why don't you... stay here with Brier? You can keep watch."

Peony blinked, some argument seeming to get lost behind her general meekness. "You don't want me to help you?"

Rosette huffed as she took a seat in Brier's lap. At Brier's questioning look, she leaned back to speak in Brier's ear. "She keeps trying to follow Palmer."

Brier raised her eyebrows, watching as Palmer continued to flounder.

"Well... you would be helping, keeping watch here..." He glanced at Brier, his face turning genuinely confused at her expression. Poor boy always had been clueless when it came to women. That he likely hadn't talked to one for the entirety of his time in the Church after ending up there as a child probably hadn't helped.

"I only have one or two good shots in me at the moment." Brier decided to put him out of his misery, shifting her eyes to the woman across the room. "It would be helpful, if we have a problem here, to have someone who can tell me what's happening farther out."

Peony frowned but took her assignment without argument.

"Now that that's settled." Nico shifted the bow on his back, taking stock of what he had on him before pulling some sort of dagger from his coat and handing it to Peony. "If you need it."

The woman's dark eyes went wide, but she held onto the hilt tightly.

"Rest of us ready?" Nico looked at Palmer and Rosette.

Rosette frowned but stood up once again before turning back to Brier. "You'll be here when we get back?"

"Unless something goes very, very wrong, yes, I will be." Brier touched the side of Rosette's grimy face gently.

Rosette's smile returned as she wrapped herself around Brier's neck.

Palmer met her eyes over Rosette's shoulder, his tan face looking a little too pale. *You'll be all right?*

As long as you come back in one piece. All of you. She kissed Rosette's head before pushing the girl back. "Do what Palmer says."

Rosette wrinkled her nose unhappily, but she nodded.

"And be safe," Brier finished and finally met Nico's eyes. "Really."

He offered her something that could have almost been called a smile

173

before checking his weapons a final time and turning for the doorway. "Come on. Time's wasting."

After a final hug, Rosette scampered forward.

We'll be fine. Palmer offered his own small smile. Then he left Brier and Peony alone in the little broken house.

CHAPTER TWENTY-THREE

"Y OUR VISIONS ARE WORKING AGAIN?" Nico's strides were stretched out as if he couldn't bring himself to walk any more slowly.

Palmer tried to keep a hold on Rosette and match the other man's long strides. He admitted, "Not entirely."

"You can feel that box thing, though?" Nico finally glanced at him.

Palmer hesitated but hopefully recovered before he sounded unsure. "We should go to the amphitheater again. I should be able to trace it from there."

"You're sure about that?"

Palmer raised an eyebrow.

"All right then." Nico sighed, once again turning up the hill that led to the amphitheater.

In the bright day, the standing arches marking the entrances into the theater seemed to offer less shelter than they had the previous night. The trio stopped at the last row of houses, pressing themselves close to one of the walls as they looked out over the expanse. A few cultists moved by, their heads down as they mumbled prayers, but the expanse was otherwise empty.

"I'm guessing it's not here if this is it," Nico said, voice low. "There would be guards of some kind."

Palmer watched the expanse, feeling a vision try to come to him, but it was too weak to offer much outside of a wider look at the cultists walking past. He shook his head. "We can go around the side and try to get down to where that machine was."

Nico nodded and pulled out an arrow, twisting it between his fingers as though he weren't completely comfortable with it. He moved the bow off his shoulder as he looked at Rosette. "You think you can cover me if there are guards down there?"

"Cover?" Rosette frowned.

Nico ground his teeth slightly but explained, "Fight any guards I can't."

"Oh." Rosette nodded. "I can do that."

Nico released a breath then glanced at Palmer. He shook his head and mumbled to himself. "Well, it's a step up at least."

Palmer refrained from commenting.

"And once more." Nico turned, keeping close to the houses as they circled the amphitheater.

The little broken house remained unnaturally quiet as they waited. Brier sat against the wall to one side while Peony sat in a corner on the other. If the other three were struggling, Brier couldn't feel a thing. And it did nothing to help her mood. Not when she was stuck sitting inside while all three of the people she cared most about in the world were off trying not to get themselves killed.

Picking at some of the dirt under her nails, she glanced up through her eyelashes and studied the woman across from her. Brier didn't think she'd looked up once since the others had left. Perhaps it wasn't entirely Palmer's fault he'd missed Peony's interest if Rosette was right. Brier wouldn't have been able to pick the woman out of a crowd if they'd met under different circumstances. Shifting against the wall, Brier attempted to keep a little of the annoyance she was feeling out of her voice. She didn't especially succeed. "What are you doing here?"

Peony looked up, seemingly shocked that Brier had spoken to her. "Me?"

"I imagine I'm not above talking to myself at this point," Brier said, "but yes, I was asking you."

Peony blinked, eyes still wide. "I... came with Rosette."

Brier wasn't sure if the woman was scared or dim. Either way, it wasn't helping Brier's tone. "I know that. I meant why are you here in general. Nico, Palmer, Rosette, they're all my friends. You and I, we've talked maybe twice. I doubt you risked your life coming here on my account."

"All due respect, signorina, but I would have been risking my life just as much by staying."

Brier raised her eyebrows. It had been a long time since anyone outside of a military uniform had called her "signorina," let alone a woman who had no reason to truly assume Brier was her better. Not while they were both sitting around in a ruined city, dirty and tired, in fabric that barely constituted clothes. Brier accepted it all the same. "You survived this long, obviously."

"Yes, but Palmer..." A flush worked its way up Peony's neck under her tan skin.

Brier stopped short from copying Rosette's huff. The woman was entirely, undoubtedly infatuated with him if just his name turned her red. Somehow keeping her tone relatively pleasant, Brier prompted, "Palmer...?"

"He was very kind to me." Peony looked down at her hands. "It's been a long time since a man has been."

Her irritation lessening just a fraction of a degree, Brier managed to tip the corners of her lips up into a smile. "Palmer has the innate urge to take care of everyone he meets, it seems. It's very sweet until he swings paternalistic."

Peony frowned. "Paternalistic? Like... fatherly?"

"It's a manner of governance that is benevolent but spends quite a bit of time justifying unilateral decisions as 'for the governed's own good.' I have to imagine it works much better on a large scale where there are several who could benefit from such governance than in personal relationships where everyone is perfectly educated." Brier offered a quick smile at Peony's expression. "I had many friends who were studying to become politicians."

Peony continued to blink, looking immeasurably confused, but she shook her head. "He's never seemed... paternalistic."

Brier tilted her head slightly. "How much time have you spent with him?"

"Well, not much."

"Try living with him for eight months, then we can compare notes." Brier pulled one of the packs near her closer, intending to poke through it if only to have something to do. The sound of glass rolling along the floor made her frown. The little vial Palmer had shown her moved in the direction she had pulled the bag until it stopped at a crack in the floor. She picked it up and looked at the clear liquid inside.

"What's that?" Peony asked.

"I'm not sure." Brier continued to study it. Carefully taking off the stopper, she sniffed it. It didn't smell like much, just the faintest whiff of something metallic. But something about it was vaguely familiar. Her mind tried to place it, but the hint of a memory was not enough. She closed her eyes, looking for anything else that could spark the familiarity in her mind.

It hit her. The baths they had once forced her into one summer while trying to cure the symptoms she'd suffered before being able to control her powers. That same slightly metallic smell had soaked into her skin, lingering for days, fighting with the rot that had followed her through each summer of her childhood. The metallic smell from the water they had brought from...

She opened her eyes and looked at Peony. "Did you come through Cittamuarta on your way here?"

Peony's brow furrowed for a split second before she nodded.

Brier pulled the vial back enough to look at it once again. "I think it's water from the baths there."

"Bath water?" Peony's frown deepened.

"Or from the hot springs that feed the baths." Brier lowered her hand slightly. "Palmer said an old woman gave it to him on the way here."

Peony swallowed, the slightly terrified look sliding back into place. "If someone did, I wasn't there."

Brier didn't bother to ask more as she looked at the water. They'd had her soak in it when she was eleven or so, trying to get rid of her headaches and the smell. The slight improvement had hardly been worth the cost of getting more water to the Augarian or sending her to Cittamuarta for the summer. They'd never had her drink it, though. But if it had been helping Palmer with his powers, it stood to reason that it might help hers.

They were opposites, true, but they worked in unison. When she'd been broken, so had he. So if that vial had helped him…

The frustration of being useless drove her to be reckless. She tossed the rest of the water back then held her body tense as she tried to judge if anything had happened. The room suddenly pitched forward, as it had the first time she'd ended up in one of Palmer's visions by accident. The fuzzy, distorted images, all tinged oddly blue, didn't make sense. She looked around. Palmer, Rosette, and Nico were walking down the steps of the amphitheater, making their way to a large box on one side of the sunken stage. She blinked, trying to make the image clearer, but it slid entirely. Stone faces suddenly looked back at her, arranged in a hazy circle. The room spun, and Brier caught sight of a man with a box in the background before the view zoomed out. The room looked nothing like an amphitheater but a good deal like part of a temple.

Suddenly, the temple cracked. One side blasted out as though a cannon had been shot from the inside. Dark soot hung in the air as the building started to crumble. Then the roar melded with the screams of the townspeople.

Her eyes flew open. The cracked house around her seemed just as blurred for a long moment before reality came back in focus.

"What?" Peony asked, searching Brier's face with perhaps the most attentiveness Brier had ever seen from the woman.

"They're in the wrong place." Brier breathed, her heart racing.

"What?" Peony repeated.

Brier didn't answer, trying to push her mind out, to find the weak connection she'd recovered. *Palmer?*

She waited then tried again after a few seconds, but Palmer didn't reply. Her agitation growing, she forced herself up to standing, unsure if the dizziness was the effect of the vision or just the lingering weakness. But she could stop it. She had to. "We need to go to the temple."

Peony blinked, seemingly searching for words. "Palmer wanted us to stay here."

"He's not having a lot of luck with that order as of late, apparently." Brier flexed her hands, trying to judge what she could do. Energy sparked there. Enough, at least, if she could get into that room with the faces from the vision. She looked at Peony. "You can stay if you like. I'm going."

Peony made a face, but she nodded, brushing herself off as she stood.

The bow twanged next to Palmer's ear. One of the guards at the bottom of the amphitheater cried out. Hissing unhappily, Nico grabbed another arrow as he glanced at Rosette. "Looks like the others are yours."

Rosette ducked forward with a smile as Nico loosed two more arrows. The third struck the screaming guard in the center of his chest, finally bringing him down.

Nico shook his head. Grabbing from his dwindling supply of arrows, he stepped forward. "Need more practice."

Palmer saw Rosette bring down the other two guards from ten feet behind them. Trusting Nico to warn him if he saw anyone else coming, Palmer moved up to the machine on the far side of the stage. The light drizzle had coated the large black box, making it shimmer. If it hadn't looked so ominous, it would have been beautiful.

"What is it?" Rosette came up behind Palmer and poked her head around his leg.

"Something we don't like." Palmer let his hand hover over one of the sharp corners of the box, down to the crank on one side, then the wires on the other. "Are you all right?"

"Fine," Rosette chirped, holding up her hands. The red in the center of her palms was a little deeper than it had been earlier. "It's tickly."

Having seen what had happened before, he couldn't bring himself to think that color change was a good thing. He focused on the odd white-silver metal that had been used to make the machine's wires. The knot in his stomach pulled tighter.

"Getting anything, Tash?" Nico asked, his back to them as he continued to watch the edges of the theater.

Palmer finally let his fingers touch the black case. A jolt passed through his fingers, as strong as the one he'd experienced when healing Brier, making him jerk back.

"Well?" Nico asked.

The vision hit so suddenly, it pitched Palmer forward. Blue and grainy, it seemed to come from outside his mind but was somehow connected—

Brier. It had to be. He tried to focus but got only a stretch of stone faces. And a dome. He looked back at Nico. "The temple."

"The box is at the temple?"

Palmer nodded.

"Are you sure?"

"This time, I think so," Palmer said, feeling the rest of the odd blue vision fade into nothing.

Despite the cool air, Brier's thin shift was soaked in sweat after the exertion of reaching the first of the connected houses. She rested a hand against a wall, trying to keep her vision from blurring once again.

"Are you sure you can do this?" Peony whispered, standing just a few steps behind.

Brier nodded and scanned the area in front of them. A man in brown robes stood in front of a large group dressed in the same type of clothes as Peony and Rosette, his arms raised as he projected some sort of sermon—one of the doomsday prophets Leone had spoken about, perhaps. Brier's eyes fell on a cloak lying behind one of the women on her knees, praying. Looking back at Peony, Brier motioned. "Can you grab me that? Maybe we can use the crowd for cover."

Peony swallowed unhappily but did as she was asked, slipping toward the cloak nearly as well as Rosette might have. With just slightly less finesse, she slid the cloth away from the woman and retreated once again to the safety of the boxy houses.

Brier actually managed a real smile for the woman this time. "Good work."

"You pick up a thing or two on the street." Peony offered the cloak to Brier.

Brier wrapped it around her shoulders quickly, feeling the rough fabric scratch wherever her shift didn't cover. She ignored it and pulled the hood as far over her face as she dared without looking suspicious. "We need to make it inside the temple. We can skirt the crowd. That should more than likely get us to the stairs."

"You're *sure* you can manage it?" Peony asked.

Brier didn't bother to look at the other woman, settling into the scratchy cloak. "I'm going to have to."

With the prophet well into his tirade, the crowd barely seemed to register Brier and Peony slowly making their way along the edge. Brier kept her eyes straight ahead, trying to block out everything else. Moving up the short set of steps to the temple, Brier finally glanced back and found Peony right on her heels. She looked into the dim temple. The space was surprisingly empty, considering the crowd outside. She addressed Peony, "Keep watch here. Get me if people start coming in. Especially the man giving the sermon."

Peony frowned, but she nodded once again then turned slightly to look out at the crowd.

Taking a deep breath, Brier moved farther inside, her eyes slowly adjusting to the light. In relatively good shape compared to the rest of the town, the temple, which looked small from the outside, felt gaping inside. Empty arched alcoves lined the walls, and the only light coming in seemed to be from a square door on Brier's left and a large oculus in the center of the domed roof. Her eyes followed the beam of light in the center of the room and landed on the large stone statue. The woman, who resembled the statues she had grown used to seeing in the Augarian, was draped in cloth. Unlike the statues in the old Augarian temple, the woman stood alone, lacking the rest of her pantheon. Brier flicked her eyes around the empty alcoves. Only seven. Not enough for a full pantheon, if that had once been their purpose. Perhaps the statue had always been alone.

Hearing the noise swell outside, Brier forced herself forward, following the curve of the wall toward the side doorway. Though the trip took much longer than it should have, she finally made it. She leaned against the doorframe, trying to catch her breath. In direct contrast to the gaping circular room, the rectangular door opened into a tight hallway, all angles and sharp corners, with light coming in from cutouts along the ceiling line, just high enough that all Brier could see out of them was sky. Taking a final deep breath, she continued forward, trying to find the room she'd seen in the blurry vision.

She turned another corner, and an open door looked back at her. More stone bodies filled the space beyond it. Brier picked up her pace, not pausing until she stepped onto the threshold. Familiarity washed over her. Not blue, not blurry, it was undoubtedly the same space with the circle of statues all staring at the middle, their heads nearly brushing the low ceiling. She pulled the hood of her cloak back slightly to get a better look. The five statues were perhaps the lone statue's mates. Why they had been moved into the little room, though, she didn't know. The odd feeling that they were all standing as a tribunal, however, left her uneasy.

"*Dolcezza.*" The voice from a far corner of the small room snapped Brier out of her thoughts. Orris Adessi stepped slightly to the side, allowing her to see only his left side past the bodies of the statues. "I was wondering where you'd slipped away to when they reported you'd somehow disappeared. You are apparently an exceedingly difficult woman to kill."

Or to get to stay dead, more accurately. She held herself stiffly, her already-exhausted muscles protesting. Still, she refused to rest against a wall again—not in front of Orris Adessi. "That doesn't seem to be from your lack of trying these days."

"An unfortunate necessity. Believe me, I consider you quite a delightful girl, all things considered. With a truly admirable amount of perseverance. You just had something I needed."

"I don't think anyone *needs* the power to destroy the world." Brier's eyes continued to move between the man and the box.

"These are all things you really never should have had to worry yourself about, *dolcezza.*"

"You don't know what you're playing with." The words came out before she could stop them as the energy in the room pulsed.

He laughed lightly. "I think I know better than you. I have been studying all this since before you were born. It's part of why I came to the Augarian, you know. The stories of the woman with the power of the gods who had led to the *Innatos'* fall before her death. It just took some time to figure out that what I'd been looking for had been right under my nose the entire time. You weren't exactly whom I would have thought it would want."

Brier flexed her fingers by her side, trying to judge if she had enough energy to attack from this distance. Her eyes went back to the box. She could aim for that, assuming she didn't believe that would be just as likely to end the world as whatever Orris had planned. But not knowing what it was made of or the specifics of what—or who—was in it made destroying the box more dangerous than just aiming at Orris and missing.

"I really have no desire to kill you, *dolcezza*, now that it's not a necessity. You're already cured. You can go off and have a completely ordinary life. Go and marry my son, if you're so inclined. It seems he'll be set on that idea no matter what I say at this point." Orris glanced at the doorway behind her. "I assume he's somewhere nearby?"

"And ready to kill you." Brier let Orris believe Nico was much closer at hand than he likely was.

Orris just continued to smile. "He may have been trained well, but if he couldn't bring himself to kill Leone already, I doubt he could kill me. He's still my son."

"And has spent the past two months hating you for what you did to me."

"I suppose we'll see." Orris looked less than troubled as he turned back to the box. "Now, if you will excuse me, *dolcezza*, I'm sure there is a crowd outside, growing impatient to see their promised god."

"They're waiting for the end of the world, by all accounts." Brier stalled, just a moment longer as power began to burn in her palms. "And you could be delivering it if you open that box."

"So dramatic." He sat somewhere behind one of the biggest statues—a large bearded man made of pure-white stone—maneuvering something blocked from sight. "I promise you everything will be fine as long as you stay out of my way." His hand went to the side of the box, revealing some sort of wire running up his arm.

Brier clenched her jaw. She was out of time. Shuffling to the side, Brier tried to see Orris once again. A soft whirring started, stirring a memory deep in Brier's mind. She ignored it and held up a hand. Her powers were still too weak. The closest statues rocked slightly, but nothing else happened. Taking a deep breath, she closed her eyes and gathered everything left in her. Her skin burned, energy crackling to the surface as the whirring grew louder. She sent all of it straight into the ground. The entire world seemed to lurch, sending Brier tumbling to the floor. Her head hit the tile. Flashes behind her eyes blinded her before the room came back into focus. The statues fell. Light streamed in, just for a second. Then the walls came down, kicking up dust, thick enough to blot out the sun. Brier curled up on her side, arm protecting her face. She remained there, too spent to move.

CHAPTER TWENTY-FOUR

"How are there this many gullible idiots in the world?" Nico murmured, looking at the crowd around the temple.

"I don't know. These past few doomsday prophecies have been closer than most." Palmer scanned the temple entrance, wishing he'd never had to give credence to the stupid prophecy about the Augarian coming down. His eyes fell on one of the women, and his stomach bottomed out. "Is that Peony?"

Nico's eyes flicked to Palmer then followed his gaze. He frowned. "What's she doing here?"

Palmer shook his head and looked down at Rosette. "Rosie, give us a distraction to let us get over there."

Rosette nodded and disappeared into the crowd. A few seconds passed, and the prophet was still ranting about the end of days. Then a man in the crowd fell. A low buzz went up near the site as the woman next to him dropped, also convulsing on the ground.

"I think that's our cue." Nico started forward.

Running up the last few steps to the temple, Palmer didn't bother with stealth as attention shifted to Rosette's handiwork. Peony glanced at him briefly, seeming half distracted by the fits across the way before she looked back, eyes wide. Palmer spoke before she could. "What are you doing here?"

"Brier said... I'm watching... I... she said you were in the wrong place..."

"Brier's here?"

Peony pointed into the temple. "She went back there."

Palmer started forward. The energy building in the air made his hair stand on end before he had a chance to look around. "Oh no…"

Someone shouted behind him, but he didn't stop. Following the charge in the air to a square door, he turned the corner. Then the entire hallway jerked under his feet. The wave of energy pulsed through the ground and shot up Palmer's legs as he tried to catch his balance. His hands went out, trying to push it away as the hallway began to crumble. Light flashed in the room ahead of him. He ran as best he could then stopped in the doorway, using the frame as a natural brace when the entire building tried to tear itself apart.

Slowly, the wave passed. Not trusting the ground to stay stable, Palmer didn't release his hold on the doorframe as he coughed. When the rumbling began to subside, he finally dared to open his eyes. He squinted through the dust to take stock of the damage.

"Tash?" Nico's voice filtered in from somewhere farther back, mixed with the wailing in the distance.

Palmer attempted to block out the crying. There was more than enough to handle in the demolished temple before he worried about anyone outside. He turned, scanning the pile of rubble that made up the hallway he had just been standing in. Palmer opened his mouth to respond.

"Nico?" Brier's voice came from the opposite direction, soft, a little dazed.

"Brier?" Nico's voice moved a closer.

"I'm here," she answered.

"So am I," Palmer cut in. "By the doorway," he added, peering in the opposite direction. The former building didn't look any better that way, but something had propped up the ceiling in places, making the rubble in that direction appear at least a little more navigable. "Are you all right?"

"I have a statue on my leg," she answered. "Other than that, better than I could be?"

Palmer looked toward the blocked hallway. "Adessi?"

"Fine enough. I'm entirely blocked off, though. I'll have to go back."

"Go ahead. I can get forward." Palmer wondered if it was odd that all of them seemed relatively unscathed despite the building being in shambles around them. But then again, Brier had been able to pick and choose who was most affected by her power, even when she couldn't consciously decide where it struck, so he didn't know what to expect.

Nico didn't answer immediately, but he finally agreed, leaving Palmer to try to work his way toward Brier.

After Palmer climbed a few haphazard piles, Brier came into view, pushing against a stone torso that looked to have once belonged to a sculpture of a young man. She looked up, face gray with dust. "I'm sorry. Orris Adessi was—is somewhere over there. I was trying to stop—"

"What are you even doing here?" Palmer moved forward, barely glancing the way she pointed. If Orris was still in the room, he was either dead or unconscious. No one else seemed to be making a sound.

"I drank your water." She stopped pushing at the broken torso, blinking a little too long as she tried to focus on Palmer. "In the vial. It gave me a vision. An odd one. But it told me you went the wrong way."

"So that's what that was." Palmer knelt, trying to get a good grip on the stone. "Help me push."

Brier grimaced but placed her hands near his. With both of them working, the stone shifted enough for them to get it off her leg. She tried to move it but cried out.

"It might be broken." Palmer tried to decide if he could touch her without hurting them both.

She pulled up her ripped shift and grimaced at the already-bruising lump in the middle of her shin.

Palmer looked down, his hand already going toward her leg as if it had a mind of its own.

"Don't." Brier shook her head before grimacing again and parroting Palmer's own thoughts. "It'll just hurt both of us."

"I'm not leaving without you, and it's try to heal you, or that." Palmer met her eyes. "I can't exactly help you out without touching you, and you're not going to be walking by yourself with a broken leg."

Brier opened her mouth, shut it again as she swallowed, then looked across the room. "He was over there, with that box. I didn't have the power to direct anything..."

"Explain later." Palmer took a deep breath, steeling himself before pressing his hand over the lump. Brier gave another sharp shout as her pain seemed to leech up his arm, burning as much as it had when he'd brought her back in the first place. He held on as long as possible but had to release her as it began to flood his chest. He panted, pulling his hand back. "I'm sorry. I can't—"

"I told you not to in the first place." Brier released a strained breath. "You're going to kill yourself at this rate if you keep trying to heal me."

"I wouldn't try if I thought it would kill me." Palmer sat back, breathing heavily as he tried to dispel the pain.

"If you thought I was dying, you've all but told me you would." Brier offered him a small smile as she pulled her leg up cautiously and prodded at the spot, which at least seemed smoother.

"Is it all right?" he asked.

"Sore, but you certainly helped." She placed a hand to the back of her head quickly before letting it drop to her side again.

"Good." He watched her. "Did you hurt your head, too?"

"Banged it when I fell, but it's fine."

"Once I'm all right again, I'll work on that."

"Don't you dare, Palmer Tash." She held his eyes. "You need to take care of yourself first for once."

"I thought we figured out taking care of you *is* taking care of me at this point."

She released a breath, face unhappy, but she didn't argue with him. She glanced around at the rubble. "I'm sorry you're always having to clean up my messes."

"Destruction and creation... I think it's part of the job description." He managed something that hopefully looked like a real smile.

She gave a nearly real smile back, then her eyes dropped to his shoulder. "That's healing too?"

Palmer looked down, realizing for the first time that his shirt had torn over the left shoulder. Blood soaked the fabric where something must have scraped him. He pushed the fabric aside. Whatever cut had been there was already knitting together into a fresh pink scar. "Yeah, it's fine."

She gave a soft laugh. "You didn't even realize you'd been hurt, did you?"

"Seemed like there were bigger things to worry about, I suppose."

She tilted her head, holding his eyes. "Please don't die for me, Palmer. I'm serious. I couldn't live with myself if you did."

He hesitated, thinking his words through. If things ever came down to her or him, he would take the hit without a moment's thought. "How about I do my best to keep us both alive?"

"Palmer." She frowned. "Really."

"What do you want me to say, Bri?" He shook his head. "That I'd let you die to save my own life? I can't, because I wouldn't."

She held his gaze for a final moment before she looked at her hands, letting his statement settle over them. The stone around them groaned as bits and pieces fell. The wailing outside began to fade into a general din of misery. Brier spoke over it. "Do you remember back when we were with Gully? Before we left his camp outside Latysia for the battle?"

Palmer tried to follow where she was going with the change in topic. He just nodded.

"What were you going to tell me?"

Palmer's eyebrows furrowed slightly. "What?"

"When we were standing out there, before leaving for the battle, you were going to say something," Brier specified. "I cut you off."

"Oh." Palmer felt a flush trying to work its way up his neck at the memory—the last time they hadn't known if they were going to both come through things alive. He opened his mouth to answer but couldn't get the words out. "I... suppose it doesn't matter right now."

"No?"

He shook his head, interlacing his fingers. "I'll tell you some other time."

Brier gave a small smile, looking at him for another moment before speaking. "I love you too."

Palmer's eyebrows shot up as he tried to respond. Nothing came out.

"Unless I entirely misread that." Her smile grew. "Then, I suppose it's just 'I love you.'"

Wise, stupid, or entirely idiotic, Palmer couldn't stop himself. Catching her cheek, he kissed her. The energy sparked, hers flowing toward him as much as his did toward her.

Her hands went to his chest, pushing him back. "Palmer..."

He met her eyes.

She pulled away an inch to look him over. "You're not hurt...?"

He shook his head. He actually felt... better. "You?"

She placed a hand on his cheek lightly. No spark shot between them. She smiled. "Apparently, we've found a better way for you to heal me."

Palmer felt the flush starting again. He stood and looked around the mostly destroyed room, trying to ignore it. "Do you think you can walk now? We probably shouldn't stay here long if we can help it."

"I feel the best I have since you brought me back in the first place." She pressed herself up, a little more slowly than normal, but otherwise seeming fine. "I obviously need to have you kiss me more often."

The burn reached his ears.

"You'd think you've never kissed me before, Palmer. Has it really been that long?" she teased, her good humor dying off as she looked around. "I really outdid myself this time, didn't I?"

"Blood doesn't seem to be raining from the sky yet, so I don't think that's true." Palmer glanced at the patch of sky visible through the wreckage. It was still overcast, perhaps, but not the ghastly red it had turned at the Augarian. He scanned the rest of the rubble, looking for a way out. "If we're careful, we could probably dig out—"

The energy flux cut Palmer off cold.

He snapped his head toward it. "Brier..."

"I've got it," Brier murmured, eyes on part of the wall behind her. Slowly, the rubble there flaked away, leaving a hole just wide enough to climb through along the ground. She looked back at him. "Do you think you can make it? I don't want to weaken it too much. The roof seems like it's barely hanging on."

Palmer nodded. He wasn't that much larger than she was. Getting down on her knees, Brier pushed herself through. Palmer followed. His shoulders nearly caught just for a second before he managed to squeeze out of their small rubble cave and into the panic that seemed a little too familiar. Only, unlike the people fleeing the Augarian when the ground had begun to open, the penitents who hadn't been swallowed by a crevice or crushed by rubble were on their knees, rocking as they cried, prayed, or both. One look at Brier's face said what she thought of that; a mix of horror, surprise, and disgust played out over her features.

Placing a hand on her back, Palmer pushed her toward the ruined houses. The closest was damaged but not much worse than it had looked before the quake. "We should probably go back for our packs. With any luck, Adessi's found Rosette, and they'll be headed back that way as well for us to regroup."

"Was Rosette in the temple?" Brier looked at him as if the thought had only just hit her.

Palmer shook his head, still directing her forward with his hand low on her back. "She was in the crowd outside. And if the past is any indication, that blast more likely helped her than hurt anything. She's always benefited from your powers."

Brier didn't seem entirely convinced, but she nodded and moved with him down the street, leaning slightly into him, even as they left the worst of the earthquake damage. Wings flapped over their heads, and a raven landed on a building a little ahead of them. Brier slowed, her face screwing up. "No..."

The bird tilted its head, studying them for a moment before it swooped to the ground. Cerise took form and looked between them. "Nice of you to announce yourselves. We've been circling, trying to track you for days. Goebel's been having a hell of a time trying to get a read on either of you. And travel is dreadfully dull when you're stuck with someone going by land."

"Goebel's here?" Brier frowned, glancing around.

"Well, after Kos here told me you'd been blacking out"—Cerise motioned at Palmer with her thumb—"I figured you could use him. Though I *can't wait* to hear how you ended up here. You both have such a talent for getting yourselves into trouble. I love it."

What did you tell her? Brier's voice popped into Palmer's head, loud and clear.

"Can we get inside first?" Palmer answered both of the women at once. "There's a cult back there still thinking the world is ending."

Cerise began to laugh. "Can't. Wait."

CHAPTER TWENTY-FIVE

B RIER PULLED AT HER SHIFT, trying to ignore the pressure pushing down inside the little room. Even if Cerise seemed caught in one of her annoyingly good moods in the wake of all the destruction, Goebel made the very air dire. His lips pressed into a tight line, he listened as Palmer summed up the events of the past weeks. Brier remained silent, looking the man over. Somehow, Goebel seemed to have aged five years in just the few months he'd been away. The gray that had been only at his temples now peppered the rest of his dark hair. With as timeless as the man had always seemed, his transformation didn't sit well with her. Perhaps losing his brother, Reinhald, had affected him more than Goebel had let on back in Latysia. Or perhaps he was just making up for Cerise seeming to have forgotten about the death entirely.

As Palmer finished, Goebel uncrossed his arms, seeming to consider everything for a long moment before speaking. "And what was in the box, then, if he obviously didn't get Brier's powers?"

Brier hesitated, unsure whether she should mention Marina to Goebel because of the history he'd had with her before Marina's death. If Reinhald had anything to do with Goebel's already-haggard appearance, hearing about his dead girlfriend would only make it worse.

"We're not sure, exactly," Palmer supplied, masterful as always at avoiding the truth without technically lying. "The problems Brier had in the Augarian seem to have been from bringing back some remnants of other powers from whatever Orris did to her under the library in the battle. It seems likely he got those, and they were enough to make him think he had Chaos in general."

"He told me I was 'normal' now, before he began to mess with the box and... everything else happened," Brier agreed.

"And where's the box now?" Goebel asked.

"Under the ruins of the temple, I'd suspect." Palmer glanced at the doorway.

Goebel frowned, studying Palmer more carefully now. "You don't know?"

"My visions haven't been working properly," Palmer answered. "Not since Brier's been hurt."

A thought hit Brier. "Have you tried since... you healed me? I feel relatively fine now."

Palmer's eyebrows rose, as if he hadn't considered it himself. "I haven't gotten any flashes of anything."

"Perhaps you're still blocking things out," Goebel suggested, crossing his arms once again. "Try bringing up that information specifically."

Palmer hesitated, but then the energy in the room buzzed, seeming to ricochet around the four of them—the three with their own powers and Goebel, with the ability to control others'—before flowing outside. Palmer pressed his lips together before speaking again, keeping his eyes on a blank space on the wall. "The box is still there, though I can't see inside it. They left that when they dug Orris Adessi out."

Brier's body tensed. "He's alive?"

Palmer considered it for another moment then made a face. "Maybe? He's not dead, I don't think, but... it's odd."

"What kind of odd?" Goebel asked.

Palmer just shook his head. "I don't know. Maybe I'm still healing myself?"

Goebel studied him for a final moment before nodding toward the door. "Could we speak for a moment?"

Brier tensed and felt Palmer do the same as he glanced at her.

"Just in the next room?" Goebel looked at the chunk of wall that was missing between the little square house and the one behind it.

Palmer didn't look pleased at the idea of splitting up once again, even for just a few yards, but he nodded. Tension kept Brier's shoulders pulled tight. She didn't attempt to dispel it as she was left alone with Cerise.

"So." Cerise broke the silence after a beat as she checked her nails. "How exactly did Kos 'heal' you? Doing something fun, I hope?"

Brier frowned. "What?"

"'Since... you healed me?'" Cerise did a weak imitation of Brier's voice that made her sound like an eight-year-old girl before returning her tone to normal. "That was a very *meaningful* pause."

Brier rolled her eyes. "You couldn't give us five minutes before starting in on that?"

"I waited a full half of a conversation. And I have to say, it was killing me." Cerise smiled, looking up with just her eyes. "Was it finally his turn to die?"

Brier shook her head, all but sure Cerise was being crude. "Don't you have something better to do than poke fun at us? You could actually be helpful for once."

"Oh, I'm always helping. Others just never seem to realize it." Cerise sighed, glancing up at the broken piece of roof. "Just watch. Another couple minutes, and Goebel and your boyfriend are going to pop back out here and tell me to go fly over to find that box. Never ask, mind you. Just 'go fly there now' like it's no trouble to me."

Brier kept her face blank, watching the woman.

The corner of Cerise's mouth tipped up into half a smirk. "Stop toying with the boy, whatever you've done. He's been in love with you... well, as long as I've known him, at least. Was rather hoping you'd figure that out on your own."

Brier started to answer, but then Cerise was gone, the raven flapping through the gap in the roof before Brier could blink. Huffing, Brier looked back where Palmer and Goebel had gone. She decided to give them two more minutes before going back there herself to see what was happening.

Palmer stepped into the back room, beginning to question if it was a separate house or meant to be part of the one he'd just left. With the wall cracked as it was, he couldn't tell. His mind flickered, but the information caught as though a net had been thrown over it. He met Goebel's eyes.

The man gave a weak smile. "We should probably keep that under control until we've worked out exactly what's happening with all of this."

The restraint Goebel had placed on Palmer's powers weakened, but Palmer stepped away from the man. Goebel had never given them a reason to not trust him—even if Reinhald had—but after the past few months, distance felt safer.

"So what's been happening?" Goebel asked.

"What are you doing here?" Palmer returned.

"Cerise said you needed me," Goebel answered simply. "If your powers haven't been working correctly, I'd say she was right."

Palmer glanced back at the other room before meeting Goebel's eyes again. "Why did you just want to talk to me, then? Brier's been struggling as—"

"You were still trying to suppress your visions, weren't you?" Goebel took a step forward as he dropped his voice. "Even when we were training you at Ruhegipfel."

Palmer didn't answer.

"And in the battle? You stopped your visions entirely there."

Palmer swallowed. "There was too much happening. I couldn't keep them and fight at the same time."

"Because you didn't train yourself."

Palmer locked his jaw. "Maybe I would have let you train me if I hadn't seen what happened to Marina."

The woman's name seemed to knock the wind out of Goebel. His face reacted before he could stop it. Even after decades, Marina's death obviously still haunted him. He swallowed then spoke, voice low. "Marina was... she wanted to fight. She'd always wanted to fight. She was... the other Chaos."

Palmer frowned, repeating, "The other Chaos?"

"The stories aren't all the same. The myths, even when the names stay. There's no saying how each incarnation will react. You're the same gods, but the world requires you to be human, as well, and those personalities change. Kindness, sorrow, anger, determination, there is no saying who you will become once you've joined with a body. I..." He took a deep breath. "I loved Marina. I did. More than you could possibly imagine. But in all the stories you read about Chaos... she was the vengeful side.

She destroyed because she could. Because whatever was in her made her vengeful. *Brier*, though. She destroys because we can't help her. Because *you* can't help her."

"You think I haven't been trying?" Palmer's voice turned deadly.

"You haven't because you won't practice."

"My powers haven't been working!"

"Because you're letting her powers control yours."

"Palmer?" Brier moved into the crack between the rooms. She looked between him and Goebel. "Is everything all right?"

Palmer nodded, forcing himself to release some of his annoyance before he spoke. "Just give us another minute."

Brier continued to flick her eyes between them before finally settling on Goebel. "Cerise has gone to look for the box."

"We'll be right there." Goebel offered her a smile.

I don't like being kept in the dark, Brier's voice filtered into Palmer's head, though she didn't look at him.

I'll fill you in. Just a minute.

Brier frowned, but she moved away, leaving just the tension in the air behind her.

Palmer looked back at Goebel, keeping his voice low but hard. "She's not trying to control me."

"No, but she is more powerful than you," Goebel said, copying Palmer's tone. "And these disasters she's causing, they'll continue to happen as long as that's true."

Palmer bit the inside of his cheek, turning the words over in his mind. "So what do you suggest?"

"You actually let me train you." Goebel stepped close enough that Palmer had to tip his head back to keep eye contact. "You can both come back to Ruhegipfel, at least through the summer, and you can properly train. Maybe then you'll be able to just call the visions you want and not have to completely shut down because you can't stop everything coming to you when it's important."

Palmer released a breath through his nose. "Let's all try to get out of this alive first. This is a doomsday cult. We still don't know if they're right or not."

197

Goebel held his eyes for a long moment before stepping back. "Brier?"

She appeared around the corner as if she had been waiting.

"Cerise went to look for that box?" he asked.

Brier nodded. "She said you were going to ask her to anyway."

Goebel gave a weak smile and clapped his hands together. "Then let's get to work."

Rosette slipped around the side of the temple, ducking under and around rubble to get into the destroyed temple. After stepping onto a clear piece of tile, she stopped and looked around. One of the walls had crumbled halfway, and the dome was missing. New stones were scattered around her. Rosette smiled. Everything had broken once again.

Except that statue. She tilted her head. Climbing over a pile of what might have once been roof, she stepped up to the statue. Voices made her hide before she could study it. She peeked around the statue's skirt, watching two men pick their way through the rubble toward the front of the temple.

"One over here, too." The shorter man kicked some of the rubble out of the way.

"Alive?" the taller one asked.

"Don't know." The first crouched. "It's a girl. Rather pretty, actually."

"Are you sizing up corpses?"

"Not a corpse." The man stood again. "She's breathing."

The taller man moved back toward the other and looked at the woman on the ground. "Well, gather her up. They said anyone in the temple."

Rosette slipped farther behind the statue, but the men didn't so much as look away from their work, pulling the woman out of enough rubble that she should very well have been dead. Squinting, Rosette got a better look. Her stomach bottomed out. Peony. She shouldn't have been there. But of course Brier had to have been in the temple. No one else could have brought it down the same way.

The men shifted back toward the front, but carrying Peony made them clumsy. Rosette went the opposite way. If Brier was nearby, she would have to be in the middle of the worst of it. And if the energy in the air said anything, the worst of it was the destroyed rooms on the side of the rest of the temple. A scratching sound made her pause. Pursing her lips, Rosette moved closer to a loose pile of rubble. Some sort of energy was behind it—if not entirely Brier.

Another chunk of rock fell out of the way, and the rest shifted, tumbling down. A spike of pain shot through the air, but otherwise, the man there—Nico—seemed fine, if curled slightly to protect his head from the rubble.

"You're too big," Rosette said, still watching him. Once the rocks finished shifting, Nico looked up. She smiled at how dirty he was; his blond hair looked gray from the dust and grime. "*I* could get around no problem."

"Well, aren't you special," Nico mumbled, brushing himself off as he stepped out of the rest of his rocks. "Did you see Brier come this way?"

Rosette shook her head. "She did this."

"Really? You don't say."

Maybe he still needed to be kicked.

Nico fixed his eyes on her, sizing her up quickly before scanning everything around them. "We should get out of here. Tash would go back to the house with our packs, more than likely."

Rosette could agree with that. And Nico was a good fighter—and always angry, which was fun when he didn't make Brier and Palmer fight. She supposed she could hold off kicking him. Instead, she let the buzz in the air soak into her skin for another moment. "They have Peony."

Nico looked back at her. "What?"

"The men digging out the temple. They found her."

Nico considered the information for a split second then moved on. "Let's figure out where Brier went."

Whether or not she had to listen to him, Rosette followed along, her muscles feeling light and springy. Even with his scratches, Nico seemed to be moving fine. Rosette tilted her head, looking at the black glow that seemed to radiate from him in the middle of all the other energy, low enough that it almost looked like a shadow. "Did she help you too?"

"What?" Nico barely spared a glance at her before he moved to the buildings still standing across from the temple.

"Brier," Rosette specified, easily keeping up. "So you wouldn't get hurt."

He slowed just beyond the first line of houses and shot Rosette a questioning look.

"You have Nothing on you." Rosette pointed. Nico glanced down but didn't seem to see what was right in front of his face. Not that surprising, Rosette supposed. Most normal people missed *everything*. Another voice cut in before he could speak.

"Some gentleman. Strolling along and leaving a lady to struggle with this thing all by herself." Cerise appeared behind them, a large black box in her arms.

Nico's eyebrows furrowed. "What are you doing here?"

"Good to see you, too, Nicolas." Cerise shoved the box into Nico's arms, brushing herself off. "Just be a dear and bring that thing, won't you? You don't look too hurt."

Nico continued to frown as Cerise strolled forward.

"Well?" She glanced over her shoulder. "Keep up. They're all going to give me a very hard time if I come back without that thing. And sadly, not in a fun way."

Nico shook his head slightly, looking at Cerise, then the box, then Rosette. She shrugged and bounced after Cerise.

CHAPTER TWENTY-SIX

"ANTIMONY," GOEBEL SAID AS HE studied the white-silver metal lining the sides of the carved box Cerise had recovered.

"Antimony?" Brier asked.

"The lining." Goebel didn't look up. "It's an odd thing to use. As far as metals go, it's very soft and overly brittle. It must have taken quite some work to make this."

"Why use it, then?" Nico asked.

Goebel released a breath and shook his head. "There are some stones and metals that have certain properties that can enhance or diminish energies, so I'd assume they found a similar use for it. Unfortunately, I don't know much about it. As I said, it's not easy to work with. You don't find it often."

"I suppose I should just try to stay away from it, then," Brier said, sitting on the blanket she was using for a bed. "I don't have good luck with the things Orris Adessi's alchemists invent."

Palmer snorted but otherwise remained silent in his own corner of the room. She'd nearly suffocated in the frozen smoke the alchemists had invented last time. And their machine, whatever it was, had killed her. Again. Orris Adessi had found people very good at killing her, and who knew when Palmer would hit his limit for bringing her back?

Eventually, everyone found their own places for the night. The little ruined house felt rather full with the half dozen of them strewn across it—even if Cerise had decided to take her raven form to roost above the rest of them.

Finally, once everyone else was asleep, Palmer closed his eyes and let the information bounce around his mind. But whether it was a lack of training, generally weakened powers, or something about the metal itself, he got nothing new. He released a breath and scanned the people in the room instead. His mind caught on Brier.

What are you doing?

Her voice sounded clear in his head, and he smiled. Even if Goebel didn't believe they were "balanced," they were working again, one way or another. *Just thinking.*

About anything in specific?

Palmer considered his answer before shaking his head. *Nothing especially helpful.*

From her spot in the corner with Rosette, Brier sat up. Palmer felt her moving even with his eyes still closed. *Can you sense if anyone is outside?*

He opened his eyes and looked at her shadow across the room questioningly but checked if he felt anyone else around. *If there are, I can't sense them.*

Brier shifted and got her feet under her. *Walk with me? I need some air.*

Palmer hesitated, trying to get a sense if there was anyone he was missing nearby—any fervent cultists or guards—but he came up empty. Getting to his feet, he nodded. As he worked his way around the sleeping bodies stretched across the floor, Brier followed silently. Neither of them spoke until they'd reached the street. Palmer watched her out of the corner of his eye. "Are you all right?"

"As far as I know." Brier glanced into the matching shells of houses that they passed. Keeping her voice soft, she said, "It doesn't seem like I'm possessed any longer, at least."

"But are you all right?"

She pressed her lips together as she stopped beside the house on the corner. "What did Goebel want to talk to you about today?"

"Why do I feel like this is a trick question?" He came up next to her, letting her change the topic.

"What trick?"

"Don't tell me you weren't listening." He offered a small smile.

"I didn't hear all of it." She stepped through the uneven doorway and turned into shadow again before the moonlight hit her on the other side.

"He doesn't think I'm trained well enough," Palmer summarized. Whatever she had heard, it would be enough to keep her from thinking he was holding back. "He wants us to return to Ruhegipfel with him when this is all over."

"So I stop killing people?" She turned back to look at him.

Palmer hesitated. "So I can control my powers better."

"So that I stop killing people."

Palmer frowned, shaking his head. "None of this was your fault."

"All of this was my fault." She angled away from him and went back to studying the new space. "How many people died today?"

"Brier—"

"I want to know." She met his eyes, voice strong though quiet.

Palmer swallowed, looking around as he hesitated. The roof was entirely missing, and it had been for some time as far as he could tell. Nothing but a stretch of cracked columns lined the edge of the hard, flat floor—*concrete*, the word came to him—before dropping off into a small space with a tree growing in the middle. More damaged than the house up the street, it had no doubt been grander before the city had turned to ruins.

"Palmer." Brier frowned.

He brought his eyes back to her. "I haven't counted."

Brier released a breath and stepped past the row of columns. "You could, though. Now that your powers are working some?"

"Do you want to torture yourself?" He watched her from his spot in the middle of the room.

She moved up to the tree and touched its twisted trunk. "Those people died because of me. The least I can do is acknowledge that."

Palmer still considered refusing, but Brier wouldn't let it go until she had an answer. He reached for the information and felt it bubble up from somewhere in the back of his mind. So they had that going for them. "There were just over a hundred people in the camp by the river this morning. There are thirty or so now."

Brier's head snapped toward him, her eyebrows reaching for her hairline. "That many died?"

"Died or fled," Palmer said. "Seems some were willing to die if the world ended. Not as much if it was just an earthquake."

"Not very good cultists." Brier looked back at the tree.

"The thirty down there are praying to you more fervently than ever, if it makes you feel better."

Brier scoffed, tracing the curves of the tree with her fingers. "Do you think it would do any good if I told them to save their breaths?"

"Depends if you're bringing down another building at the same time or not, I imagine."

She shook her head. "Seems rather pointless now, doesn't it? Praying. Perhaps they could 'pray' for me not to kill them, but I have no say over their souls or what happens to them if they do die. At this point, I couldn't even honestly tell them if they had souls, if they asked. As far as I know, we are nothing more than animals cursed with understanding our own mortality."

Palmer measured his words, finally stepping to the edge of the concrete as he watched her. "Marina and Clover are obviously still around. We're still around."

"We're special cases." Brier shifted slightly, her face mottled by the moonlight coming through the silvery leaves. "I'd have been dead for fourteen years at this point if none of this had ever happened. I would have suffocated in that fire as a little girl, and that would have been the end of it."

"Brier—" Palmer stepped into the little courtyard and moved in front of her.

"I just don't know what it means for the world if *I'm* all there is to believe in." She finally met his eyes, the brown seeming black in the dark.

He touched her cheek lightly as the leaves rustled over them. Even his darker skin shone silver as the moon hit it again. "You're not alone in this, you know."

She watched him, face troubled.

He took another small step forward. "I'll always be here with you."

She opened her mouth, as if she were going to argue, but then just offered a sad smile. "Perhaps I should just get them all to pray to you instead, great creator and all."

"If we listen to the myths I read at Ruhegipfel, you came first. Something came from Nothing, not the other way around."

"And if we listen to the old Seers, from what I remember from services, the creator supposedly created the destroyer." Her body leaned forward, just an inch, nearly touching his. "Perhaps the entire world has your problem to some extent. We have too much information when it comes to some things and no way to filter it."

He traced his fingers along her cheekbone. The earlier painful sparks were gone, and he could still feel the energy building between them. The air in the small gap between them charged, dangerously maybe, but he couldn't bring himself to pull back.

"What?" she asked softly.

"I'd like to kiss you." He let the words fall out, not bothering to judge them.

She seemed to just stop herself from laughing. "Do you need permission now?"

He still didn't lean forward—too much was suddenly moving through his mind. He blocked it out as best he could, but the last memory stayed a beat too long. The night she couldn't remember. The night she hadn't really been her. The night both he and Nico had kept from her. He let his hand drop and leaned back far enough to snap the tension urging him forward. "There's something I need to tell you."

All humor dropped from her face. "That doesn't sound good."

"No, it..." He couldn't think of a way to end the sentence. Could barely think of a way to start a new one. He took a different approach. "Do you still want to marry Adessi?"

Her eyebrows furrowed, creasing her forehead. "That isn't telling me something."

"Just... answer that first."

She hesitated, chewing on her bottom lip for a moment before she shook her head. "If we're going to be honest with each other, part of me wishes I could. That we could just pretend nothing had changed. But that hasn't been true for a long, long time. He's one of my oldest friends—well, actually, he is my oldest friend. No qualifier. But I don't know if we would have been good for each other, even if this hadn't happened."

Palmer worked his way through the words, coming up with, "No?"

205

She shook her head. "But you still haven't told me anything."

He caught her hand, interlacing his fingers with hers. He spoke softly. "I really don't want to tell you."

She tried to pull back. He tightened his fingers around hers to stop her from closing herself off at his reluctance. She'd never easily accepted him keeping things from her. She released a breath then looked up, waiting to speak until he met her eyes. "Is it that bad?"

"I don't know about bad," he said. "But I can't imagine you'll necessarily find it good."

"You're going to drive me mad if you insist on dragging it out much longer."

He took a last second before dropping her hand himself. He could force himself to say it, but he couldn't force her to stay. "I know what happened the night you ended up on the roof."

Her eyebrows furrowed again, but she remained quiet.

"When you got drunk," he continued, "Marina managed to take over your body. I had a vision of it. You were there, arguing with Cerise, and then there she was. People saw your body, but it was her."

Brier's expression contorted, like she was fighting to remember something.

"Bri..."

"Keep going."

Palmer cleared his throat. "Marina took control of your body. And then *she* went and found—"

"Nico," Brier whispered.

Palmer hesitated. "Do you remember?"

"No." She shook her head. "Not really. There's just something in my head... I'm missing something."

"Do you want me to continue?"

"She slept with him?" The words barely came out, more like a thought than a true question. She met his eyes. "*I* slept with him?"

The words hit Palmer a little too strongly. He still felt the need to defend Nico, for whatever reason. "He had been drinking too, that night. If that matters."

"But..." Brier shook her head as she rested back against the tree.

"But he wouldn't. He made a point, repeatedly, that he wouldn't when we were drunk. He's been saying that for six years."

Since she'd been thirteen? Palmer couldn't stop himself from doing the math. True, Nico would have been only a year older, but Palmer hadn't even talked to a girl for nearly a decade six years ago. He forced himself to focus and stop comparing just how different his life had been from the ones everyone just across the piazza had lived. "You weren't acting drunk, from my vision. I don't think he knew. He didn't agree when he thought you were."

"But he didn't tell me." Her voice began to rise.

"He didn't want to hurt you." The words came out before Palmer could think.

"Did he tell you that? Or did you see it?"

"A mix of both."

Brier's eyebrows rose. "He told *you* and not me?"

"You were already having your problems. I'm sure he thought he was protecting—"

"You," Brier snapped, turning back on him. "Both of you. Always deciding what's supposedly best for me."

"Bri—"

"You don't get to decide that, Palmer Tash. Either of you. Especially not when it's about my own damned body!"

"Brier, calm down." He held his hands out and checked behind them. It didn't feel like anyone was out on the street, but if her voice got much louder, he doubted that would remain the case.

"You promised you wouldn't keep things from me." She lowered her voice, though the bite remained. "Back in Lantello. You *promised*."

"I'm telling you right now," he argued.

"And how long have you known?"

He hesitated for the briefest moment before answering. "Not until after you were unconscious."

She searched his face. "You'd swear to that?"

Technically it was the truth. He hadn't *known* anything for certain with the odd visions. He'd only suspected. And who knew? It could have turned out to have been Cerise after all. Then what good would it have done, upsetting her over an odd flash of a vision? "I drank some of that vial while we were on our way here and saw part of what happened. Adessi confirmed the rest when I brought it up, at least as much as he ever talks to me. And he truly did seem remorseful, knowing you were drunk enough not to remember any of it."

She studied his face, finally deflating. "You're really defending him?"

Palmer made a face, pressing his lips together before speaking. "He might be an entitled ass, but he does care about you. Deeply. I can respect that."

She sucked in a breath then blew it out again as she took a seat at the base of the tree.

"He wants you to be all right. That's what we both want."

She looked up at him. "Just remember I don't need either of you to be my father."

"I don't think either of us wants to be." He took a seat next to her.

"You do a crappy job of showing it sometimes." She rested her head against the trunk, staring at the branches above.

A vision fought to the front of his mind, an entirely useless one, all things considered. Maybe he really did need more practice at controlling them, at least while he was getting used to the block being gone again. All the same, Palmer indulged in it for a moment before he looked at her. "Do you actually want to know why he said no? When you were drunk that first time?"

Brier looked at him, lips pursed. "I don't know. Do I?"

"Just if you were wondering," he said. "Since it popped up and I *promised* not to keep thing from you."

She seemed to weigh her words but nodded. "All right?"

"He'd been with someone else earlier that day and had a feeling you'd react poorly if he did anything with you and that got out. After that, he was rather stuck."

Brier's eyebrows furrowed. "He'd been with someone else?"

Palmer nodded.

"Whom?"

Though he'd seen only a short clip of a vision, there was no mistaking those black curls. He still considered lying, whether or not he'd made a point of honesty. He sighed. "Carmella Huerta-Rey."

Brier twisted toward him, eyebrows raised. "He slept with Carmella?"

"No." Palmer didn't question the information as it came to him. "He didn't want to chance getting her pregnant. But she was more than willing to do other things for him, apparently."

"Like what, exactly?"

"Please don't make me focus on that." Palmer grimaced. "I could have gone my entire life without seeing the flash I did." He already had more than enough of Nico Adessi's sex life bouncing around his head.

Brier released a breath through her nose. "What was in that flash, then?"

"Do you *really* want me to tell you that?"

Her jaw worked, then she settled back against the tree. "No. I suppose not." She picked at a thread on her ripped shift. He started to speak, but she cut him off. "I'm not sure if I should be insulted or not that he apparently wasn't worried about getting *me* pregnant."

"Well, did he know you couldn't?"

The silence swept over them as Brier went stiff. She looked at him. Any color she'd had drained from her face. "What?"

"Oh." The thought hit him a second too late. "*You* didn't know."

"I, well..." She swallowed, blinking a little too quickly. "I haven't had... things I'm not entirely comfortable discussing with you, in all honesty, in months. Not since before Ruhegipfel, actually. But with everything else the doctors said might be wrong with me growing up, they never said that."

"I'm sorry." Palmer shifted uncomfortably. "There were definitely better ways of bringing that up."

Brier took a shaky breath, placing a hand low on her stomach, and remained silent long enough that Palmer wondered if he should offer to leave for a moment.

"Bri—"

"It's part of all this, isn't it?" she said softly.

Palmer hesitated. "What?"

"Part of who I am. *What* I am... I've found out worse things. I guess."

He didn't answer, waiting for her to work through it all on her own.

Another moment of silence passed, then she gave a somewhat sardonic laugh. "I suppose I should be glad things didn't go back to normal, huh? All the reasons I'm entirely unmarriageable keep stacking up the longer we talk."

Palmer shook his head. "Plenty of men would still marry you, if that was what you wanted, I'm sure."

Brier looked at him, the leaves once again leaving her face dappled in silver. "You?"

The word took a second to register. He coughed when it did. "Or Adessi," stumbled back out. "I don't think he would care."

"Contrary to how he acts at the moment, I think even he wants children." Brier shook her head. "It's engrained in his psyche as an Adessi, no doubt."

Palmer nodded.

"You wouldn't?" she asked after a beat. "Want children, I mean."

Palmer attempted to lighten the mood. "We already have one, don't we? She's about seven and enough of a handful for me by herself."

"True." Brier laughed lightly.

Palmer nodded, letting a new silence, slightly less awkward, settle over them.

"But you'd be happy with that?" Brier asked. "Just me and Rosette for the rest of your life?"

He offered a smile. "I can't think of a better life."

She smiled back, her fingers slipping over his. "Careful, Palmer Tash. That nearly sounded romantic."

He looked down at their hands resting on the ground. "Is that a bad thing?"

"I'm just remembering when you were barely able to talk to me."

He released a breath and forced himself to pull back before the draw to touch her grew too strong again. "We need to get back. We don't want to leave the others alone too long. And if Rosette wakes up and finds us gone, she may very well start a plague."

"Things have been quiet since everything this afternoon. I don't think Rosette would be too worried about us."

He scratched the back of his neck awkwardly. "I might have already left her behind, twice, by slipping out while she was sleeping."

"Palmer!"

He offered his only defense. "I was trying to keep her safe."

"By abandoning her?"

"We were obviously going back. Once we found you."

Brier shook her head. "You lost your parents. How would you have felt if you were left behind again after that?" She watched him then sighed when he couldn't find anything to say. "I love you, Palmer Tash, but you are a gallant idiot half the time."

He opened his mouth to object, but she kissed him before he could utter a word.

Pulling back, she looked at him for a final moment before standing. She offered a small smile. "I suppose we should get back, then. Considering."

Blood pounding through his ears, he nodded. "Yeah. We should."

CHAPTER TWENTY-SEVEN

B RIER RAN HER FINGERS ALONG the wall behind her, following the crack in the plaster. It felt like only a few days ago that she'd been looking for destroyed rooms in the palace, places that would be no worse for wear if she lost control of her powers. Now she'd found an entire city that was already destroyed. And dedicated to her, no less.

"You still can't sense anything about it?" Goebel looked up from the cracked box, which all the men were once again circling.

"I can't even feel you helping." Palmer shook his head. "It's like the metal is absorbing anything before it gets to me."

"I'm going to guess Brier was right—that doesn't mean anything good." Nico crossed his arms and took a step back from the other men.

"Most likely not," Palmer agreed.

Brier continued to move her fingers back and forth, even as the plaster began to flake from the friction. Pressing her lips together, she kept her eyes on the men. Actually telling her something, without prodding, was progress for Palmer. She gave him that. But she couldn't help but suspect he had known something before. And even if he hadn't known, Brier couldn't imagine how he could stand around as if he didn't feel it in the air. At least after keeping something like that from her, Nico had the good manners to avoid her eyes as much as possible.

"If it's a magic thing, it shouldn't affect me." Nico's voice shook Brier out of her thoughts. "I can go when we find them."

"But if it means someone is now controlling 'a magic thing,' you're the least protected of any of us," Palmer returned.

Rosette and Cerise appeared at the doorway. Their scouting for Orris and the others apparently hadn't offered much. Wherever the cultists had placed Orris, it seemed none of their abilities could help them find him now.

But the thought hit. Brier looked at everyone in the room. Cerise, Rosette, Palmer, Goebel, her—they were all "special," leaving Nico as the odd man out since... She looked at Palmer. "Where's Peony?"

He glanced over with a frown. "What?"

"Peony," Brier repeated. "She was at the temple yesterday. She's not here now."

Palmer looked around as if just noticing someone was missing.

"They took her out of the rubble," Rosette piped up.

"Who's Peony?" Goebel asked.

"A girl who was with us," Palmer said quickly, keeping his eyes on Rosette. "'They' who?"

"The men," Rosette said. "They said they were supposed to take everyone they found in the temple somewhere."

Brier arched an eyebrow and looked back at Palmer. "Can you sense *her*?"

Palmer blinked, letting his eyes drift off to the side as he worked. "There's an old palazzo. Near the top of the hill. Near the amphitheater. They have set up some of the injured there."

Nico's body went tense. "Including my father?"

"Maybe?" Palmer shook his head. "I still can't feel him, whatever they've done."

"They possibly could have surrounded him with antimony, as well," Goebel said.

"Then I'm definitely the one who should go," Nico said, turning to the weapons sitting in the corner.

"I'm not sitting here." Brier shook her head. "I'm doing better, which makes me stronger than any of the rest of you."

"Unless that metal stops all your powers," Nico said, truly meeting her eyes for what felt like the first time since she'd recovered.

She forced him to hold it, making her face just as hard as his. "Then give me a sword."

"Do you even know how to use one?"

Brier narrowed her eyes slightly. "I had one for the Augarian battle."

"Though you barely knew how to hold it," Cerise added, as helpful as ever.

Brier shifted her glare to the other woman. "I can handle myself."

Goebel stepped in. "Cerise and I can fight hand-to-hand—"

"As can I," Nico interjected.

"—so it makes the most sense for us to go."

Brier continued to frown. "Try to stop me going, and just see what happens."

The eyes in the room shifted back to her.

She kept her eyes on Goebel. "You said it yourself, Palmer isn't as strong as me. Are you *both* going to waste your efforts trying to keep me here today?"

"I'm coming too." Rosette stepped forward.

Brier bit down her gut reaction to say *no*. If she didn't intend to be left behind, she couldn't expect Rosette to stay.

"We still don't know what we're up against," Palmer said, voice cautious.

"I'm still not staying," Brier said. "And you've seen what happens when you try to make Rosette."

Rosette beamed, taking her place against Brier's leg.

She could get hurt. Palmer glanced at Rosette's hands, though from what Brier had seen, the odd rash had gone down over the past day.

All of us could. Brier placed a hand on Rosette's bony shoulder, trying not to rub the rough fabric more than necessary. "All of us can do something. We might as well play to our strengths."

Goebel scanned them all, his eyes lingering on Nico for a moment. Then he sighed and looked down at the box in front of him as he ran a hand through his hair. "I suppose we should work out a plan, then."

Trepidation built in Palmer's stomach. He could feel Peony, but why, he wasn't sure. Something had changed about her, making her glow, as if she were calling out to be found. Maybe she was. Whether or not she had known what the actual kidnappers were planning, Palmer imagined he owed her some sort of apology for forgetting about her entirely. More than once. Especially if she ended up being the reason they found Orris Adessi.

The location of the large L-shaped palazzo near the river on the east side of town came to Palmer as easily as any information had in months, but when he tried to see anything inside it, all he got was Peony and whatever odd buzz she was giving off.

Cerise circled overhead, cawing once before drifting behind another building to their left. Goebel followed her with his eyes then turned to the rest of them. They followed the raven before he needed to direct them.

"Three men out back," Cerise reported before they had all made it around the corner. "Few more by the front door. Not much other security from what I can see from above."

"There must be more inside," Nico said. "They have to know we're still in town. My father or cousin I would assume, at the very least—whichever of them is currently conscious."

"Still probably best for us to go around back." Goebel began to plan.

The voice was lost as Palmer's mind lit up all at once. Orris Adessi—and something else—appeared out of a vacuum. Palmer tried to get a reading, but the image was shaky as the shape moved around inside the palazzo.

Brier looked over before anyone else seemed to notice Palmer's expression. *What is it?*

Orris Adessi is awake. Palmer didn't mince words. *And it doesn't feel like he's alone.*

Brier hesitated. *Marina?*

I'm not sure, but... Palmer made a face.

"Anything you'd like to share with the rest of the class?" Cerise's voice broke Palmer out of his thoughts.

"What?" he and Brier asked together.

Cerise smirked. "If you were planning to argue that you can't speak telepathically, it probably would have been best not to speak in unison like that. Just for the record."

"Telepathically?" Nico frowned.

Cerise looked at him. "It means—"

215

"I know what it means," he snapped.

"Ah, just didn't know that's what they were doing?" Cerise looked back at Palmer and Brier. "See, I only get vague whispering, and it's really quite rude to leave people out like that, I hope you know."

"Orris Adessi is awake," Palmer said before Cerise could stir up too much trouble. "I could suddenly feel him in there."

"How far in?" Nico asked, distracted for the moment.

"One of the back rooms. Toward the middle of the long side," Palmer reported.

Nico didn't wait for Goebel to start planning before he began issuing orders. "We head in the back. Rosette can help with the guards outside." He looked between Goebel and Cerise. "Which of you two feels better going in with me?"

"I will," Brier cut in before anyone could answer. She continued quickly, before Nico could object, "It's why I'm here. I didn't walk all this way to wait somewhere else."

Nico shook his head. "If your powers—"

"If they don't work, I'll get out again." Brier wouldn't let him finish. "I'm a grown woman."

"All right then." Cerise clapped Brier's shoulder. "So Cay goes in. I take it Kos will want to, as well, then?"

"I will." Goebel shook his head. "I can watch her and fight if need be. You, Palmer, and Rosette can keep a perimeter. With any luck, there won't be many inside, and we can keep anyone else out."

"Thoughts, Kos?" Cerise looked at Palmer.

He pressed his lips together. The thought of letting Brier go without him did not sit well. But it didn't seem likely he would be able to change Brier's mind, and he wouldn't do much better to protect her than Goebel. He nodded once. "Be careful. He may not be alone."

Nico brushed it off. "I can handle—"

"Palmer means he might be possessed," Brier said, pressing her hand to her middle as if voicing the possibility made her nauseous. She continued in a rush, "Marina was in my head for a while, but she's not now. I don't know where she might have gone, but..."

"It's a possibility," Palmer finished when she didn't seem able to.

"Who the hell is Marina?" Nico frowned.

216

"A previous incarnation of Chaos." Palmer went with the simplest explanation. *Goebel's old girlfriend, the woman you actually slept with...* All the other ways he could describe Marina were more than they had time to get into—especially when Goebel already looked like he'd been hit in the stomach from Marina's name. If Goebel and Nico were going in with Brier, they couldn't be distracted. "Just be careful. If she's possessing him or anyone else in there, who knows what that means he could do."

"Powers?" Cerise asked.

Palmer looked at Brier to see if she knew what the specters could do. When she shrugged, he could only shake his head. "No clue."

"Great," Nico said. "That was almost helpful. Now let's get this over with."

Brier watched the guards by the front door fall, one by one, though Rosette never left her little hiding place nearby.

"She does like doing that," Nico murmured. He shifted the weapons on him in a way Brier was starting to recognize as a stress-induced twitch than a necessity. Brier let her fingers touch the pommel of the dagger he'd given her. She would likely be as useless with it as she had admittedly been with a sword. At least this time, she didn't have any plans to use it. The town was already in ruins. If she had to add to that, then so be it. Nico let his hands drop to his side and looked at her. "You're sure about this?"

"Why? Are you planning on letting me die?"

The corner of his mouth twitched, and the near smile was almost enough to let Brier ignore some of the tension lingering between them. She supposed it was for the best. If she did die again, they could spend her final minutes pretending they were the same friends they'd always been. He looked forward again. "I'll go in first. I can take anyone just inside while you figure out if your powers work. If there are any problems at all, get out of there. I'll take care of it."

And get yourself killed in the process. Brier still let him move forward, grateful he couldn't hear her thoughts. He pushed open the door, and Brier heard a shout followed by one gurgled scream. Then another.

"Clear," Nico called.

Brier stepped inside, with Goebel close at her heels, and her stomach twisted. Two men lay in thick puddles of blood, their throats slit. And she suddenly understood the sickening gurgling sound. She glanced at Nico, but he had already sheathed whatever blade he had used and had an arrow nocked as he scanned the rest of the empty hall.

"Brier?" Goebel asked.

She started out of her thoughts.

"Do you need to leave?"

Nico glanced back at her, but Brier shook her head, flexing her hands. "I'm fine."

"All right, then." Goebel's hand hovered just above the small of her back as he guided her forward.

Brier let Nico lead, doing her best not to watch too closely. He had been dressed as a soldier when she'd returned to the Augarian, but she supposed she had never actually seen him fight. She'd assumed his father had forced him to trade his academic robes for a soldier's uniform, and Nico had given the same piddling amount of gravitas to both of them. Seeing the two bodies behind them and his carefully measured movements ahead of them, though, she suspected he might actually have *been* a soldier while she was gone.

Her vision blurred, just for a second. She blinked it away. As odd as everything had been the past few days, she couldn't help but blame the building itself. Something about it was affecting her. She flexed her hands again. Her powers seemed to be working, but the world around her seemed both brightened and dulled, as if she were looking at it through colored glass. She looked for any offending windows, but any glass that had ever been in the openings was long gone.

Goebel dropped his voice. "Are you certain you're fine?"

Brier nodded. "I'm—"

A round of gunfire made her jump. Goebel pulled her back as Nico ducked around the corner ahead of them, pulling out another arrow.

"We found more guards." He glanced at Goebel and Brier before leaning out just enough to get off another shot. A volley answered.

Projectiles took chips out of the wall closer to Nico than Brier liked. He didn't so much as flinch. Ducking out, he shot another arrow.

Brier took a step forward. Goebel caught her arm, but she shook him off. "I can handle it."

Whether or not he believed her, he let her go. She moved toward the corner then jumped back as another volley sent pellets pinging around the hall.

"Bri." Nico glanced at her, keeping his back to the wall as he loaded another arrow.

"Let me see," she ordered.

He frowned but shifted.

Letting the power gather in her fingers, she moved to the corner behind him. Time to see what she could do.

"Try to catch them while they're reloading," Nico murmured.

With a final breath, she swung out enough to see the four guards standing at the end of the hall. She threw a blast as they started to level their guns. It caught. The men flew back, the one in the center falling to pieces as his torso disappeared. Brier grimaced, but there was no blood. She looked back at Nico. "Keep going forward?"

He looked down the hall. His eyebrows rose for a split second before he nodded. "A little late to turn back now."

Without waiting for either man to lead, Brier started down the hall, maneuvering around the body parts. The sooner they found Orris Adessi, the sooner she could stop destroying things. Brier hoped those would be the only men she had to hurt.

Shots echoed from behind her. Nico and Goebel had already spun toward them by the time Brier turned.

"Go." Nico motioned to her sharply then moved against the wall for cover.

Brier headed the way Palmer had said, toward the center of the palazzo. Despite the fighting farther back in the hallway, the rooms in front of Brier were eerily silent. She slowed as her heart pounded in her ears. The odd patches of bright and dull grew stronger, everyday colors turning jewel toned. She turned a corner and stopped dead, staring at the closed doors ahead of her. Even chipped, the red and green paint seemed to shimmer like crushed rubies and emeralds. She swallowed and forced herself forward. That had to be where she was headed.

The door creaked unhappily as she pushed it open. A last breath, and she stepped through. Pain shot behind her eyes, strong enough that she had to close them. Slowly, the saturation of color died back down, returning the room to normal. She flexed her hands as she recovered. Her powers flickered slightly but did not die. Her sight back, she looked around. Even without the oddly bright colors, the room was undoubtedly grand—a throne room, perhaps, or a space meant to impress visitors to the palazzo back when Venchia had been a thriving city. Her eyes caught the veins of metal running through the walls. Inlaid in intricate geometric patterns, it looked decorative, but Brier wondered if that was the case. If Orris Adessi had worked out what metal could affect their powers, Brier assumed others had, as well, even if that knowledge had been buried for over a millennium, along with the rest of the ruins.

"Fascinating, isn't it?"

The voice made Brier jump. Her hands came up as she turned toward the opposite door. Orris Adessi studied the glinting patterns then tilted his head with an odd jerk. He looked back at Brier, his entire body moving a little too stiffly to be natural. He tapped his forehead with another quick movement that nearly made it look like a twitch. "There's something in here about it," he continued, the cadence of his words all wrong, "but I'm having a hell of a time getting through his memories. I don't think his mind is as compatible as yours."

The power sparked in Brier's hands. It faltered as the metal in the walls conflicted with her body's involuntary urge to rid the world of that unnatural... thing. She could feel the death attempting to leech into the room. Or her. "Marina?"

"Unfortunately." Orris... Marina looked at her hands. "I didn't have much choice in bodies. I really don't know how Cerise stands being men. They're so... disgusting to be inside." Marina wrinkled her nose, the expression grotesque on Orris's stiff face.

A chill passed over Brier's skin, something she hadn't felt since Sage Visentin's death in Lantello. She spotted the shadows starting to gather along the roof. Obviously, she wasn't the only one ready to destroy whatever Marina had become. If Orris wasn't dead already, he was certainly dying. Brier pressed her own powers down and forced the death in the room back out.

The door slammed shut behind her, snapping Brier's concentration.

"Dominik?" Surprise leeched into Marina-Orris's voice.

Goebel turned sharply at his given name. Nico pulled another arrow.

Marina flicked her eyes between the men. Her surprise at seeing Goebel faded as she began to laugh. She looked back at Brier. "Nik and Nic? See? We do have the same taste in men."

"I'm sincerely hoping he is possessed." Nico pulled the bow taut, aiming it straight at Marina-Orris's chest.

"Now is that any way to treat your father?" Marina shook her head, tilting off balance once again. "Though this body seems to be giving out on me without any help."

"Marina?" Goebel's entire body worked as if he couldn't quite bring himself to believe it—even with advance warning.

"So it seems." Marina looked over her host form before meeting Goebel's eyes again. "Though you don't look especially happy to see me."

Goebel's face remained frozen with shock or horror, perhaps both. He glanced at Brier.

Marina's rigid face went dark. "Prefer it if I still looked like her, would you?" She scoffed. "Ready to just replace me with her, I'm sure."

He started, "Mari—"

"I know about that night in the library. The both of you." Marina jerked a rigid arm up to point. "I've seen her memories just fine. I should have known. You were already willing to replace me there."

"What?" Nico kept his eyes narrowed.

"He was talking about having lost *you*," Brier argued, not bothering to explain the entirely innocent kiss Goebel had given her at Ruhegipfel while breaking down about Marina. "How—"

"How I was brash, isn't that right?" Marina cut in, starting across the room with stiff, twitchy steps. "How I 'got myself killed' by not being as sweet and special as little Brier Chastain. The little girl all the boys want to come save."

"Marina—" Goebel stepped forward at her approach.

"You fought for her. You fought for her when you wouldn't even

221

fight for *me*." Marina's hand flew out, sending black energy streaking across the room. Brier tried to catch it on instinct. Goebel flew back and hit the door with a crack. Brier returned a blast of her own, another flash of color blinding her as the power left her fingers. The energy hit. Marina tipped and hit the ground. Coins from Orris's pockets scattered along the tile with the momentum. She groaned and rocked slightly but stayed down. Brier glanced behind her. Goebel grimaced, hand on his stomach, but he seemed to be in one piece.

The ground rumbled. Nico's bow loosed before Brier could turn back. Marina grunted as the arrow hit her shoulder. The ground opened as energy shot into the rest of them. Doubling over, Brier tried to absorb the tainted energy into her body. Another wave passed through her, bringing her to her knees as rubble started to fall.

"Now that's better." Marina's rough voice carried above the aftershocks. Brier hissed, releasing the energy with the breath. Rubble and coins scraped across the ground as Marina pushed herself upright. "Just us girls."

Brier's eyes flicked back and forth, not letting Marina out of her sight for too long as she tried to see Nico and Goebel past the rubble. Neither seemed to be moving. She pressed her panic down, meeting Marina-Orris's cloudy eyes. "That body is dead, Marina."

"Why do you think I need yours back?" Marina forced herself onto her knees. The death along the ceiling swirled, agitated. Brier's second of distraction was enough. Marina's hand flew out. Brier ducked, protecting her head with her hands. The energy glanced off her and ricocheted around the room. Blast after blast followed, each more erratic than the next. Marina took a shaky breath as her body slumped with exhaustion. "This would be easier if you would just let me finish this."

Brier lifted her head, starting to speak. The words died in her throat. Half cracked, the metal still in the wall pulsed dangerously. Her eyes widened. "Marina…"

"How is it fair? How? You died. I died. But everyone helps *you*." Marina continued to pant, but she raised her hand.

"Marina. Don't—" Brier scrambled, trying to stand.

Another blast left Marina's hand. And everything went still. Silence hit Brier's ears, as loud as a gunshot, before it shattered. The wall went to pieces. Rubble sprayed across the room. Brier threw her hands out. Most of the debris dissolved before it could hit her, but her own powers flickered every time the metal pelted her as it fell. She curled into herself, fighting to breathe through the dust. Coughing as the rubble settled, she looked up. The room around her was gone, bent bars of metal the only thing holding bits of roof above her head. And that didn't seem stable enough to last for long.

She twisted. The door behind her was blocked. Along with any sign of Nico and Goebel. Her throat constricted. She forced herself to ignore it. Until she knew what had happened to Marina, she wouldn't be able to help anyone else.

A pile across from her shifted. The rubble slid, scraping against itself, as Marina pulled herself to the top. Brier recoiled. Already damaged before, the body Marina inhabited was nearly unrecognizable. Blood had congealed into a purple stain covering one side of her head where a stone had flattened the skull. The opposite arm had come out of its socket, dangling unnaturally as Marina fought to move. She looked up, her eyes milky. "The quicker you destroy this body, the sooner I will need a new one, *dolcezza*."

Brier's skin crawled at the nickname. Any sign of the real Orris leaching out through his walking corpse couldn't be good. Not in the middle of all of this. "Marina..."

"You aren't strong enough, Marina." A new, lighter voice came through the carnage. Peony appeared through a gap in the room, maneuvering gracefully through the destruction. "That body or anyone else's, you wouldn't be able to stay alive long. It's madness to keep trying."

Marina twisted as best as her destroyed body could and looked at Peony for a long moment. She laughed. "I was wondering where you'd gone, Clove. You obviously found a better body than I did."

Brier flicked her eyes back to Peony, looking for any sign of her mother inside the girl.

"This one isn't dead." Clover-Peony shook her head. "Just unconscious. And I fully intend to return it, once this is done."

Marina scoffed and shuffled toward Clover. "Return it and do what? Go back to floating through oblivion?"

"We're memories, Marina." Clover stepped over a chunk of metal, careful not to touch it. "You can't survive in a corpse. Just look at you."

"I won't have to for long." Marina jerked the loose arm toward Brier.

"You're nothing more than an echo of her power. An echo of Nothing. It's time to move on."

"Because you have?" Marina sneered.

Clover bent, picking coins out of the debris. "I already told you I was returning this body."

"Then why haven't you already?"

"Because you're still here." Clover moved toward Brier.

"Just stay out of this, Clove." Marina's voice turned dangerous.

Clover pressed the coins she'd collected into Brier's palm. She frowned but didn't ask at the look Clover gave her. Tightening her fist, Brier felt something scrape her palm. She looked down. The ring Rosette had stolen—and Brier had been wearing at one point?—sat in the midst of the rest of the gold and silver, its green stone glowing gently. Brier blinked then watched Clover move back toward Marina.

"That body is decomposing." Clover kept her eyes forward. "And that means you are. You stay in there, you're not going to be you for very much longer. Your mind will go with his."

"That's why I need her." Marina attempted to move her arm again, though it rose only a few inches.

"Force her out, and her body will start to die, too. You'll have to keep jumping from body to body to body. And how long do you think it will take Palmer to figure out how to capture you outside of a body?" Clover glanced at Brier then back. "You might have destroyed that book, but you hurt her and—"

"Her attack dogs will come after me?" Marina's knees started to fail. "I think I can handle it."

"They'll figure out anyone with the right metal and stone would be able to catch you midair between bodies," Clover continued, voice level. "And you're already about to be forced out any second now. Assuming you don't want to take some of that man's mind with you."

Marina grimaced, her hands shaking. "I'm not... dying... again."

"You're already dead," Clover insisted.

The convulsions grew worse. Marina fell to one knee, deep-purple energy gathering just beneath the corpse's skin. And the stone in Brier's palm grew warm. Brier looked down, all the pieces starting to fall together.

Throw it. Clover's voice filtered into Brier's mind, so soft that Brier questioned whether it had been there at all. *Now.*

Orris's body began to flake apart as the purple light dissolved it inch by inch.

Now, Clover's voice insisted.

Grabbing a piece of the antimony from the ground for good measure, Brier took aim. The corpse's flattened skull cracked open, and the death in the air rushed toward the rising light. While the cacophony blotted out everything else, Brier threw it all. The coins scattered, some hitting the tile, some dissolving with the rest of Orris's body, but the ring hit straight on. The light shuddered then constricted, scattered by the metal and gemstone as they drew in the energy. The metal holding the roof began to quake. Brier fell backward, twisting to avoid a chunk of plaster. Something exploded. The crashing disappeared behind the ringing in her ears. And the roof came down with the darkness.

CHAPTER TWENTY-EIGHT

"PALMER..." ROSETTE BOUNCED ON THE balls of her feet.

"No." Palmer sent her a look he hoped was severe before going back to watching the building.

"But I can help..." Rosette whined.

"You are helping by staying right there." Palmer glanced up as Cerise returned.

The raven flapped back to their hiding place by the door and changed back to human form. "Sounds like there's plenty of action inside, but I've kept anyone from going for help so far."

Palmer didn't ask exactly how.

"Palmerrrrr..." Rosette pulled at his pants leg.

"*No,*" he repeated. "We stick to the plan."

Rosette pouted and crossed her arms.

Smiling, Cerise nudged the girl. "Dad's such a killjoy, isn't he?"

The swell of energy cut Palmer off before he could reply. His own powers attempted to flare to life, making the hair on his arms stand on end.

Rosette's body tensed next to him. "Someone's dying. Someone special."

Palmer nodded, turning to face the building head on. His mind searched for Brier. Building chaos toward the center of the palazzo forced him back out. He had to assume she was there, but she certainly wasn't alone.

"Well?" Cerise looked at him.

He frowned. "What?"

"Do we go in?" Cerise glanced at the building, the tension in her shoulders saying she felt the energy as well.

Palmer frowned at Cerise asking for his input about anything.

Cerise looked down at him. "Without Mom around, your powers outstrip any of us. What do they say to do?"

Palmer blinked, jarred by the seriousness of Cerise's tone. And somewhere in the back of his mind, it registered. Chaos and Kosmos. The start of the universe and parents of the other gods. Perhaps using parental names had been Cerise's way of legitimizing who they were all along—in her uniquely Cerise-like way.

The ground rocked as something exploded deep within the palazzo. Palmer looked down at Rosette. "Let's go."

Rosette smiled and dashed ahead before anyone could stop her.

"Ah, to have that kind of energy again." Cerise shook her head as she pulled the sword from her belt. "Ready?"

Palmer nodded, going for his own sword, even if he likely would be relying on Rosette and Cerise until they found Brier and whatever energy was still pulsing in the air.

Bodies littered the frescoed hallways—whether that was Rosette's doing or Nico and Goebel's, Palmer didn't know. He tried not to look at them, focusing on making his way forward. Rosette darted up ahead and disappeared around a corner. Cerise stayed closer to Palmer's side, ready to take on anyone Rosette missed.

They moved quickly. The only guards Palmer saw were already dead by the time he passed them. Still, the pressure in the air pushed down on him, making his head feel heavier and heavier as he neared the center of the villa. He turned the corner and froze, his vision graying out.

The power snapped back, nearly throwing Palmer off his feet in the vacuum. He caught himself against the wall, breathing heavily as he blinked. When he regained his vision he saw daylight streaming in through where there had once been roof. The opposite wall wasn't much more than rubble. But the doorway straight ahead had remained standing. Looking for Cerise, Palmer forced himself away from the wall. He caught her eyes and motioned to the doorway. Cerise nodded once and followed.

The low groan made Palmer pause before he crossed the threshold. Whatever room had once been there was gone. Some combination of tile, metal, and masonry blocked the rest of the space from view, but not the feeling in the air. That Palmer felt far too well.

A chunk of stone slid from a pile after another grunt. Palmer turned, spotting the man mostly covered in debris. "Adessi?"

Nico winced as he forced more of the rubble off his body. "I'm fine. I think."

Palmer moved over to him and worked to dig the man out. "What happened?"

"She could use powers." He pulled his leg free with another grimace. "The last Chaos. In my father."

Palmer nodded then hesitated as he saw a purple-black glow shimmering across Nico's legs. "Marina. Did she hit you?"

Nico shook his head. "The place started to come down. That threw me back, I think. But Goebel..." He twisted to look behind him.

Palmer looked over in time to see Cerise digging through rubble where Nico had motioned. Hoping she could help Goebel, Palmer looked back at Nico. "And Brier?"

Nico's face went grim. He looked at the wall of rubble separating them from the rest of the space. "On the other side of that."

Palmer swallowed, but there was nothing to be done about that. The sooner they got Nico and Goebel out of there, the sooner they could look for Brier. He turned back, eyes going wide as Nico moved to stand. "Wait—"

The ground shook again as the black light shot down Nico's leg into the earth. The building trembled, but nothing else fell.

Nico froze. "What the hell was that?"

"Whatever Marina was controlling, it's stuck to you." Palmer glanced at Nico's other leg. The energy there swirled as if looking for a place to be absorbed.

"What do I do?" Nico remained still.

"Thank whatever gods you believe in that it didn't dissolve you the second it made contact." Palmer shifted carefully, assuming whatever had protected Nico from Marina was the only thing still keeping him alive. "Hold still."

Nico didn't argue. Starting at the man's knee, Palmer sent his own energy down Nico's leg, trying to force the swirling energy to dissipate—ideally without destroying anything else. It pressed back, dark and unnatural but weaker than anything he had so far dealt with. Maybe that was the other reason Nico still had all his limbs attached. It was Brier's power, corrupted. The energies finally cancelled out, and the black disappeared with an unhappy hiss but no more shaking.

Palmer released a breath and looked back up at Nico. "Now that you aren't going to kill us all, the rest of you all right?"

"I'm not sure about 'all right.'" Nico shifted, waiting for Palmer's approval before he folded his other leg under him. His hand went to his side as he grimaced. "But it's nothing I can't handle."

"I can heal you, you know." Palmer watched as Nico struggled to stand.

"I'll manage."

"Kos," Cerise cut in. "If you're done chatting with your boyfriend, we could use your help over here."

Palmer twisted, spotting Goebel's gray-streaked brown hair past Cerise's shoulder. "How is he?"

"Alive," Cerise reported, shifting to give Palmer space next to her. "He seems less banged up than Nicolas over there, but... look."

For having been buried under a pile of stone and tile, Goebel looked surprisingly untouched. No bruises or blood that Palmer could see. Not even the layer of dust that coated everything in the room affected him. But still, the man didn't move. His eyes stared blankly into space.

Palmer pressed his lips together, trying to determine what to do. The faintest purple-black glow ate into the rocks covering his stomach and legs. Palmer began to dig. "Help get the rest of him out."

Cerise seemed to inflate, not fully morphing but making herself larger so that she could pull the rocks out of the way more quickly. The more they uncovered, the more Cerise slowed. She finally sat back on her heels. "Gods..."

The purple energy swirled, as it had over Nico, but it was managing to eat away at Goebel. Most of his shirt was gone over his stomach, and the skin along his center was starting to go translucent.

"Do something." Cerise looked at Palmer.

Like what? Palmer refrained from asking. He flexed his hands and, with nothing else to do, forced energy down Goebel as he had with Nico.

The energies clashed. The swirling became more vicious as they fought against each other. As pain began to radiate up Palmer's arms, he sent a final blast. The floor lurched as the energies concussed. He let go, pulling his hands back to his chest as he looked down at the man.

"Well?" Back to her normal size, Cerise watched Palmer's face.

Palmer looked Goebel over and frowned. "I think I got the dissolving to stop. Maybe. But I don't know. The power on Nico was easier to get rid of."

"I didn't take a direct hit," Nico supplied. "He did."

Palmer nodded and glanced back over his shoulder. Nico still wasn't standing straight, his hand pressed to his side. His ribs were bruised, if not broken. Those would have to be healed once Nico stopped being stubborn enough to try to push through it. But that was an argument for another time. Palmer turned back to Cerise and nodded at Goebel. "I'll have to try to heal him somewhere away from here. Do you think you can carry him out?"

"Of course." Cerise didn't hesitate in the slightest.

Of course. Palmer wasn't sure why he'd asked. She could always turn into someone stronger if she needed. He worked out the plan in his head as he talked. "Look for Rosette on the way out. And help Adessi if he needs it."

"Where am I going?" Nico frowned.

"You need to lie down before you puncture a lung." Palmer left no room for argument in his tone.

"And you?" Cerise asked.

Palmer released a breath, looking at the wall of rubble in front of them. "What else?" He turned back to Cerise. "I try to find Brier."

Something tingled along Brier's back, gently stirring her awake. She forced her eyes to open. Once again, she found herself in a cave made from the rubble of a formerly grand building. That she hadn't been crushed yet, as often as she brought buildings to ruin, truly had to be some sort of divine providence. Light filtered in through the cracks, leaving the little cave mottled in shadows. She let her head drop to the side, and her eyes slowly focused on the shape sitting a few feet away.

It all came back to her. Marina. Clover. That hideous corpse. Brier sat up, getting a better look at the woman next to her.

Clover rolled the ring back and forth between her thumb and pointer finger. Green streaked her face every time the light caught the stone. Her eyes moved to Brier as the ring stilled. "How are you feeling, *cara*?"

"Surprisingly, not awful," Brier said. "You're still... not Peony?"

"I was waiting until you woke up so I could give you this." Clover studied the ring for a final moment before holding it out to Brier.

Hesitantly, Brier reached out to take it. It didn't burn, shatter, or do anything it seemed likely to do after the fight she'd been through. It just sat placidly in her hand. She looked back at Clover. "Marina's in...?"

Clover nodded, studying the stone. "It seems the universe has been conspiring to be rid of us. Palmer finding the necessary book, you getting that ring..."

Brier pressed her lips together. "The one that I... that Marina burned that night?"

Clover nodded again. "It had exactly how to exorcise us from your head. Step one being transferring us into something nonliving." She motioned to the ring.

Brier glanced back down at it. "And then what?"

"I'm not sure. She didn't let me see beyond that before she had it dangling over the fire." Clover stood. "You'll have to ask Palmer to recreate it for you. Hopefully, his powers will be working better now that Marina and I aren't getting in the way."

"And what will happen to you?" Brier asked.

"Oh, I'm going in there, as well." Clover smiled. "This poor girl needs her body back—it doesn't especially like me in here while she's still living—and I'm more than ready to move on. It's been... well, how old are you now?"

"Nineteen in a few months."

"So it's been over eighteen years I've been lost in the ether with Marina. I think it's time for both of us to move on."

"Move on to what?"

Clover smiled. "Well, that's the big adventure, isn't it? What truly is the hereafter? I'm rather excited to see."

"Even if there's nothing?"

"I've grown to appreciate Nothing." Clover touched Brier's cheek lightly. "You—both you and Palmer—have done such amazing things. More than I think Marina or myself would have been able to, even if we had been willing to work together. But more and more, I think that's how the universe works. It chooses what it needs and fights to keep it that way, no matter what the rest of us might have to say about it. It's time for Marina and me to move on, wherever that might lead."

"But we're supposed to be the universe," Brier said. "Kosmos and Chaos. And I, at least, have nothing even close to a plan."

"But something still chose you. Out of all of the other millions of people it could have chosen, it chose you. Why do you think that is?"

Brier shook her head. "I haven't a clue."

"Perhaps, but you can't say it didn't. It even waited for you, after Marina died. There were years before either Chaos or Kosmos reincarnated. And they chose you and Palmer. Two children, on the same day, who ended up living two hundred yards from one another. You can't tell me that wasn't planned."

Brier opened her mouth to object, but Clover stumbled before Brier could get a word out.

"I really do need to give this body back before I kill her." Clover caught herself as a light-golden glow started around Peony's skin. "Just remember to have Palmer divine that book again. It'll have everything you need to release us from there for good."

Brier frowned, looking at the ring in her hand. "You're going to trap yourself inside it as well?"

"It's that or back to the ether with me." Clover gave a resigned smile. "Hand it here?"

"There has to be—"

"Brier, I've made my peace. It's what must be done, and I am more than willing to play my part."

Brier frowned, but she couldn't argue with someone who actually seemed to have faith in something. Forcing herself to lift her hand, Brier offered up the ring.

It barely touched the glow around Clover's palm before the energy snapped. Light flashed then flowed into the ring, the air crackling around it. Peony's body went stiff, and the ring fell from her flat palm as the light poured out of her. Getting to her feet to go for the ring, Brier ended up catching Peony instead as the woman crumpled, her glow entirely gone. The ring hit the floor, sounding much too heavy for even such a large stone, but it remained there, still once again and looking entirely benign.

"Brier?" Palmer's voice filtered through the rubble somewhere behind her, sounding panicked. So he'd felt the energy, too.

"I'm all right." She didn't pause to consider if she actually was or not. She looked down at the limp woman in her arms. "I'm not sure about Peony, though."

The panic turned toward confusion. "Peony's with you?"

"She's unconscious." Brier didn't bother to explain before laying Peony the rest of the way to the ground and turning to the ring.

"I'm trying to find a way through."

Brier picked up the ring by the band and studied the stone. A shade darker than she remembered, it seemed otherwise unchanged. She would never have known anything was inside had she not seen the spectacle with her own eyes. Carefully, she slid it onto the ring finger of her right hand, waiting to see if anything happened.

"Brier?" Palmer tried again.

The ring seemed safe enough. Nico would just have to wait a while to get it back. She glanced at Peony as she answered Palmer. "Try to make it through to here. I don't think I can carry her as dead weight. I'll see if there's some exit the other way."

"Stay there," Palmer said. "I'll find you."

She released a breath. If there was anything she didn't think she could do at the moment, it was stay. Not there. "I'll be fine. Worry about Peony."

"Brier..."

"I'll be fine." She scanned the rubble across from her, looking for where the most light was coming in—where the rubble was likely the thinnest.

"Brier, please..." His voice was already turning more resigned.

And with a final glance at the green stone on her finger, Brier started forward. "I'll see you outside."

CHAPTER TWENTY-NINE

THE SUN HAD SET BY the time Brier made it out of the rubble she and Marina had left behind them. Still covered in dust, she stepped through a doorway and out into the growing twilight. If everyone was all right—if *she* was all right—she didn't know, but she couldn't bring herself to stop and think quite yet. If she stopped and let her mind catch up to everything that had happened, she might not be able to keep going on. Clover believed in her plan. Believed so completely, it had given her peace. But Brier didn't know if she could do the same. Not when she was nothing more than a not-even-nineteen-year-old girl fumbling her way through keeping the world from ending.

She stumbled over a new crack running across the ground. And she wasn't even doing a particularly good job at that. The world likely would have ended twice if she had been left on her own.

Following her feet, she ended up at the top of the amphitheater. She half wondered if she should be worried. No good had come from being near the place so far. But everything remained silent. Any guards who'd been there earlier were long gone. Even the little tents all the cultists had kept down by the river were half trampled, with no fires out front. Venchia had been abandoned. Again. But that seemed to be her current lot in life—to fight for an abandoned city.

Instead of apprehension, exhaustion finally caught her as she stood there, looking over the expanse. She released a long breath and took a seat on the top row of the step-seats that made the theater. Who knew what had happened to the ancient Venchians? The ruins had been ruins long before the Augarian had been built, but perhaps that meant Venchia was the perfect city for her—where new destruction would be lost among the old decay. Living among ruins was better than turning full, vibrant cities into empty shells at the very least.

Brier felt Palmer's approach before she heard his footsteps. She kept her eyes on the empty stage and dead countryside.

Palmer came up beside her. "It would be nice if *somebody* started listening to me when I told them to stay put."

The corners of her mouth tipped up into a smile. "Perhaps you need to start telling us to go places instead so we'll end up staying when we ignore you."

Palmer sat next to her and looked out across the expanse.

She waited a moment before speaking again. "Is everyone all right?"

Palmer released a breath through his nose before beginning. "Cerise is. And Nico. Whatever's been protecting him so far more or less protected him from what Marina hit him with. He's a little bruised but nothing life threatening. Rosette's slipping around the ruins too quickly for me to actually speak to her, but I'm going to assume that means she's fine."

"You didn't keep her with you?" Brier finally looked at Palmer, her eyebrows furrowing.

"I didn't have much say in it." Palmer ran a hand through his hair. "She's getting to like using her powers a little too much. Someone's going to get hurt if she keeps it up. Her or someone else."

"I'll talk to her. I think we've been leaving her alone too much." She would track Rosette down as soon as her legs were willing to move again. Knowing Rosette, she was probably ferreting around, looking for shiny things to play with. Brier only hoped the girl didn't cut herself on anything. "Goebel?"

Palmer paused a little too long.

Brier's body tensed. "He's not all right?"

Palmer made a face. "Nico was protected from what Marina did to him. Goebel... his own powers must have helped some, but he took a direct hit."

Brier wet her lips. "Is he dead?"

"No." Palmer shook his head. "But he's... faded some."

"Faded?"

"Like his body was slowly dissolving." Palmer made a face. "I think I managed to stop it for now, but... I don't know."

Brier pressed her lips together tightly, trying to stop herself from analyzing the information too much. So she would talk to Rosette and then see Goebel. "And Peony?"

Palmer nodded, looking straight ahead again, as if he couldn't bear to hold her eyes. "We got her out of the palazzo. She seems to be all right, overall, though she's unconscious, as well."

"Clover was in her," Brier said and continued explaining before he could ask, "like Marina was in Orris. Only Clover left before Peony's body gave out."

Palmer frowned. "And where are they now?"

Brier held up her hand to show him the ring. "In here. Clover said you'd know how to get them to pass on."

"Me?"

"It was in that book I burned that night," she said. "You just need to figure out what was in it."

Palmer released a shaky breath. "I suppose we'll hope Goebel is all right so he can train me more like he wanted."

Brier returned to studying the town around them. "I don't think we should go to Ruhegipfel."

"No?"

Brier shook her head. "At least I shouldn't."

Palmer pursed his lips. "Did you want to go back to Latysia?"

"No."

He studied her face. "You don't want to stay here, do you?"

She didn't answer immediately. Brier needed to stay in a city she wouldn't destroy, at least for as long as people kept making her fight. And they seemed likely to keep doing that for a while longer, no matter what she wanted. She released a breath. "This isn't finished, you know."

"What isn't?"

"All of this." She motioned widely across the shadows of the ruins and trampled tents. "All this anger and fighting and death... it isn't over. You can't tell me it is."

"Ruhegipfel is a stronghold," he said. "People would have a hard time reaching us there."

"We go to Ruhegipfel, and we're under Goebel's thumb." Assuming he wasn't as good as dead. "We go to Latysia, we're under Gully's. I'm done listening to orders."

Palmer took a moment. "We could both use more training, Bri."

"So we need advisors," she said. "Perhaps mentors. Not a commandant. I'm sick and tired of being ordered around by people who either think I'm a little girl who can't take care of herself or a weapon to pull out whenever they can use me." She paused. "I need to be somewhere I can figure things out myself. Without other people telling me who I should be."

He tapped his fingers on his thigh. "And that somewhere is..." He motioned to the amphitheater with his other hand. "Here?"

"It's a ruined town hosting a doomsday cult," Brier said. "I can't think of many better places for me."

The tapping continued for another moment before it slowly tapered off, then Palmer sighed. "We better figure out what sort of supplies they have here, then. There isn't exactly a market nearby."

She glanced at him. "You're willing to stay? Just like that?"

"I was willing to walk a hundred and however many miles with a man I border on tolerating most of the time to come find you, Bri. You didn't think I'd be willing to stay?"

She smiled at him then forced herself to stand. "Then let's go find that daughter of ours."

OTHER BOOKS BY JESSICA DALL

Raining Embers (Order and Chaos: Book 1)

ABOUT THE AUTHOR

Jessica Dall finished her first novel at the age of fifteen and has been hooked on writing ever since. In the past few years, she has published novels such as *The Copper Witch* and *The Paper Masque*, along with a number of short stories that have appeared in both magazines and anthologies.

In college, Jessica interned at a publishing house, where her "writing hobby" slowly turned into a variety of writing careers. When not buried under her own world building, character sketches, and manuscripts, she works as an editor and creative writing teacher in Washington, DC.

She can most often be found with her overworked laptop and too often ignored husband wherever there is Wi-Fi.